Kitty Sutton

Penny

From the time Europeans landed in North America, the People were forced out of the land they had known for generations. By the nineteenth century, the United States had pushed them into the remote and undeveloped area known as Indian Territory and promised them food and protection that never came. Plagued by the loss of their ability to farm and hunt, the lack of food and shelter, the disease brought by the White Man, every tribe suffered losses so great only the memories of the survivors could document the dead. This story, taking place among the Cherokee after the Trail of Tears, is a story for all the People.

"Once again Kitty Sutton has spun a magical tale in WHEEZER AND THE SHY COYOTE. New villains are preying on the Native peoples struggling to build new homes in Oklahoma (Indian Territory). Wheezer's 'people' are drawn inexorably into a dangerous web of intrigue as they struggle to stop the insidious whiskey trade. With his 'people's' lives on the line, Wheezer and the curious new friend Yellow Eyes, a shy coyote, to break the case open. Steeped in Native American history and lore, WHEEZER AND THE SHY COYOTE is a worthy successor in the Mystery from the Trail of Tears' series."
-Kathleen O'Neal Gear and W. Michael Gear – New York Times Best Selling authors of *PEOPLE OF THE SONGTRAIL*

What are people saying about *Mysteries From the Trail of Tears?*

At once moving, heartbreaking and life affirming. Wheezer and the Painted Frog is a story of the human will to survive. The adventures of Sasa and Jack are fun and interesting. How they form their relationship and become each other' family is a lesson on the way we live with other denizens of our earth.
-Karen Doering, Amazon reader

One of the aspects of Wheezer and the Painted Frog that I enjoyed the most was the clever way in which the author, Kitty Sutton, has managed to weave a history lesson into the fabric of what is a delightful mystery novel... and who can resist a story with an eager and exciting dog as the hero?
-David Makinsin, Amazon reader

This is a moving story that instantly captured my heart. Never verbose or preachy, this tale flawlessly captured the flavor of the West, and the bigotry of the times. Yet, it is written in

an inherently upbeat style that had me cheering for the good guys, and booing at the no-good, low-down, greedy bad guys. I also cheered for Wheezer, my favorite character. This book is the first in a planned series of mysteries. I am looking forward to the next one by this talented new author.
-*L. Jenkins, Amazon reader*

As I said at the beginning, this book brought me back to the love of my childhood and youth, and I must say that reading Wheezer's story, the Cherokee people story, Sasa's story, captivated me as much as the best novels by Zane Grey and Louis L'Amour managed to do so many years ago. I definitely recommend reading this book. You'll feel the richer for it
-*Annarita Guarnieri*, author of *Cats: Instructions For Use*

Kitty Sutton

Wheezer And The Shy Coyote

by
Kitty Sutton
Illustrated by Kitty Sutton
Published by Little Buffalo Arts Publishing

Cover art: Kitty Sutton
Copyright 2018 Kitty Sutton
and Little Buffalo Arts Publishing
ISBN-13: 978-1-7321496-2-5
ISBN-10:1732149623

This is a work of fiction. Although it is based on real historical events, some characters have been created for the sake of this story. Actual persons have been included, based on documentation of their presence at relevant events, but actual dialogue is speculation, used to enhance the dramatic tension of the story. Certain words and dialects are used which are representative of the point in history in which this story took place, and should be viewed as such.

In an effort to present the broadest view of the events happening in this period, the author has condensed the time line so that some events may not appear in their proper sequence, year or season. Any mistakes made, or omissions of other pertinent events happening during this era are purely the artistic license by the author and may be taken up later in this ongoing saga.

Dedication and Acknowledgments

I would like to acknowledge the helpful members of the writing community who gave encouragement and advice to my work. They are Susan J. Welker, Pico Triano, Denise Sinn and Christine Case-Leng.

I would like to dedicate this book to my helpful and steadfast husband of forty-one years, Jim Sutton who is a descendent of the Cherokee Old Settlers who voluntarily came to Indian Territory before the forced march.

And I would like to make a special dedication to Jehovah God, who will right the wrongs of the past and set matters straight concerning mankind. He will cause his promises, to rid the world of evil, to become reality. And, all those who have died, righteous and unrighteous, will be brought to life, and will have the opportunity to inherit a peaceful earth as Jesus promised.

Preface

It was a hot, breezy, but humid afternoon the day Kathy visited the Old Fort Museum in Fort Smith, Arkansas. Why did they always have to take these kinds of trips in the hot summer months? Already tired of hearing about old this and old that, the past was long dead, and she was more interested in the here and now. She barely heard the guide as they walked along the path that lead them past the oldest site of the earlier fort built on the land they called, Belle Point. The Arkansas River lazily flowed past them. Just looking at it made her feel sleepy. Kathy wanted nothing better than to head back to their motel room, luckily just a few blocks away on Garrison.

Ira was all eyes and ears. It had been that way ever since he found out that he was Cherokee Indian. In fact, not just a little, but enough that he qualified to get his citizenship card from the tribe. So, it was natural that he would want to know as much as he could find out about the area. She would give him that, but how long does someone have to look at the old river before they saw enough? Ira turned to see Kathy waiting on the walkway. He had crept closer to the edge of the river bank, and was examining where the river had taken a chunk out of the side of the shore. He motioned for her to join him, and she reluctantly acquiesced. As she got closer, she was able to hear the guide continue her rehearsed spiel.

"The river banks have changed many times over the years, but less so since the dams were put in, which have regulated the flow somewhat. We still get high water sometimes which eats away at the sandy bank, but then deposits it somewhere else further down," said the guide.

Kathy got closer to look, a little worried about the side of the bank collapsing under them. Just before she looked away, a glint of sunlight played on something along the shore. She saw it in the corner of her eye, and she quickly looked back.

"What is that?" she asked the attendant, pointing to the object.

"Oh, probably some trash from upstream. We sometimes have to go through and clean the banks from all the garbage that gets swept up here."

Kathy looked a little closer.

"I don't think it's trash. It's half buried in the bank," said Kathy.

Curiosity was one of the things that got Kathy into trouble. Once something intrigued her, nothing would stop her from checking it out.

"It looks as though it has a handle on it. I am going to reach over the bank and pull it out," said Kathy.

"I'm afraid I can't allow you to do that, miss. Our insurance does not cover exploration on our grounds. You could be hurt, or you could fall in," said the guide, all the while, Kathy was down on her hands and knees moving closer to her target, taking no heed to the guide's warnings.

"Don't waste your breath," said Ira. "She's pretty bull headed. Always has been, at least for the last forty years of marriage."

Ira chuckled at the guide's consternation.

"Almost there, ugh... ugh," said Kathy as she tugged on the handle of what looked like some kind of old crockery. "Got it!"

Kathy crawled back up the bank and presented her prize to the guide.

"What do you think it is?" asked Ira.
The guide looked it over first, then Kathy took it from the guide's hands.

"It's a jug of some sort; it even has a cork in the top. Ira, can you pull this cork out with that corkscrew you have on that fishing tool you keep in your pocket?" said Kathy, boredom and lethargy utterly gone from her mind.

"Sure, Honey, got it right here," said Ira, as he pulled out the screw from the combination knife, corkscrew, file, bottle opener, screw driver and pliers tools in one.
POP!! The cork came free with a good bit of tugging. Without getting any closer to the mouth of the jug, they could smell the aroma, which was enough to burn the little hairs out of their noses.

"What the…?" said Ira, holding it out as far as his arm would reach.

"I know what this is," said the guide. "This is an old jug of Indian whiskey! What a find. And imagine, it was right here under the dirt the whole time."

"What do you mean by Indian whiskey?" asked Kathy.

"Well, back in the early 1840's, there was a big struggle here at the fort and the town. They called it the Whiskey Wars. Selling whiskey to the Indians was strictly against the law, but the townsfolk made and traded it to the Indians faster than anyone could keep them from it. Yes, as I recall, there was a lot of violence connected with it as well. Yes, a lot of history right here in this old jug. I better get this to the curator at the museum. They may want to look for more. Who knows, this may have been an old stash hidden right here just waiting to be picked up. Heaven knows why it wasn't…

Sasa with her friends

Chapter 1

She sniffed the air picking up the tangy odor of fresh meat, but she saw no animal in sight. She rarely came this close to the settlement of the two-leggeds, and she crouched close to the ground with anxiety. Every guard hair of the fur on her back was standing up, but she was not sure what the danger was or where. Her belly growled savagely; it was sometimes difficult to carry a litter of pups when snow still clung to the tall brown grass in the open meadows.

She had always been an excellent hunter, but she had stayed home in the den, waiting for her coyote mate to come back with food. It was taking too long for him to return and she was ravenous with hunger, so she slipped out of the den, her belly hanging low, almost ready for the spring when she would produce her litter in the fine, warm den the two had prepared.

Again, the wafting odor slipped past her nose, and the saliva began to form on her tongue, collect around her canines and then drip from her mouth. The need to feed was the most important thing, nothing else mattered, and it began to override the feeling of danger that had cautioned her before. Now, she crept forward, not seeing anything ahead, only the smell to lead her on, and then there it was, just lying in the snow, a fresh piece of succulent red meat. The closer she came to it, the more enticing it became. One last look around in all directions caused her to relax somewhat, and she took one more step to place her paw on the slab of meat so she might rip a chunk off and gulp it down right away. Later, she could drag it away to a secluded place to feed at leisure, but her burning need was upon her then and nothing could stop her.

Snap!! She jumped, but her body did not obey. Somehow, she was caught; something held her paw, squeezing it, biting into her fur and flesh, blood beginning to drip on the bright white of the snow.

No matter how hard she tugged, or bit at the hard, solid thing that held her close to the ground, she could not get away. She yipped and howled, tugged and jumped to no avail, and finally she slumped next to the thing that tormented her. Slowly she began to lick her leg where it was being held tight, but it did not staunch the flow of the dripping blood. Her paw had become numb now, and she began to tremble with cold and fear.

Then, far across the meadow she saw movement. A tiny dark speck coming closer, but she did not have to see it clearly to know what the movement was. Just the way it moved she could tell it was a two-legged coming straight to her. She tried again and again to achieve release, but it would not budge even the slightest bit. As the figure approached, she saw it carried a dark stick across its arm, walking right up to her, bold and sure.

"Ah, I see I caught ya. Ya won't be stealing any of my sheep now, will ya?" the two-legged said as it looked down on the poor beast. But she did not have any idea what it was saying, or what the noises meant.

"A good clean catch. You would have never gotten away, the teeth have split the bone of the leg, but thankfully I won't need your legs when I skin ya. I can sell your pelt and what a nice pelt it is to. In fact, I have not seen one so nice, mostly white. And I see I caught you just in time too. You're carrying a load of pups in ya, and I don't need any more trouble. Yes, a fine day of trapping this has been," the two-legged said.

As she watched, crouched down baring her canines at him, frantic to get loose for all she was worth, the two-legged brought the dark stick up to his eye, "click" and the world went black.

*****

He watched the big house quietly, not moving a muscle, nor flicking an ear. His yellow piercing eyes watched; his nose watched; yes, and even his ears watched. The small figure on the lawn held something in her hands while she seemed to stare intently at it. The coyote had no idea what this human was doing, but it interested him just the same. He came to this place every afternoon now for weeks. Sometimes he would stay a short while, or sometimes it would be half a day. Then he would slink out of sight, back to his den, his empty den.

The coyote and his mate had occupied that small hole in the hard ground. There is where they raised their

3

pups, several litters of them. She had always been there, then she was gone. At first he looked everywhere for her. He checked every hole in the ground, every pasture where they used to wait for sick buffalo calves to stumble by, every stream where they used to play at the water's edge, and even in places he knew she would never go. Like the increasing number of human dwellings springing up here and there, especially beside the big river, but he knew if she had gone too close to those dwellings, the two-leggeds would have killed her the moment they spotted her in the tall grass. He mourned for her, ached for her warm fur against his in the night. He missed playing with the pups while he and his mate taught them how to hunt.

She had been a splendid mate. He appreciated her beautiful silver tipped cream fur, unusual for a coyote. His was a mixture of tan and gold with white under his jaw, his fur was tipped in black. He always knew she was special, and, as coyotes always do, they had mated for life. Now his days were aimless wanderings. Trying to hunt, but finding all the places he went reminded him of her, at least until the day he happened by the large white house where the girl lived. He had accidentally gotten much closer to the human's dwelling place than he normally would have. The girl human had been outside, sitting on ropes tied to a thick branch of a large tree, swinging back and forth, on and on. Today she had her friend with her, a dog. He could tell they were friends, just by the body language of the dog. They played in the yard as the dog yapped a shrill bark, begging for the chase to begin. He could read those movements, like a language among all canines. The dog had not noticed him, he was still too far away, but his eyesight was keener than even a dog, as long as he stayed quiet and hidden, like now.

There were other things that he could read in the body language the dog displayed. Every day he learned something new about the dog and his friend. He learned that the dog trusted the human completely, and also that he was her protector. The dog would, most likely, fight to the death to protect the girl. He remembered he would have done the same for his mate, had he known she was in danger. And by the girl's movements, he could see that she had a deep feeling for the dog. He wondered what it would be like to have a human for a friend, but it was almost too much to consider. The plain fact was, humans killed coyotes, and that was that. The coyote was not sure exactly how the humans killed his kind, but it was usually accompanied by a loud bang. Sometimes something would hit the ground hard beside him, and it made him run all that much faster. He had seen other coyotes killed in that manner, so he always kept his distance from human kind. Until the day, he saw the girl.

There was something about her that drew him to this spot to watch every day. He should have felt fear, but fear was totally absent from his mind. Instead, he felt a longing. Watching her play with the dog puzzled him greatly. He understood play; his mate and pups would romp and play with him while the sun still shone, then when it did not, the hunting lessons began. There was something different in the play between the girl and the dog which kept the coyote pondering, day after day. Was it possible that this human did not kill coyotes?

Looking at the gray overcast sky, smelling the breeze he could tell water would soon fall on his head, so he crept on his belly away from the house and the girl, then trotted away to his lonely den. He would be back tomorrow to carry on the vigil, for what reason he did not yet understand.

*****

Wheezer paused momentarily, gazing out at the fields beyond. The coyote had been there again. Wheezer

5

noticed him many days while he was out with Sasa, playing chase in the yard. The coyote puzzled him. He did not feel threatened by this wild animal that came almost on a daily basis to sit in the grass and watch, just watch. Wheezer was, of course, curious, but something told him, it was not the time to make an introduction. There was something sad in the way the coyote held himself. However, Wheezer had not known very many coyotes, so it was difficult to tell for sure. Wheezer hoped he would come in and play, but the coyote never came any closer, never gave him a chance to make his acquaintance. Wheezer turned to chase Sasa around the tree once more. She would tire out before he did, because he could play this game for a long time.

*****

Sasa finally sat down on the porch of her new home in Van Buren, Arkansas, out of breath. Her glossy blue-black hair clung to her cheeks and neck, which glistened in the late afternoon sun. She patted her soft cheeks dry with the hem of her calico skirt, then fanned herself with her hand.

"Whew, Wheezer, I can't run any more. I just can't," said an out-of-breath Sasa.

Wheezer flew around the tree with the swing two more times before he noticed Sasa was not chasing him anymore. He ran, full tilt for Sasa sitting on the stairs, coming to a screeching halt, planted his elbows on the ground with his bottom high in the air and his short tail wagging at such a pace, it was a blur to try to look at it.

"Come on Wheezer, you win," said Sasa.

"Arf! Arf! Grrrrrrrrrr," replied Wheezer.

Wheezer was not ready to take "no" for an answer, so he ran up the couple of steps to Sasa, grabbing hold of the tie that laced her apron, and gave it a firm tug. Without much effort, it fell from her waist.

6

"Shame on you, Wheezer. That is mine. You don't have to wear aprons, or even clothes, but if you did, I would not pull your things off of you," complained Sasa. Wheezer's answer was to turn in circles so quickly it was amazing that he could stay upright.

"Oh all right," said Sasa with a grin as she got back up to give chase for one more time around the yard, gaily laughing while Wheezer smiled from ear to ear, running and romping with delight, always able to stay ahead of her easily.

This was a far cry from what her life had been such a short time ago. She and her Cherokee family were part of the thousands that walked all the way from their homeland in the east to Indian Territory the year before in 1839. The Cherokee people named this forced removal from their homeland, Nunahi duna Dlo Hilu-i or 'The Trail Where They Cried'. She had arrived there with her parents and little brother Usti Yansa; his name meant Little Buffalo. He died not long after their arrival, but she still felt the hurt and pain of it.

Life is so different now, she thought. She was extremely happy with the new things she was learning from Miss Anna, and she could truly want for nothing, living here in Jackson Halley's large house, but it was decidedly different from her life with the Cherokee. Jackson said she could go and visit any time she liked, it was all up to her. She made the choice, no one forced her when Jackson offered to make her his ward and educate her so she could later help her tribe. But nothing was the same here. No groups of children playing stick ball in the grass; no old grandmother to teach her the old stories of her people. When all was said and done, there were good things and bad to each choice. She chose the one that would help her people the most, plus there was Wheezer. She could not ever leave Wheezer. She owed him her life, and he was the one who found the painted toy frog, the one that was used to murder her little brother after it was painted with rat poison. That little Jack Russell Terrier had won her heart, and she would always be loyal to him.

Wheezer had belonged to Jackson before Sasa rescued him out of the forest east of their camp. Jackson had had a fire at his ranch with an explosion of stored gun powder. At that time, Wheezer's name had been Jack, but she named him Wheezer after she found him at death's door from a snake bite. Jackson had as much right to Wheezer, and she even more so. She could never take Wheezer from Jackson, and she would never leave Wheezer, so the decision was already made. She would stay and learn. Every morning she had classes with Miss Anna, which was an exquisite joy to her, but there were things that were troubling her.

Sasa finally slowed to a sluggish walk and sat down again on the steps of the house. Wheezer seemed to know this was the end of the chase game for today, and dutifully sat down beside her.

"Ah, Wheezer, I am worried. Did you know that when I go to Anna's house across the river and behind Fort Smith for my lessons, I am yelled at by the people on the ferry? They call me names I don't understand, and they say a Cherokee should not be allowed to come to that side of the river and walk through the town like I owned it," Sasa told Wheezer.

Wheezer pricked up his ears, listening with intent. As Sasa poured out her worries, Wheezer placed a gentle paw on her knee.

"I know you worry, but I have to learn all I can about the white man's world. Jackson says, someday it will be particularly important for my people. I am worried though, because the men from the fort look at me like they can look right through me. Some holler for me to come over to them and talk, but somehow I do not think that is what they want. And the town's people will not talk to me. They refuse to let me come in their store unless Jackson or Anna is with me. Then they are forced to allow me in because they don't want to lose Jackson as a customer. He is one of the few people around here with money to spend. And that is only because of his mule breeding. Fort Smith pays him extremely well for his mules, but I don't think they like me or the Cherokee that are in business with Jackson to be over here.

"Jackson says they can't do anything about it. It is his land, and I am legally his ward."
Wheezer took his paw off her knee and cocked his head the other way, like he was asking a question.

"Oh, a ward is like being adopted, uh... like I am Jackson's family," said Sasa as she patted Wheezer on the head and looked directly into his amber-brown eyes. Then he smiled.

Sasa knew there could even be worse things happen if she did not learn the ways of the white people and use that knowledge to protect them from evil, greedy whites, bent on destroying them.

She leaned her head back against the tall white pillar that held up the tall portico. She absently smoothed down the wrinkles in the skirt of her tan and white calico cotton dress, while Wheezer crept up to lay his head on her lap. She placed her hand gently on his mostly white fur and stroked rhythmically while she thought.

Last year she had been in dire straits. It was hard to believe that she had survived that horrible forced march from her home in the East. She did not want to remember the cruelty she experienced each day of that miserable journey, but it was something the mind refused to put away.

It seemed a terrible nightmare when she thought of the day the soldiers came to her family's log cabin. She had been helping her mother set the table for the evening meal. Her father had not come home yet, and they were hurrying to have it ready for him when he came back from his fields. Her family farmed not a small plot of land in New Echota, now part of Georgia. Sasa had not gotten to go to the missionary school there because she was needed at home. Father said that Usti Yansa (Little Buffalo), her little brother, would be the first to go and learn both the white man's letters, and also the fairly new Cherokee written language. It was important to her father that at least one of his children be educated as Chief John Ross had been. That is why he spent many hours in the fields, education cost money.

Just as her father came through the door, she could hear horses coming quickly up the road to the cabin.

"By order of the U.S. Government, you must vacate your home now," someone yelled at the house.

Father turned, with surprise written over his face, as the white soldiers stormed into the house. They pushed us out of the front door by the point of their short knives on the ends of their guns.

"Where are we going? At least let us take our coats or a blanket and some food," Mother cried.

"No, leave it all where it is. Nothing belongs to you, now get or I'll shoot!" replied the soldier on the horse.

"Sir, these are just children. Please let us take what we can for them," Sasa's mother pleaded.

The soldier on the horse hesitated a moment, "You have one minute, and only one. Grab only something to cover yourselves, nothing more."

Mother scrambled to the cupboard where she kept the quilts she had made through the years. In all, they were able to take one blanket for each, plus mother made sure all had socks which she swiftly stuffed between the stack of quilts. Then, out they marched, leaving the pot over the fire to burn, leaving every item they owned, some passed down from the ancestors of Sasa's family, never to be seen again. Later, Sasa heard from a neighbor who was taken a few hours later, that their house had been emptied, all put in a pile in the front yard and set ablaze, or was carried away by the soldiers. That was when she knew, down in her gut, she would never see that home again.

That trip took months. Every day, people died, every day someone began to be sick, and you could almost count the days to their end. First day, shivers. Second day, deep cough. Third day, breathing difficult. Fourth day, allowed to ride on the wagon, and on the fifth day, dead. Some days there were so many dead, the soldiers refused to wait for them to be buried. She saw mothers carrying their dead babies, refusing to just leave them by the roadside. Most of those mothers died, as well.

Every day was filled with dread. The soldiers that were there to guide them and who were supposed to help them, turned out to be evil men, some of them thought nothing of killing an Indian. On one of the coldest days of the march, she had been walking with a woman and her three children. The oldest girl, who was a couple of years younger than Sasa, was helping her mother carry the baby while the mother helped her young son along the trail. He was just a toddler and he was a chubby boy, so it made it difficult to carry him, mile after mile, and his little legs could just not keep up with the group. The soldier nearest them came by on his horse, and hit them with his crop, but it only made the boy cry and stumble to the ground. Sasa wished she could wipe out the memory of the next thing that happened, but she knew it would be there until the day she died.

The soldier must have gotten too irritated, and tired of pushing that family along as the toddler could not go as fast as the soldier wanted them to go. After riding by slowly on his horse, staring meanly at the little boy, he passed them, and for a little while, she heard nothing. Then, the sound of a fast moving horse coming up behind alerted them a soldier was coming, but there was no time to react. As the soldier trotted by, he leaned down and grabbed the boy's chubby arm, swung him like a rag doll, and bashed his head against a tree. The sound his skull made when it crushed was a sickening watery thud. After the mother saw what the soldier had done, she took her new baby and buried it under her clothes so that the soldier could not grab at it. But, it ended badly for that family anyway. The woman and both of her other children died of sickness, or heartache as far as Sasa could tell, not too many days after that day.

Sasa never understood why she lived. Why she made it to Indian Territory and lived when her parents and little brother were dead. But then she remembered that she almost did not make it.

After they arrived in Indian Territory, the man that murdered her little brother had been looting the food allotments along with many men from the east. She was blessed to have Jackson Halley to take care of her. That first winter in Indian Territory, over one thousand Cherokee died of starvation. Even though they solved who was looting the allotments, men who were now dead, the looting continued to happen throughout Indian Territory. Sasa realized she could have been one of those poor starving people who died last winter if it had not been for Jackson and Wheezer. So, she must show her appreciation for the gift of life from the Creator, and do what she can, to be a good Cherokee and help her people.

While she rested on the porch step, Wheezer sat up quickly, directly in front of her, a smile plastered over his intelligent face with his short, stubby tail wagging furiously. Then, from inside the house, Sasa heard the cook holler, "Supper's on the table, come an' get it!"

"We better hurry, Wheezer. If we are late, she will put our plate away, and then make us eat it for breakfast, cold," said Sasa, as she scurried into the house through the red oak doors, with Wheezer at her heels.

Wheezer thought it made no difference if the food was hot or cold, he liked it either way. Masey always had a bowl of food ready for him when she called for supper. You didn't have to tell him twice to come eat.

"I am coming, Masey," said Sasa, as she ran to the pantry behind the kitchen to wash her hands. As she dried her hands on the linen cloth hanging beside the square zinc tub where they washed the vegetables, she could hear the voices of Jackson and Arch coming from the dining room. She briefly checked her appearance in the small mirror that hung on the wall beside the doorway, then smoothed her crumpled apron before going into the dining room.

As she entered the room, she quietly walked across the blue and blood red Turkey rug on the hardwood floor. Taking her seat at the handmade maple table and chairs, just as Anna had taught her, she kept her arms from resting on the table. She had said it was not mannerly for a lady to place her arms on the dining table, even though men might do it with impunity. There was still so much to learn, but Sasa was determined.

"Yonaguska is dead. It happened last year in April, and we are just now hearing about it," said Jackson Halley. "Some of the headmen and chiefs heard about it this last winter, but I am sure they did not think to tell us. We are not exactly on the path to Fort Smith from their homes and camps. He died in April 1839, just after the last group arrived in Indian Territory." Sasa and Arch stared in astonishment.

"How, how did we get word?" Arch murmured quietly. His somber eyes looking off into the distance through the dining room window, while Sasa looked stricken to tears.

"It was related in a letter and order for fifteen more mules to be broken as mounts, which I received yesterday from the commander at the Fort. Ah, Sasa I am truly sorry. This information will not bode well for the Cherokee."

Sasa slowly slipped her napkin from the table, absently unfolded the linen, not saying anything. She knew how this news could hurt her people. Yonaguska was a powerful Chief among the Cherokee; indeed he was a legend. He had seen many wars with the whites and had always been a steadfast spiritual leader for his people and found peaceable ways to resist the onslaught of the white.

He had said the whiskey, rum and spirituous liquor was making the Creator angry with the People for weakening themselves with the "Black Drink", and that the People must not drink it anymore. His whole village had to agree to give it up. He had his son, a white man adopted as a boy, Will Thomas, write out the pledge, and had all of his people of the town of Qualla make their marks as agreement. All the Cherokee knew what that pledge said, "The undersigned Cherokee, belonging to the town of Qualla, agree to abandon the use of spirituous liquors." As the story went, liquor and drunkenness were almost unheard of in Qualla before the forced removal to the west. Sasa wondered why the Creator allowed blow and blow to hit her people. Had he abandoned them? Now that Yonaguska was dead, who was there to remind the people of what the spirituous liquor could do to the Cherokee Nation? She was startled out of her reverie.

"It is as if all restraint has been lifted from the People," said Arch, his temper showing by the darkening of his already tan face. "Once we were under one Chief Of All and our great men of vision like Yonaguska who reminded us of our spiritual duty. We strove to put away our uncivilized ways, but now we seem to be in complete chaos. Our young men will trade anything they lay their hands on, just for a cupful of very bad whiskey," he growled, balling up his fists and banging on the table top, making the silverware rattle.

"Arch, I don't know what we can do about it when the town's merchants and soldiers take part in selling it right under the nose of Stuart," said Jackson. Irritation etched deep in the lines of his forehead, but compassion dwelt there, as well. He wanted to help, but this problem seems gargantuan compared to others that faced Indian Territory.

"But, Jackson, our young men are so depressed; they look for anything that will relieve their despair. Sure, we caught a small part of those who stole the allotments of food and supplies from the Cherokee last year, but it has not stopped it completely, not by a long shot. There has been no progress within the Cherokee Nation after the murders of those members of the Treaty Party, the headmen who signed away our land in the east. And the fight over who shall govern the Cherokee Nation is all consuming. There are too many factions wanting their own way. And while they dither the weeks and months away, the whites, little by little, turn our young men into drunken wrecks, and our agents steal our allotment right from under the nose of government," said Arch. He knew that his best friend and business partner wanted nothing more than to help the Cherokee. Jackson had proved it over many years of association.

Sasa did not speak, she just listened, absorbing the words and arranging the problems in her mind like a jigsaw

puzzle. In fact, that is what she did with any large problem that came her way. She never panicked, but always
stopped to pull the various pieces of knowledge and clues
together until she had a clear picture of the problem before she tried to find the solution. But, this was more than
just a problem. This hit her personally, for she was working
to learn all that she could, so she might save her people in
some small way. Her large round eyes were lowered, but
evidence of extreme thought could be seen by the flicking
of her dark, long lashes against her brown cheeks. Would
she be too late?

Wheezer slunk under the table to sit at Sasa's feet.
He could feel the tension in the room and knew something
was making his humans unhappy. He slicked all his hairs
down against his body, tucked what little tail he had under
and drooped his normally pricked up ears down. He placed
a paw on her knee, and she gently patted it. Then he lay
down at her feet, and proceeded to lick Sasa's ankles. This
was his way of bringing comfort and support to her and
she understood it. There was nothing Wheezer would not
do for Sasa, and the feeling was duplicated in her. *I may
need you my friend, if the time comes,* she thought. *We
must find a way to be of help to the People.*

*****

Jackson Halley sat in the library of his home listening to Sasa and Wheezer play in the yard. He had tied his
sandy brown hair, simply gathering it to the nape of his
neck, but he had unconsciously run his fingers through it
while in thought and now several loose strands fell across
his chiseled tanned cheek bones. His blue-gray eyes were
partially hooded by his heavy lids as he rested his chin in
the palm of his hand with his elbow firmly on his desk amid
his business correspondence.

He had essentially taken the girl as part of his family, his ward, and an immense responsibility it was, too. He had not actually thought it out when the necessity had been thrust upon him last year over in Indian Territory. That was when he had met Anna Edwards, the daughter of the Indian Agent in the interim camp for the Cherokee removed from the East. He had been drawn in to investigating what was happening to the food stuffs that were to be provided to the new arrivals. What he found was a web of conspiracy, and then death. The man Anna had not known well as her father, turned out to be a most corrupt criminal, capable of killing children. Anna had turned out to be the polar opposite of her father. In fact, she had helped in the investigation and confrontation of the terrible deeds her father was guilty of.

But, *Jackson thought,* not only was she true and just, where her father was base and corrupt, Anna turned out to be someone I could love, make a home for, and have a family with. But, how can I ask her to marry a mule breeder? She is used to the finer things, fine society, glittering balls and society teas. My life is here now, and I can't go back, nor do I want that life again. I have Sasa to think about, and the city is no place for her. Not until she is comfortable with the way to behave among that type of society. If I were to take her now, Sasa would be ridiculed as a savage, and then she might never want to learn white ways to help her people. That means that if I take a wife, it will have to be someone who can make a life here with me. Anna seems like she wants to be with me, but I am just so unsure. Oh! Why can't I just ask her? Why do I clam up when she is around?

Arch, or Archibald Flint, Jackson's best friend and a full-blood Cherokee, had told him numerous times that he was being too timid. Arch was never one for many words, but when he did talk, he usually was right.

Arch had taken a pretty significant step when he came out to Van Buren with Jackson, before the removal of his people to Indian Territory. Jackson's father, Andrew Halley, had invested heavily in many Cherokee businesses for many years. Jackson worked with his father and was destined to take over Halley's Financial, headquartered in Boston, now in St. Louis, when the furor to grab the ancestral lands from the helpless Cherokee became a frenzy. Halley's almost went under. To take the burden of Jackson's salary from his father, Jackson took his savings and moved west with Arch and Arch's family to partner in a mule breeding business in Van Buren. It was already bearing fruit. With the Army just across the Arkansas River at Fort Smith, Jackson's mules were always needed, not to mention what the Army would need in the future.

Chapter 2

Poison Woman had been worried until she was sick with it. Her brother, Di Damv Wi S Gi, or Medicine Man in the English, had been missing now for three days. He had finally come back to their lowly cedar pole shack this morning. The same shack they had built in the first few days after being left in Indian Territory by the white soldiers. Built of scrap sticks and cedar poles, it barely hung together in the stiff winds of the territory. Still, it was better than nothing at all.

It had been more than a year since the long walk, and many of the People had already left the camp to settle in other places within the Cherokee allotted land. They said this place was a place of death, and she agreed with them. Medicine Man, though, refused to leave. He had said they were too old to be going anywhere now, especially since all of their family was dead, taking The Long Walk to the ancestors before the soldiers came, or during removal, and some shortly after they had arrived. The clans and the families were scattered, what was left of them, so here they sat, within walking distance to the Indian Agent's cabin.

She should feel grateful her brother still lived and had come home, but something was terribly wrong with the old, weathered man. Not a sickness exactly, but more like he had lost himself. There, he lay on his cot, stinking of the white man's whiskey, urine, vomit and feces. He had never done this before, had never allowed himself to become this filthy, but even so, she knew where the whiskey was being traded to the People. He had probably walked the few miles over the Indian Territory line, all the way to Fort Smith where the white soldiers were rebuilding the fort. The little town that had started when they built the first Fort Smith, stayed and grew some after the fort closed a few years ago. Now that the soldiers have come to build a new fort, the town is growing bigger, full of white settlers, but some of these settlers made the white man's whiskey, or as the elders called it, 'the drink that makes men crazy'. And even though these white men despised the Indians, they made a business of making them their primary customers.

Poison Woman sat beside his cot, wiping his brow with a piece of old calico, moistened with water. Her sparse flyaway hair glistened pearly white as the sunbeams played along its unkempt ends. There seemed to be more scalp visible than hair, for it gleamed brightly as well. It had been many years since she was able to put her hair in a braid. Now there was more scalp to see than hair. Once, she had been considered somewhat of a beauty, but now the lines and crevices cut so deeply into her face that even her eyelids had wrinkled.

She thought to give her brother some of her herbs, but that could be dangerous without knowing what was ailing him and for that he needed to wake up and talk for she did not want to make him worse.

As she sat next to his prone figure, she tried to reason it out. Had he not always said, he hated the white man's whiskey? It was very strange that he would come stumbling home with it all over him and sick from swallowing it. And she had never in her lifetime seen him soil his clothes with feces. Something very bad must have happened.

She sat in the darkened lodge; she had not built her customary morning fire in a hollow of the dirt floor. It still lay there cold and dirty with scattered ashes left over from the night before. Dust dancers played on the sunbeams that pierced through holes where the cedar sticks and poles did not cover. The room smelled of endless cooking fires, animal skins and the herbs she dried on the wild grapevine she had strung across the lodge above their heads. The longer she could delay beginning the cooking fire, the better; she hated the choking smoke that never seemed to make it through the gaping hole in the middle of the roof.

As she sat quietly beside her brother she noticed a slight movement of his body and in a few moments he began rocking himself back and forth. Almost like a tune on the breeze sung by a faraway soul, his chant began, gradually gaining strength, louder, then in earnest. Now she knew he would be all right, but his chant told her something else. It was a prayer to the Creator; although it had no words, she knew, in her heart, it was great sadness, which he spilled out to the one God. And it was not his death song for which she was thankful. With eyes closed, he continued his sincere prayer, tears running down onto the old quilt he lay upon. The chant filled the small lodge, and as she gazed out of the open doorway, she watched as the trees swayed lightly in the breeze, unaware of the tragedy which lay out in front of the Creator at that moment. Her realization that Medicine Man was now humbling himself before Creator in a way that was profound and important poured over her. Something must be terribly wrong, because the sound of his prayer was sadness itself, pleading and desperate.

She was unsure if she should ever ask the cantankerous old man the theme of his prayer. In fact, she knew that if she asked, she would never know; he would seal the prayer in his heart, and it would remain his own unto his death. Better that she keep her own counsel and allow her brother to tell her what he felt she needed to know.

Then the sun changed its position, redirecting the sunbeams to shine on other spots within the lodge; the trees gradually calmed to only a tremor of bright green leaves against the blue sky, and her brother opened his eyes. He seemed surprised to see her there, and wearily sat up. He smiled slightly, but a frown swiftly filled his old face. He covered his face with his hands, and then ran his fingers through what was left of his hair, sticky with something unknown. Sobs racked his body momentarily. When they subsided he looked up at Poison Woman, with tears in his eyes.

"My sister, I have been away to a bad place; I was caught by a great evil and held so that I could not move. A devil man came; he knew my name, Sister. The name our father gave to me, Deer Caller. Other men held me down while this devil man poured the white man's whiskey down my throat. For many days, they did this thing, over and over until I had no senses left. They kept me tied up so that

I could not move and when I was sick, they let me vomit on myself, and when I begged to be allowed outside to move my bowels, they laughed and forced me to sit in my own excrement," said Medicine Man.

"Brother, I am glad they did not kill you. Why did those men do this evil thing to you?" Medicine Woman knew he would not lie to her, but she needed as much information as she could get out of him, for once he was done with his talk, he would keep silent and not speak again of it. If she were to help, she had to know all that had happened.

"I do not know Sister. I walked to the fort where they sell us provisions. The soldiers were all about, and they did not look at me. Many of our young men, our warriors have gone close to that town by the fort, and there is where they buy whiskey. I sat on a rock close to the path while I summoned all the young men to come near to me. I explained about the white man's whiskey, how it had almost ruined the Cherokee many years ago. I told them about Yonaguska, Drowning Bear. How when I was a young boy, Yonaguska had been a drinker of the "Black Drink" the white men call rum. This strong drink held him captive for most of his life. How he fell into a trance, coming close to death; then, when he awoke he drank no more. He said he had a message from the Creator. He said, "The Cherokee must never again drink whiskey. Whiskey must be banished." And how he proceeded to ask his town of Qualla to make a pledge they would never use spirituous liquors again. He made them sign with their mark as they do in a treaty, the whole town. And how those Cherokee never could be conquered by the whites through their whiskey. And that how almost no one ever broke their promise, if they did the punishment was the lash. He was a revered prophet of the Cherokee, but he died last year.

"I told them how it would ruin what pride they had left in their clans, their families and tribe. I think some listened, because I saw some turn away from the whiskey traders and start for home. That is when white men grabbed me; they covered my eyes and stuffed a rag in my mouth. I don't know where they took me, except that it was a white man's building; I felt the wood planks under my feet. That is when the devil man came with a white man's voice. He said I must stop my talking to the young men. He said he would show me what I was missing and forced me to swallow the whiskey. I did not know if it was day or night. The man came many times, again and again, he forced his whiskey down my throat. If my stomach threw it out, he would make me drink again until my eyes closed and I slept the sleep of the dead.

"Today I woke up in the field outside of this camp, like I had only dreamed it, but I know that it happened, which means our people are under attack by something worse than walking the Trail Where They Cried, Sister."

She gazed down at his sodden clothes, surprise on her old, wrinkled face. Not wanting to believe and yet knowing it was the truth. He smelled like a rotten egg, and she was thankful that she was old, and her nose no longer turned up at bad smells.

"We can go to the Chiefs. It is a long walk, but they can stop the town's people. They will talk to the soldiers and ask their leader to make them stop," she said with confidence in her words.

"No Sister, it cannot be. The Chiefs of the Cherokee are all fighting amongst themselves. They are fighting for who will get to stand on top of this pile of buffalo dung they call Indian Territory. They have no time to worry about us; each side is plotting to take the leadership from the other. Meanwhile,

24

some of our families have no homes, no food, no guidance. Is there any wonder why the Creator cannot hear the People, since they do not speak with one voice?" Medicine Man did not speak these things very loud, but his eyes showed the bleeding within his soul, the horror of the already dead and the calamity that would come again upon them.

Poison Woman knew it was true, and she thought, All the People know of this fight between the ones they call the Old Settlers, Cherokee who came before the forced march, against the new, much larger group who walked the Trail Where They Cried, including the Over Everyone Chief, Chief John Ross. The Old Settlers have been here a few years and have gotten used to following their own counsel. Now the larger majority of the Cherokee people come walking in and assume that Chief John Ross would speak for them all. Thus, began a terrible struggle for power. And even the group for Chief Ross is splintered into other fighting groups. So much so that a year ago, several of the signers of the Treaty of New Echota were murdered. Everyone knows that they were murdered because they had signed that bad treaty, the treaty which forced all the Cherokee to walk away from their homeland.

Bitterness reigned against them because during that forced march, their nation lost at least 4,000 of the People in death along the way. Once these men, who had no right to speak for all the Cherokee, had signed, they picked up their own families and hurried to Indian Territory with help from the U. S. Government; they traveled in comfort with no loss of life, and this caused much fighting.

Medicine Man nodded his head as if he knew her thoughts, then said, "With all of the Chiefs fighting between themselves, there is no one to guide our young men. So, they wander over to Arkansas to see what this white man's whiskey is all about. There is something about that drink that holds a young man hostage, and as long as he has something to trade, he will keep drinking. If he has no more to trade, he will eventually steal it from someone else even his own family. This drink does not seem to affect white men the way it does the People. I am afraid, Sister. I am more afraid than I have ever been in my lifetime."

Although Poison Woman did not speak, she, too, was afraid. Afraid of the one thing that her brother had said through all of this. The fact that the devil man who had attacked him had known Medicine Man's before-time name. No one outside of the tribe knows that name. To speak of the Medicine Man's name was the utmost of disrespect. It only meant one thing; someone, within their own people was helping the white men destroy the People, and that man would truly be evil.

Medicine Man rose from his cot and left the shack. Poison Woman knew where he was going. He would go to the nearby creek to wash himself, his clothes and hair. He would cut up a nearby Yucca plant, pound it on a flat rock to get at the soapy pulp, and make a lather to clean himself. Because of his age, she knew he could not do this alone, so she rummaged around in the shack for something for him to put on while she dried his wet clothes. She also grabbed the quilt he had laid down on which was now soiled and must be cleaned as well, and followed him to the creek. They would return later, and then she would finally light a fire in the hollow place on the floor so that she might cook him some broth, and also prepare some herbs to help him.

But herbs would not help solve this problem for the People and Poison Woman, old and wrinkled as she was, would have to find someone to help, help them all before the Cherokee nation was no more, destroyed from within and ravaged from without. She felt sad and desperate as she hurried out of the shack to minister to her brother in silence.

Chapter 3

Meanwhile, to the north, above Indian Territory, a warrior had proceeded carefully, making sure he did not happen upon others in the area. He had walked from the northern plains of Kansas Territory. He would have liked to believe that he was doing this as part of a quest to find a spirit helper, but that was not needed, he already had one. It was a quest, though, but of what he still had no idea. He ached for some insight into where his future was taking him. In many ways, it was good that he was a loner, not caring for the company of many people, or a village, or even a family. He preferred it that way. Now and then he would become melancholy, wishing he had someone to talk to, but he never found anyone who would accept him as he was. It was not his fault that he was born with the blood of two sworn enemies raging inside of him. His mother, Chatawinna, Left-Handed Woman, had been a young Lakota Sioux who had been captured by the Siksika, a tribe of the Blackfoot who had swooped down from the upper Big River, the river the whites called Missouri, to steal ponies and slaves. When he was just a boy, she told him that she had been forced to become the wife of a Siksika warrior; within a few years, the tribe had considered her part of the Blackfoot. When her husband became lazy and refused to hunt, forcing her to beg for food from his parents, it shamed her and his people. So she placed his things out of the tipi. Which meant, of course, she was divorcing him.

Then she was free to do as she pleased, and so she provisioned herself and walked out of that Blackfoot village to find her people, the proud Lakota. She rejoiced in her people; her father had been on the Big River when the two white chiefs came, bringing gifts and stories of a Great White Father, of villages so large you could not see the edges, with a people so numerous they were beyond counting. He did not believe them. His mother said that later, her father had begun to think he had been wrong, for they began to see more white men. The chiefs of the Lakota decided to discourage these interlopers from coming up the Big River, but the white men possessed a wondrous weapon, a fire stick that could kill a warrior, many bow shots away.

Finally, they decided to make begrudging peace with some of the whites who came to trade goods they had never beheld before. After all, these white men only wanted buffalo robes, a thing so plentiful the Lakota could never run out of them. What the Lakota wanted most were the fire sticks of the whites.

His mother, Chatawinna, had so many relatives in her village he should have been a fortunate boy. But it was not to be. When she walked back into her village alive and with a child as yet unborn, the love of her relatives cooled. Even after she told them what had happened to her. As far as they were concerned, it would have been better if she had died. When he was born, his mother did not have the help of the village women, for she was bearing a child with their dreaded enemies' blood in him.

After many months, the chiefs called Chatawinna into the council lodge. It was time for the naming ceremony. He could hear his mother telling this story to him over and over.

"This was the day I had been waiting for, many moons we waited to see if you would live. No child is given his child name until we see his strength. I was so young, and as yet, I had no husband of my own people, the Lako-ta. Even though I was pretty, no young men played their love flutes for me outside my lodge," said Chatawinna, re-membering the scene with sadness.

"Chief Lone Horn himself was sitting in the place of honor. I was terribly frightened and could not speak. When the shaman took you from my arms to examine ev-ery part of you, my heart began to pound, and I felt dizzy. I was afraid they might cast us out, but they did not do that. Chief Lone Horn took you from the shaman Wa Ek-tuza (Forgets Things), held you high above his head, and pronounced you 'Sunkmanitu', meaning Coyote.

"I stared in disbelief. Coyote is 'the trickster', no one names their son after him, but here we were in front of the chief-over-all saying my child's name would be Coyote. I be-gan to weep, for there was nothing I could do. Not only did Forgets Things make this your child name, he said this would be your forever name which could never be changed.

"Then, Forgets Things handed me the leather pouch you now wear around your neck. He said it was a piece offering from the village so you would always remember that they treated Coyote kindly instead of casting you out. He said you would be accepted, but that our people would always be on guard because you have two nations in you. One good and one bad, and like coyote, you might play tricks on your village, some funny or some hurtful," she said. And then his mother would say, "This story does not have a good or bad ending, it is still being made." And then she would grow quiet.

Coyote remembered all the years of growing up in his mother's village. He always had thought of it as his mother's village, not his. From the beginning, he kept to himself as he learned all he could from his mother. Then one summer, Forgets Things came to their lodge and asked Coyote's mother if he could come to learn from him. She was highly honored; Coyote was not so happy. He did not want to be a shaman. He did not know what it was he wanted. But, one did not turn down an offering from the village shaman.

So, he learned many things from this man, things that maybe a father might teach his son; how to survive in the wilderness alone, where his place was among the animals of the earth and some things that a father would not know to teach a son; things about Wakan Tanka the Great Spirit and all the other gods who played a part in a warrior's life. Forgets Things also went a step further and taught Coyote all he could remember of what the Blackfoot believed about the same things.

Coyote enjoyed learning about herbs, plants for food, medicine and plants for ceremony. There seemed to be no end of the things he learned from the shaman. It was aiding him now on this lonely wandering of his. Then, one spring day, old Forgets Things summoned Coyote to his lodge, for a purpose unknown. He obeyed promptly as he was taught, but upon entering the dark and gloomy interior of the shaman's tipi, Coyote could see a change in the appearance of Forgets Things.

The shaman motioned Coyote to sit before the tiny smokeless fire while he supplicated the Creator for guidance. After cleansing himself with smoke, then doing the same to Coyote, he sat wearily across the fire from him; only then began to speak.

"Coyote, maybe you have wondered why a man who is not your father would take you into his lodge for these past years and teach you many things. Maybe you have worried that Forgets Things was trying to make you a shaman. But, I am here to say to you, Coyote, that those things are not the reasons for our work together," said the shaman.

Coyote listened with a building excitement. He thought that finally now he would know what his purpose was going to be on the earth.

"Coyote, you are now a young man, and I am a very old man. It is time for me to leave. The responsibility given to me by Wakan Tanka on the day of your seeing ten summers," said the shaman, "is now complete."

Coyote automatically began to ask a question as he had done so many times while learning from Forgets Things, but the shaman held his hand up to stop the boy's speech.

"I know what you are going to ask Forgets Things. I am here to say that I have asked the same questions myself and was not given an answer. I will tell you all that was given to me. Many times there were some in the village that wanted me to throw you out. They wanted to blame you for any bad thing that happened to them. I was not allowed to do that. No. There have been plans made for you which I do not know. So I was made to think that you were of two nations for a good reason and that you were not a bad omen for us, but would someday be a good one for both your peoples. I was also made to think that you needed as much as I could teach you in the ways of survival, for you will leave this village soon, just as I will leave it soon as well," said the shaman.

Coyote took in this knowledge with a horrible fear sweeping through him. Where was the shaman going? Where was he going? Were the People driving Forgets Things away? Before he could utter any of his concerns, the shaman answered just as if he had asked.

"I am going the way of my ancestors soon, and when I am gone, you will no longer feel at home in your mother's village. It is then that you will go on a great quest. I do not know how long this quest will take. It could take your entire life before you know what it is you were to learn. I do not know which way you are to go, but what I am sure of, is that the two nations within you are important in some way that I am not allowed to see. When you fulfill your quest, you will know, and you will also know what it is you must do after that. There will be no need to fast for a dream like the others, for this is something that you will learn by living it, not dreaming it. And so, tonight we will sweat together, and eat together. Then I am giving you all of my packets of medicine plants. Also, my white man's steel knife and my best buck skin hunting shirt and leggings. I will no longer need these things, for my own son is dead. I will also give you my paint pony, riding saddle, and lastly my pipe and tobacco. They all must go with you. You will take these things tonight so that all the village can see and know that I have given you these things myself, and no one will take them away from you after I am gone," said the shaman, as he began to look tired and weary.

"Grandfather, I do not want you to go away, and I am not yet ready to leave my mother. Will you not need your pony and your pipe tomorrow when you give thanks to Wakan Tanka? Will I not be here tomorrow, to sit at your side, to learn more about the medicine plants?" asked Coyote with true pain in his eyes.

"Coyote, you will be here, my son, but I will not. That is why you must take these things now to your mother's lodge so the whole village can see that this is what I have said. Then you must come back so that we may take one last sweat together, for truly I am made to believe that I have given you all that you need to complete your quest," said the shaman, as he motioned for Coyote to be about his request.

With a heavy heart, Coyote lead the white and black paint pony loaded with the items the shaman desired to give to him, through the village to the very end of the lodges where his mother's lodge stood. All eyes were on him. He glanced behind once and saw the chief go into the shaman's tipi, and he knew what the chief would be told. But, Coyote had so many questions, and most could not be answered here in this village with these people. He knew then that he would leave.

When the old Forgets Things died, Coyote found he had very few friends in his mother's village, so he said his good-byes to his mother.

"Mother, do not look at me that way, please, I must go. I must find the answer to the questions that burn in me. I must complete the quest just as the shaman taught me. I know now that I will never fulfill it if I stay here," said Coyote.

"My son, will I ever see your shining face again?" said Chatawinna.

"Mother, have you thought about why it is you do not have a husband yet, here in your own tribe?" he asked.

"Maybe your mother does not want a husband," she blurted.

"I know that is not true. It is because I am here. I remind them of their powerful enemy the Siksika. Every time there is an attack, they look at me. Every time our village has to move so the Siksika will not find us, they glare at me. I am the one who makes their hearts bad. When they look at me, Mother, they only see them, the Siksika, and their hate blinds them to the one who stands before them.

"Mother, you were just a girl when the Siksika took you from your people. You are still young, and can have more children. Ones that the tribe will accept. If I go away, you will have suitors. Many warriors will pay court to you and play their love flutes outside your lodge. Even if you were only the second wife and not the sits-beside-him wife, it would be better for you. I want to know that I helped bring you one thing that is good, and it can only be given to you if I go," Coyote smoothed her blue, black hair as he reassured her. Left-Handed Woman finally saw the wisdom of it, and helped him to prepare.

Coyote was careful as he traveled through the lands south of the Lakota, also called the Teton Sioux. And there were also other bands of the Sioux nation, but Coyote knew that other tribes not of the Sioux were all considered bitter enemies. He could have been half-blood of any other tribe and be just as hated in his mother's village. That meant that he must be wary of meeting anyone who might notice him, a lone Lakota, and think him easy prey, and a target for vengeance. But he was not afraid, for Forgets Things had been extremely thorough in his training. It occurred to Coyote that the shaman took on his training because he knew the boy would leave and follow a different path than either half of his blood. The shaman had never spoken of it to Coyote, until the night before his death, but now that he was walking south, out of Lakota lands, and traveling the opposite direction from the Blackfoot, he knew Forgets Things had trained him specifically for this journey.

In the seventeen years of his life, he was able to watch his mother's people, as if from afar, terrorize, kill and mutilate those of other tribes. In fact, it was required before becoming a man and warrior to count coup against the enemy. That could be anything from stealing their ponies, stealing their women and children to an all-out massacre of a village. It did not actually matter what tribe a warrior chose to unleash his brutality on, he would receive war honors from the chiefs and gain status within the tribe for carrying out these things.

Coyote's heart, though, was not made that way. He was of exceptional height, being part Blackfoot, and well-shaped. He did not lack strength or ability. He was just as adept at combat as the other young men. He learned everything the other boys learned and because he felt unaccepted he excelled at everything, unknowing it would make him even more disliked by his peers. He could be just as hard and determined as they. However, there was one thing they had in abundance that he lacked. He lacked hate.

Coyote saw the world in a different way. He wondered. Why is it that the Sioux had to attack neighboring tribes, why is it necessary to spill so much blood? It is not different with the Blackfoot either. Would it not be better for all the tribes to work together? If they all got along, could they not establish trade to help them all live better lives instead of welcoming death? What honor was there in warring on women and children? Why did his days have to be filled with this training to kill? Was that what all their gods demanded of the tribes?

Whenever he spoke of this to his teacher, the shaman, he had never received an answer. His teacher would always shake his head sadly from side to side. Then one day when Coyote was twelve summers, he did answer.

"Coyote, there are things I cannot tell you. These are things you must come to know yourself. You have your feet in two nations. You must decide which is the path you will follow," said Forgets Things.

"But, grandfather, what if I do not want to follow either path?" asked Coyote.

"Only Wakan Tanka knows these things. I cannot help you. The answer is hidden from me," said Forgets Things, who then turned silent.

And so, the only explanation he received was what the shaman said that last night with him. It was when he began to think this way, that he had become restless and began wondering what other lands and peoples lay over the hills and past the plains. Now, here he was, walking, riding and thinking, unable to come to terms with the questions floating around in his mind.

He thought of his mother as he walked and rode ever south, hoping all the while she would be well and happy. For himself, he had to find the place where he was meant to learn, a place where he could explore for the answers to his questions, but he did not know where he might find that place. Coyote would keep trying until he did, or die trying. What other choice was there?

* * * * *

Sergeant Willis was not in a happy mood. Yet again, the Fort Smith commander stood in his way, and was making it difficult to get the rotgut whiskey across the border into Indian Territory. Of course, the captain had no clue, however, that every time he plugged a leak, Willis would make sure another would spring up, and once again whiskey would get on over to the Indians.

Willis had been a lifer in the U.S. Army, mostly cavalry, until he was ordered here to supervise the care and keeping of the mules and stock they needed to rebuild the fort. The previous fort had been just west a bit at Belle Point. But, they kept having too many of their officers and soldiers die from the ague. *Heck, even that dad-blamed Army doctor took sick and died,* he thought. They were sure it was from that vermin infested swampy land over there, so they bought the land that butted up against the other, but was on higher ground to the east of the old Fort Smith. Now, the slow task salvaging what building materials they could steal from the old buildings at Belle Point, at least what was left after the town folk had scavenged the wood and rock for their own dwellings. Now, the building of the new Fort Smith is underway.

Sergeant Willis stood on the parade ground, looking far across the Arkansas River, pondering his problems. He was a muscular, compact sort with graying hair, leathery weathered skin, tanned, and ancient looking brown, and blue gray eyes. He looked as if he had been born in his Army uniform and boots, complete with all the dust he collected each day from walking the grounds.

"Private Dade, have you seen to the morning detail?" Willis barked.

"Yes, suh, I have, suh," said the private saluting stiffly in the bright sun of a summer day.

"Then take a detail over to the ferry landin' and unload that new cargo for the commissary, and report back to me, and be quick about it. And stop looking at me like a walleyed catfish!" Willis said impatiently.

Why did it happen when everything was going just right, Captain Stuart has to put his big foot in where it don't none belong? I swear, someday I am goin' to chop his toes

37

off if'n he don't stop it. He is supposed to be rebuilding the fort, not sticking his stinking nose into the goin's on of the town folk. It's plum messing up the whole works, *thought Sergeant Willis.*

At the private meeting in the town livery barn, he would have to tell the merchants the newest block to their efforts. He could not for the life of him see what the Army had against giving spirits to that bunch of vermin across the border; it was totally beyond him. Up until a few years ago the border of Arkansas Territory had been another fifty or so miles from where it lay now, which was right across the Arkansas River, almost at the fort's back door.

Homesteaders had already begun to settle in that area, and then what? The government done an' give all that land to the injuns and made all those hundreds of white settlers move back. There was many a nose got knocked out-of-place over that, *he thought.*

It just doesn't make a lick a sense in my book. Why didn't they just finish all them redskins off when they had the chance? Why move good white folk out of their homes and farms just to give it up to a bunch of lousy injuns? Now, I'm a-thinkin' the only thing they is good for is to make a profit off of. And maybe me and them town merchants can accomplish something else in a round-about way which the government could have done themselves if'n they had had any brains. This way might take longer, but what the heck, it doesn't matter how long it takes. Eventually, all those tribes over there will start killing one another off for something to trade to get our squeezens. Not to mention the wars that could start between all those other tribes they moved in over there. And once that happens, the government will see the error of their ways and step in, corral them all up again, and maybe march them down to Mexico where they need good slaves.

But, I have some doubts because of Captain John Stuart, who seems to be single-mindedly determined to whip up concern for the safety of the whites here abouts. Heck, they don't need any protection from the Indians. They just want to be left to their own designs. Stuart, in past years, convinced those yokels back in Washington City that there is too many dealings of contraband, namely whiskey, going across the border, but at the same time Stuart was adamantly against the reoccupation of Fort Smith. And Stuart was very much against exposing the troupes to the, as he put it, "influence of the immoral community at Belle Point, which included, bought women, saloons and the temptation to participate in the demoralizing whiskey trade", and Captain Stuart is determined to stem the tide. Well, that was counterproductive to my plans, sure enough.

But, we finally got that taken care of back in Washington City. We have some powerful people back there that a certain merchant has in his back pocket. Why he even arranged to sell his land to the government so they could rebuild Fort Smith. Yes, has just as much at stake as any of us other whiskey runners. He's been makin' a killin' on both sides of the fence for some time now, and I been helpin' him do it. The injuns are forced to come here for supplies, so we get them to turn right around and buy our whiskey with those same said supplies and go home drunk, plus we sell to the construction workers building the fort. Yes, we is all makin' a tidy sum indeed.

If I play my cards right, I should be sittin' pretty in a year to two, just as long as I can keep the lid on those Cherokee elders who want to complain about the drink coming into their country. Ha ha, I sure showed that one old injun. He won't be traipsin' over here to warn his Cherokee friends away anytime soon. And if he does, well, we'll give him a stronger talkin' to than the last time, that's for darn sure.

He was happy to be stationed back here close by that little upstart of a town they now also called Fort Smith and used to be called the community at Belle Point. It was much easier to get the whiskey into Indian Territory from here. He had been stationed at the fairly new Fort Gibson, about seventy miles further northwest of here. But, this location was more profitable by a long shot. He did not want to be in the Army forever. And Army pay was not very much, at least not enough to save anything.

At the moment, his superiors knew nothing of his involvement in the whiskey trade; he wanted to keep it that way. Well, the boss might be able to get away with just about anything, but there would be nothin' I could do if I got caught. They'd put me in the brig for the rest of my days, *he thought dourly.*

Keeping his eye on both the Army and the town merchants would have to be his priority since he stood to lose the most. There was no civil law this far out to do anything at all to the runners; he alone stood to lose everything, but, he had no intention of it ever coming to that. He would make sure of it.

Chapter 4

Anna Edwards sat at her rough pine desk in the room which had been the parlor, but was now converted into a classroom for Sasa. She had sent Sasa home for the day about an hour hence. She was taking the time now to look over an essay Sasa had written. Anna had asked the girl to write an essay about her life before the Cherokee removal. There were two reasons for Anna requesting this of her. First, she wanted to see, of course, how Sasa's grasp of English was coming, sentence composition, word root meanings, as well as penmanship, etc. The second, she would not share with Sasa. She wanted Sasa to remember the happy times, to make them real in her mind so that she could call them up at will. Anna knew that sometimes children forget a previous time after something untoward happens, and last year had been an exceptionally distressing period for her Cherokee friend indeed. Adults didn't seem to have that problem, or should she say ability? She thought that sometimes it might be beneficial to be able to lose parts of one's memories if it meant to lose the disagreeable along with it.

So far, Sasa had been an eager student. Anna and Sasa were becoming close friends as well, something that Anna would not have thought possible just a little over a year ago, when she came to Indian Territory to visit her father, Samuel Edwards. She hated her occasional remembrances of her father, but they came unbidden to her mind anyway, even though she was blissfully happy with her new life here on the frontier. However, the shame of what her father had perpetrated on the poor Cherokee was a still bitter pill to take.

Her father had been the Indian Agent for the Cherokee, and he had used that position to steal the funds that should have paid for the food, which would have kept so many removed Cherokee alive that first winter after the Trail of Tears. Sadly, because of her father and other men in the east, who had hatched their plan together, and had brought it to bear just when the Cherokee needed the help the most. It became the cause of more than a thousand deaths from starvation that winter. She would never forget the debt she felt she must pay to the Cherokee for what her father had done to them. That is one of the reasons for her staying here and making a new life for herself. She wanted to help the Cherokee in whatever way they would allow. The other reason she stayed, lived in a fine white house with white pillars made in the southern style, which perched on a hill at the outskirts of Van Buren, just across the Arkansas River. Part of her heart was there, though she doubted the occupant even noticed, being too busy with his mule breeding to think about amore.

He was a man she could look up to, and work side by side with, if he would only notice how she felt. At least Sasa was here almost daily, and Anna could hear all the things going on at the Halley mule breeding ranch any time she cared to ask. Sometimes, Sasa brought an invitation for dinner. On those occasions, Anna would dress her most feminine and accompany Sasa back on the ferry across the Arkansas for a most enjoyable repast. But, no matter how much Jackson smiled at her and engaged her in conversation, he never paid court to her, and she could not understand why. After all, was she not the most cultured woman in this part of the territory, being finished in Boston at a highly prestigious girl's finishing school? She had the most beautiful dresses and every feminine accoutrement for miles around. She always made sure she looked her most fetching whenever she was invited, but alas, no real response was forthcoming from him. He was a puzzle, but she would be patient; someday, she would figure out the way to his heart.

Until then, she was already becoming the beginning seed of society in this growing little town. To be sure, there were not very many women of consequence, only one church and an entire town of misbegotten whiskey runners and drunks. There were a few cultured people here, which was fine, but Anna was not a snob. If society sought her out then she did not mind the company, there was so little of it here. The only other women here were the ones that hung around the grog shops and saloons. Anna refused to venture into town at night for that reason. She did not want to be confused with that certain type of woman, and she had no protection save for a small lady's gun she kept in her reticule. After all, this was a border town with somewhat dubious civil law.

However, the dark side of this small settlement was a constant reminder of the terrible injustices being done to her friends in Indian Territory. She thought of the Cherokee often, and not just the Cherokee, but also the many other tribes who had been pushed onto that land, which at the time, no one seemed to want. Now, it looked as if others were, once again, viewing the land the tribes had been given, as something desirable; desirable enough to swindle, cheat, even kill for, which she well knew was happening all around her.

After the murder of her father last year, Jackson kindly allowed her to use a small cabin on his property. She had no intention of staying there for long; Anna decided she would feel more at home if she bought a property in the community at Bell Point, now called Fort Smith. She found what she wanted fairly quickly, a well-built cabin in town with several rooms. After finally settling in the bright white log cabin, she set about preparing the inside for her uses. The cabin was something of an anomaly, because even though it was made of logs, a brilliant white plaster had been laid over the rough exterior and interior, using a local rock that had been heated, then ground fine, and painstakingly applied. Once completed, a fresh whitewash was applied, along with painted pink shutters on either side of the windows; the wilderness cabin looked like a fairytale cottage. It even had real glass for the windows.

She had been surprised to find such a place in what was still an exceedingly rough frontier settlement, and was happy to find that it had been built by a Methodist missionary. Alas, he and his family never got to make use of the structure. The missionary's wife had been left back east to bear the couple's fourth child. Just as the cabin was completed, he received word his wife had died during childbirth, but the child had lived. He knew, as much as he wanted to stay and minister to this community, he had to go back and take care of the raising of his family who now was without a mother.

Anna bought the place for a remarkably reasonable sum, and was secretly overjoyed with the prospect of living in such a sweet dwelling. As she sat at the desk, smiling to herself, she was startled out of her daydream by a quick knock at her door. She quickly checked her appearance in the mirror hanging beside the fireplace and straightened a few flyaway strands of wheat colored hair before crossing to the door. It was only when she put her hand on the knob that she began to wonder who might be calling on her at this time of day. It was very close to the evening repast, although she had scarcely thought what she would make.

When Anna opened the door, she gazed upon a slim, petite woman dressed in a gray wool nondescript dress, an over worn hat on top of drab, brownish gray, frizzy hair, a small reticule on her arm, whom she did not recognize.

"Uh, Miss Edwardz?" the woman said. Anna noticed the woman was standing ramrod straight, her bloodless lips in a short line.

"Yes, I am Miss Edwards. What may I do for you?" replied Anna.

"Oh, I suppose you don't remember me. I am Mrs. Reardon. Mrs. Patricia Reardon. I live just around the corner and down, just past the livery stablez. I wonder, if you don't mind, Miss Edwardz, could I have a quick word with you?" said Mrs. Reardon.

"Certainly, please come in. I am afraid I do not have

a parlor, but I do have a small sitting room just to the right. Please do sit down Mrs. Reardon," said Anna, as she took the opposite small chair, and began to wonder at the woman because this was a singularly improper time to call as far as social courtesy went. That thought disappeared once Anna became a bit mesmerized at Mrs. Reardon's nasal intoned voice and the odd way she continued the endings of some words with a hum or hiss, as if she could not let go of the word, or that she might even explode given half the chance.

"I do hope you will forgive me, Miss Edwardz, but I heard from my neighbor that you were teaching here at your home. I have seen you at a few gatheringz, but we have not been formally introduced," said the woman, but her unusual way of holding on to the last syllable of a word along with the nasal whine, made it difficult to follow, especially when her s's all sounded like z's making an unfortunate hissing sound. "Myself, I have two children. Their father owns the Reardon Dry Goods Store along the riverfront, don't you know? I thought I might come over and see your classroom for myself, and then to ask if you would be taking on any other studentz. You see, I have all I can do to keep the house up these dayz, don't you know? However, I am on the town committee to find a teacher. I have been praying for a school," Mrs. Reardon said as her eyes scanned the room.

It was now that Anna noticed an odd smell coming from Mrs. Reardon's person. It was a sickly sweet odor, combined with human sweat and possibly horse manure. It was all Anna could do to sit and listen.

"Well, uh, Mrs. Reardon, I had not thought to run a school. I have agreed to teach one student and one student only. I don't know if I would be qualified to teach an entire classroom of children, ma'am," replied Anna who was beginning to resent the intrusion and wonder if she would be able to even eat that evening.

"Oh, but I don't see how you can make any money with just one student, Miss Edwardz. My, oh my, but this little town is beginning to grow, and with more people, there is always more children, don't you know? We need a teacher in the worst way. I just don't see how you can support yourself on one student," said the woman.

By this time, Anna was beginning to feel nauseous, not to mention irritated by the woman's speech pattern.

"Well, I am not teaching her for money, Mrs. Reardon. It is a labor of love and friendship you see," said Anna, as she took out a hankie from the small drawer of her tea table to place at her nose, while the woman continued, seeming not to notice.

"Ah, someone of your own family I presume then. Well, I always say the morez the merrier, and what you can teach one, you can certainly teach a few more, don't you know? I was not aware we had another child here at Fort Smith. May I ask who the young person is?" probed Mrs. Reardon.

Anna was becoming a bit suspicious, because she had been teaching Sasa now for a full six months. She could not fathom why this woman would not already know who she had coming to her house so often, and the unpleasant aroma was becoming unbearable. And on top of that, she had seen Mrs. Reardon at some of the gatherings and never had she had even one child with her. She was almost positive that the children were an invention.

"Her name is Sasa, and she does not live on this side of the river. She lives over in Van Buren with a very good friend of mine. I only plan on teaching her until she is caught up to her age level of study and then I believe she will be sent to finishing school after that," said Anna, as she periodically held the hankie to her nose.

"Sasahh? Sasahh, I don't recogniz the name. Sounds Swedish or something. Is she your relative?" asked Mrs. Reardon.

"No...no, she is not. Sasa is the Cherokee word for Swan. She is the Cherokee ward of Mr. Jackson Halley and a very fine student she is, too," said Anna, beginning to feel decidedly defensive.

The woman's eyes swelled in her head, and upon taking a deep breath, she griped the arms of the chair.

"You - are teaching - a Cherokeeee girl?" she finally said, letting all the air out of her lungs in one big foul smelling gush.

"Why yes, I believe she is Cherokee. Is there a problem with that Mrs. Reardon?" asked Anna knowing full well what the answer would be.

"Oh my dear Miss Edwardz. I cannot say in more strenuous termz that it is a very unfortunate circumstanz. Yez, unfortunate indeed. Miss Edwardz, I just don't think that anyone of the town will want to bring their children to be taught right along with one of those Indian people from over there, don't you know, in Indian Territory. It just will not do, don't you know? Well, if you plan on getting anywhere with your teaching, you will need to drop her as a student right away, the sooner the better" demanded Mrs. Reardon.

Anna felt like flying across the tea table at the pompous, smelly woman, but turned her head and took a breath instead, while forming what she would say and do.

"Oh, I am sorry, Mrs. Reardon, to be a disappointment to the mothers of our town. I don't know what I could have been thinking. Only that I have no intention at all of taking in any other students. I am comfortably situated, you see, as I have been well provided for. There is no need whatsoever for you to worry about my income, and as for

Sasa, she is becoming as well bred...no, I should say, she is better bred than most of the inhabitants of our comely little village here," said Anna as she arose from her chair, and then taking Mrs. Reardon's arm forcing her to arise as well, and walked her leisurely to the front door, as if she were escorting an invited guest to their waiting carriage.

"I am just thankful that Sasa has agreed to come here for her lessons, considering the fact that we have at least two or more saloons on every block, and all sorts of unsavory persons coming and going at all hours of the day and night, not to mention the whiskey peddlers plying their illegal trade to the Indians. No, Mrs. Reardon, I think I must be thankful that I have such a worthy student, and such fine neighbors. Really, you must come again, DON'T YOU KNOW? GOODBYE!" said Anna as she closed the door just as Mrs. Reardon had cleared the doorway and was getting ready to say something more. She left the woman standing there with her mouth open, her finger in the air and her hat askew. Anna chuckled as she went into the kitchen to wash her hands, then find a couple of candles to burn to disperse the odor, and to make her supper.

This will be a story to tell at Jackson's. We will all get a good laugh out of it, *she thought as she walked over to the window facing the street.* Curious, Mrs. Reardon is talking to a man at the end of the block. He looks like one of the merchants, and oh... she is pointing at my house. Yes, this is definitely something to discuss with Jackson.

Chapter 5

"I thought I told you to keep your nose out of my business, Patty. I have a mind to whip you all the way home," said Robert Reardon as they stood in the middle of the street, just down from Anna Edwards' house.

"But, Robert, I thought you said you wanted to know more about that woman and the Indian girl she haz coming there," said Patricia Reardon as Robert took a firm grip of her arm and led her down the street toward their home and business.

"I told you no such thing, you little idiot. I can learn all I need to know in my own way. Now you have put your foot in it. Don't you understand that she is the one that helped catch the men who were stealing from the food allotments last year? Let me tell you, missy, she is the type that will stop at nothing to bring out the truth of a matter. She even exposed her own father. If she would do it to him, she could do the same to us. I don't know what you think you're doing girl, but this was not part of our agreement. You are not and never will you be the society matron of Fort Smith," growled Robert as he reached their front door. Then shoving her inside he said, "You better pay me heed, Patty, or you will be right back where I found you and that is certain."

Just as he slammed the door, the new town banker and his wife on a stroll, stopped with concern showing plain on their faces.

Robert had to think fast, so he opened the door a little and spoke as if Patricia was standing their listening, "Uh, now don't ya a-worry your pretty little head no more, hun. I'm a-gonna take care of a-killin that there rat in the kitchen if'n ya just be a mite patient. No need for ya ta get all fired up, consarn it," Robert yelled then closed the door.

The couple smiled as if they now understood what the commotion had been all about. Nodding, they continued on their afternoon stroll.

Robert shook his head and thought. That was a close call. I can't afford for anyone to get suspicious.

*****

Lucius O'Malley paced behind the front counter of his feed store. He had just received word there would be another meeting tonight. He was not happy about the news one iota. Didn't these people have anything better to do than stir up trouble? Already Captain Stuart at the Fort had mentioned the sale of whiskey becoming troublesome when he was last in the store. Lucius was beginning to get

51

nervous. Sure, he was happy to make a profit in most ways, even selling whiskey to whom ever wanted it, but he was getting that old feeling of impending doom. He was afraid the captain would find out that he was supplying the corn to make the local whiskey being forced onto the natives. That same feeling he got just before he was arrested in Ireland for treason against England's Imperial government. He had fought for independence from England since he could walk, but it had all come crashing down on him that day in 1825, thanks to Peter Brennon, the old fool. Never should he have been given the names of men working for Ireland. But, there was nothing for it, now was there? For the Saints be told if anyone could have kept Peter's mouth shut when the English soldiers were holding his wife and his wee slip of a girl.

Instead of hanging Lucius, they tried to ship him to Australia and turn him over to a penal colony. Fortunately, there were a few intelligent men among the English soldiers who looked the other way while he slipped away into the night. The soldiers had arrested him at his family home at Killrock in County Meath and were taking him north and west to Galway Bay where a ship waited. But, one night, he slipped away and headed south to the River Shannon where he knew merchant ships would lay up and wait for a crew before setting sail; destination, America. That is where he knew he had to go if he were to escape Britain's long arm. He had heard that America was taking all the healthy Irishmen they could get, for they were building across their continent and needed strong workers, and a strong Irish worker he was.

He landed in New York, and quickly he found the city too crowded with immigrants who seemed to get off the boat, set their cases on the ground, sat their bottoms on their cases, and no further would they move. He could not fathom that. Not with all that land he had heard about on the trip over. Land just being given away, and so that is what he set his mind to do. And that is how he landed in this little town next to Indian Territory where the United States President saw fit to gather up all the native peoples they could find, banishing them to a land that the government thought was worthless anyway.

Once here, he found he had to dance to another man's tune. At first, it sounded splendid; easy money. Until he saw the sorrowful condition of the Indians. Especially the families that had had to leave loved ones dead or too sick they could go no further, along the trail, just to arrive here in the west and lose another thousand or so from starvation. Starvation was something he knew extremely well, yes for he had seen his own sister die that way. She was a wonderful bright colleen, she was. But, it was surprising how fast a body turns to ruin if it does not have enough to eat, then afterwards, shoved out into the cold damp of a moor with nothing save the clothes on their backs. It does not take long for a body to succumb, and his sister was just one of thousands dying of starvation and exposure in Ireland, all at the hands of the bloody English.

Now his profit tasted bitter to him. So, tonight there was another one of their secret meetings. How long would it be before the American government succeeded in doing what England tried to do, arrest him? However, extricating himself from this ghastly business was harder than it sounded, so he would have to go. But, he knew enough than to let anyone know his true feelings. If they knew, they would not wait for the law to take him, they would do the job in secret and leave his body to go floating down the Arkansas River. Once found, no one would be able to tell what had befallen him, and his reward would be an unmarked grave.

About the time he had reached the far end of the store counter, he heard the footfall of, hopefully, a customer. Lucius shook his head slightly to sweep the webs of worry out of his head, as the customer came into view, rounding the stock shelves which blocked his view of the front door which stood open in the spring evening air.

"Uh, hello Robert me boy," said Lucius, "What can I do for you this fine day." Robert Reardon was certainly the last person Lucius wanted to see. Undoubtedly, he was involved in the whiskey trade up to his ears. Robert was an easy man to like, at first, and an easy man to talk to, until it was way too late. Once he had something he could hold over your head, you would have the devil's own time being your own man again.

Since Reardon was a known family name in Ireland, he thought he had found an Irish comrade at first, but Robert swore his family had been in America for as long as any in his family could remember. However, Robert now knew something about Lucius that he did not want the Army to learn, and Robert wasn't a bit shy about pressing the point.

Because of the situation he found himself in, he put off finding a wife here in America. There was nothing he could do, at least not now, but he would have to do something eventually. Lucius had no intention of living his entire life this way, for it was Robert that had talked him into joining the town merchants in their, albeit profitable, whiskey venture. And it was also Robert that was the barrier to his quitting for good and all.

"Well now, Lucius, I just done come around to check on ya. No harm in that, is there? Naw, no harm a-tall," said Robert as he settled his behind down on a hundred pound sack of corn. "Now if I was ta begin that there meetin' to-night, would I be likely to see ya sittin' around with the others, or do ya have in mind to skip this one? I would hate to have to come round in the middle of the night Lucius. You know I needs my sleep, and I get plumb punch drunk if'n I have to go out, traipsin' all around searching for ya."

There it was, that little barb to remind him that he was not his own man. He would have to let it pass. This was just not the right time to do anything about it.

"I said I would be there, Robert. Is this man's word not worth the speaking of it now?" replied Lucius.

"Now, now, Lucius. No need to get yourself in all in an uproar. It's just a friendly reminder, is all."

Robert looked from side to side for any other customers in the feed store, found none and leaned over the counter.

"I heard that ole Sergeant Willis roughed up one of them there Medicine Men over tah Fort a few days ago. That's one of the things he's a fixin' on tellin' us all about. That, and some other things he wants took care of I xpeck. So ya come bright eyed and bushy tailed.

"Well I best be going on back to my own bailiwick before my Patricia notices I'm gone. I swear Lucius, she can be worse than any ten magpies once she gets a going. Now, midnight over ta livery, ya hear?"

Lucius just nodded his head, afraid he might say something he would regret if he had spoken even a word. Instead, he untied his apron, slipped it over his head and hung it on the wooden peg beside the cash drawer.

His last customer was the muleteer over from Van Buren, just across the river. The man always came in a hurry, but he did a good bit of business from him. Mr. Halley had settled over in Van Buren just a few years ago, bringing breeding stock with him to make some fine looking mules.

Now, that was an interesting business it is. You can't just mate two mules since mules be sterile. The only way you can get one is to mate a donkey stallion to a horse mare.

Twice a year, Halley traveled to the east, buying up starving, weak, or ill-treated mules, driving them cross country to his ranch on the north side of the Arkansas River, not too far from Lee Creek. After six months of good feed and proper care, Mr. Halley's mules were as dependable as any. And, that being the case, it was a steady business for his feed store. In fact, it had helped him to keep a better stock in the store. Today's business was fairly short, and Mr. Halley said he had a bit of other business in town and then planned to go see a friend of his.

Lucius had already taken the day's intake and stashed it in a small safe he hid in the back room behind his small office. It was not yet seven in the evening, the sun had yet to set, leaving plenty of time to go down the street to the local hash house to a quick supper. The weather was warm, the air smelled of green. Being a full blooded Irishman, Lucius always thought he could put a color to some smells and today it was green.

As he walked down the block past a sundry of houses, some shabby and some passable, as far as frontier towns went. However, the houses were not what he was looking at. In fact, he was not looking at anything at all except his own feet, not actually seeing them either. He was thinking hard about this whiskey business when he rammed right into something warm and giving, and hearing an "Ouch" in a feminine, soft voice. Quickly looking up to take stock of his blunder, he came eye to eye with the most beautiful woman in town or anywhere else for that matter, Miss Anna Edwards.

"I must say, a woman takes her life into her own hands when she takes it upon herself to sweep her own front step!"

she exclaimed as she pounded the straw end of the broom down on the walkway like she was churning butter.

"Pardon me, miss. Now I am thinkin' it is entirely my own fault. Poor soul that I am, I was lost in thought and was not watching a widow's mite. I do apologize. Have I hurt you, lass?" he asked, gazing at her eyes and feeling the world shift.

"No," she chuckled, "no I don't think anything is hurt. Just a surprise is all. I'm afraid I was not paying attention while I swept the step, so it was as much my fault as yours, I dare say," said Anna with a faint blush on her cheek.

"We have not been properly introduced. I am Lucius O'Malley, lately from Ireland and now Fort Smith. I own O'Malley's Feed, if you please. And you are?" said Lucius.

Anna was a little uncertain of the propriety of introducing one's self in the street to a male she did not know, but there seemed to be no one in the vicinity watching.

"Yes...well, I am Anna Edwards, from Boston, now a resident of Fort Smith," she said.

"Well, it is a pleasure meeting you. I am headed up the block for a bit of food. If you have not eaten, I would be honored if I could escort you to the beanery," said Lucius, wondering at his new found boldness.

Anna was a little off balance. Within seconds of meeting a man on the streets of Fort Smith, she is asked to accompany him out to eat. The idea was preposterous in the extreme.

"I do beg your pardon Mr. O'Malley from Ireland, but I am not accustomed to having whirlwind invitations from people I do not know, and I certainly would not want to accompany you to the, as you so quaintly call it, the beanery. Especially when it is more likely just another sad excuse of a place for the locals to swill whiskey. I am afraid I will have to turn such a handsome offer down," she said, all the while watching his face as, what she could only describe as, a glow creep across his fair skin, almost matching the color of his red hair.

Lucius barely heard a word she said, for standing before him was not just a lovely refined woman, but one with fire in her veins and sparks in her eyes. The cut of her tongue was like music to his ears. And he muttered, "almost as good as me mum could have done back home, she is." He had rarely seen or heard an American woman with that kind of fire in her, with a sturdy backbone as well. He would have to make sure they were introduced properly, and in polite company too. *Aye, that I can manage*, he thought, then tipping his hat, said good day to Miss Edwards, and down the street he went, with a new lilt in his step. Anna, for her part, was bewildered that the man had not recoiled at her rebuke. What happened just then, in front of her house, was a strange encounter. She turned to finish her chore.

Just a few yards away, a man had stopped his walking and had watched the entire scene as it had unfolded. The man seemed to change his mind about something, shake his head solemnly, and turned to walk the other way. Jackson Halley had planned on coming to see Anna, but seeing her in such amiable conversation with the charming Lucius O'Malley, made him lose heart.

He counted the days between visits with her. He knew he hadn't the strength to let her go and forget her, and the thought of rejection froze him whenever he considered revealing his feelings to her. I suppose I am a coward when it comes to matters of the heart. It is just as well, he told himself. I wasn't sure what to say to her anyway; chances are it would have been an imposition to show up unannounced. It looks like she has an admirer who is smiling at her, and she at him.

Chapter 6

Wheezer lay next to Sasa while she slept. A large, full moon was beginning its descent, but he could still see the open fields towards the river. Carefully, he moved to the window sill. The night breezes were pushing the curtains to a gentle rhythm and the aroma of wet earth, and new spring grass wafted past his nose on the eddies of the wind. Furtively he scanned the tall grass, now lit by the moon so well it positively glowed. His searching eyes finally settled on a particularly small object standing behind a few blades of last year's brown grass. It was hard to tell because the object was the same color of the grass. However, Wheezer's keen eyes detected movement.

He had thus been up several nights watching out of this same open window, communing with the silent creature across the fields, then lying back down next to Sasa. But something was different tonight. The form paced slowly, then would sit down, then rise, turn in a circle and settle once more. Wheezer knew who the night visitor was. If it had been any other animal, he would have barked feverishly until it went away. This, he knew, was the coyote who watched them from afar, but something was wrong. Wheezer could tell by the way the coyote paced.

Wheezer looked back at the sleeping Sasa, making sure she was asleep and safe. Then with a quick bound from the bed, across the window sill and down to the soft carpet of new green grass just outside of Sasa's bedroom window, Wheezer made for the tall prairie grass quite a way from the house. It was strange, in a way. Wheezer was not familiar with the coyote at all, but something told him that the coyote needed him.

He preceded cautiously, first a few feet, then a pause, then a few yards and a pause, each step Wheezer took seemed to make a scratching noise. He ran the last few feet, and as Wheezer got closer to the line of tall grass at the edge of the field where Jackson exercised his mules and where the grass had been trampled down to dust, he saw that the coyote had stopped pacing. It was not running away as a coyote would normally do, and Wheezer did not sense any danger in the yellow eyes that gazed back at him in the moonlight. He approached the coyote slowly, then came along side of him, doing what all canines do when introductions are in order. Wheezer carefully sniffed. The scent, musky and warm. Once that ritual was done, and they were both satisfied with each other's scent, the coyote yipped and trotted to the south with Wheezer in tow. Wheezer thought, *if we kept going in this direction, it will take us close to the river.*

The coyote did not run but did not waste time either. He kept his head down, sniffing as he went. Wheezer kept pace, allowing the coyote to lead the way. There was no wondering about being led into a trap. Trust had been established, plus they had already established their pack order. The night noises echoed off into the distance, the soft wind moved the grass before them. The muffled sounds they made with their paws seemed louder to Wheezer's ears.

The coyote slowed, and quickly crouched down in the grass, sniffing the air in all directions. Wheezer only stood with his head cocked and his ears perked up and over. Still he was alert to any signs from the coyote, warning of danger ahead. When the coyote had assured himself that it was safe to continue, Wheezer followed. After just a little while the coyote pulled up and sat quietly, looking off into a dark recess against a rocky outcrop. Wheezer could not see what was there since the angle of the moon over the outcrop was casting a dark shadow over the area.

The coyote again made a yip and Wheezer, not being familiar with coyote talk, wondered what he was supposed to do, so he put his own nose to the ground to see what he might discover, and soon he detected a faint odor. As he tracked with his nose to the ground the odor became stronger, and he forgot about the coyote while he continued on into the dark recesses where the odor was leading him. The closer he got, the more he recognized the smell, and soon he came upon something lying in the grass. Even without the moon's light, Wheezer could tell, it was something dead, but what? He approached it, but when he was hard upon it, he jumped back all of a sudden. Then he knew. He knew it was a dead human; he whirled to look at the coyote, but the coyote had vanished as if it had never been there at all.

In the dark, there was not much Wheezer could tell except that it was a man. The scent of the blood told him, it was not fresh. After scratching at the edge of the dark stained ground, he knew the blood had been soaking into the ground for some time, the air having dried some of it. There was nothing he could do. The man was too bulky to drag to the house, besides, once his eyes adjusted to the dark shadows, Wheezer could see that someone had tried to bury it with rocks. He would not be able to move them off of the body. He looked from side to side, trying to decide whether to stay or go get help. After looking back at the body one last time, he bounded through the tall grass, running as if a mountain lion were on his tail.

As he approached the house, he started barking before he reached it. He kept barking as he leaped up and through Sasa's open window.

Wake up, wake up. There is something wrong. Wake up now. Come on, I need to take you there. Wake up, *he barked, pulling the covers off of Sasa.*

When he saw Sasa sit up in bed, he bounded out of her room, down the hall and into Jackson's room to do the same to him.

Jackson, Jackson, get up. Something is wrong, help me, he barked, and when it seemed that Jackson was not getting up fast enough, he began to howl like a hound dog, something Jackson had never heard Wheezer do before.

"All right already. What in tarnation is going on, Wheezer?" said Jackson, but Wheezer was already bounding down the hall to make sure Sasa was out of her bed.

Sasa stepped out in the hall, pulling on her knitted sweater over the light dress she had just wiggled into.

"Jackson, I think Wheezer is trying to tell us something. He had been outside for a while. I think we need to see what the problem is," she shouted down the hall, as

Jackson emerged out of his room with whatever he could find to throw on.

"All right boy, calm down, calm down would you? We're coming," said Jackson.

Wheezer ran up to him and started pulling on his pant leg, tugging furiously.

"There must be something dangerous, I am going to get my shotgun before we go out there. Sasa, take the rabbit gun with you and run down to the bunkhouse to wake up Arch; tell him how Wheezer is acting. I may need him," said Jackson, "but, be careful when you step out the door. We don't know where the danger is. Meet me at the big tree by the swing. I am going out to check around the house first, then Wheezer can show us where the problem is. I just hope this is not a wild goose chase."

Wheezer vaguely heard "wild goose" from Jackson and thought, *Goose? I didn't see a goose.* And the thought quickly faded away as he accompanied Jackson around the outside of the house.

After making it around to the front much faster than Jackson, Wheezer paced back and forth, with his ears pricked up. Worried, he gazed off towards the tall grass while uttering low gravelly sounds deep in his throat; before long, though, all three of his humans were at the tree. Arch rubbed the sleep out of his eyes but was dressed in his customary skins and moccasins. His Green River knife hung at his side, and his long black hair was loose around his shoulders. Wheezer looked up at Jackson for the signal to go, but he was so keyed up that his legs fairly vibrated with his high strung nerves.

"Do you want us to bring one of the oil lamps?" asked Sasa.

"No, we better not. Even though a lot of the tall

grass is green, there is still enough of the dry grass on the ground that if a spark should ignite it, we could have a terrible prairie fire going. I think there is enough moonlight to see by. All right now, Wheezer," said Jackson, his voice lowered so as not to wake the ranch hands in the bunkhouse. "Go on boy, show us. We'll follow right behind you."

And so, they all trotted out into the tall grass under the bright but waning moon. Sasa was getting enjoying the travel, but worried, *I wonder what Jackson will do if Wheezer takes us to a downed rabbit or something.* As they made their way through the new tall green grass, Sasa could smell the fresh scents from nature around her. Last year at the end of her first summer in Indian Territory she got to experience the beauty of living on the prairie. By the end of the summer, this grass would be almost as high as a man, and the sun would bake it to a golden yellow. The breezes would cause the blades to rub against one another and make a sound as if a thousand mothers were trying to "shush" their children. The winter winds would lay it down where it eventually would become soil. Until then, it could catch on fire if someone were careless.

With her moccasins on, she quickly but silently picked her way along the bent grass path Jackson had just passed through. When they finally reached the small clearing next to the rock outcrop, the moon had shifted and had changed the direction of the shadow over the body so that the victim was partially exposed by the searching moonlight. Wheezer ran to the body and barked, but there had been no need. All three of his humans were aware of it laying there, partially covered by rock, its hand stretching out as if to plead. As Jackson made a cursory inspection, quickly finding the man's head had been bashed in from the back.

Sasa had seen much death in the last year. With so many dying of starvation the last winter, death had almost become common place, even though it had been several months. Now she stood still, not wishing to find out who the person was, but noticing the markings on the hunting shirt on the body. She gulped back her fear and murmured, "I think he is a Cherokee."

"We shall see, Sasa, and if it is, we will need to know who he is. But, you are right, the body is male," said Jackson as he bent over and began taking rocks off the prostrate form, setting them aside.

"What are we supposed to do about this, Jackson?" asked Arch. "This man has been murdered. We are still on the Arkansas side of the Territory line. You know we don't have any law here, at least not officially. Marshall Elias Rector is probably way over in Fayetteville, he may as well be in St. Louis. Even though we are outside of Indian Territory lands, Captain Stuart won't want to bother with this either. It's not army business, for one, and two, this is probably a Cherokee. I can already see the design on his buckskin shirt. None of the whites over there at Fort Smith is gonna' give a hoot whether or not one Indian got himself murdered. I mean, it has to be murder, somebody tried to cover him up."

Sasa stood watching them work; just listening, but not quite knowing anything that could help. She had never thought of her new home as being lawless. Suddenly, she felt unsafe.

Jackson made quick work of removing the stones. Arch helped to pull the man out of the shadowed rock shelter. As Arch looked down at the face, he thought he might know the man, but was not sure. Jackson looked up at Arch, noticing the strain on his friend's face. Arch just shook his head.

"Sasa, I hate to ask you to do this, but could you please look and see if you can identify him? The moon is still fairly bright yet," said Jackson.

Sasa stepped over to the body. Jackson was right, there was still just enough moonlight to see by. She looked hard at the man's face, not recognizing him, but when she began to turn her head, her eyes caught an old scar on the side of his face. She looked a little closer.

"What is it Sasa? Do you think you know him?" asked Jackson.

"I have seen this man before. Here in Indian Territory," said Sasa. "Maybe Medicine Man would know him."

"Arch, please go back to the ranch, hitch up some mules to a wagon, and maybe grab one of the hands to help us lift him up. He is a pretty big man. I think we can find a place to put him where it is cool while we send word to Medicine Man," said Jackson.

Sasa made a low moan under her breath. Arch did not move to leave, there was clearly something they wanted to say.

"What did I say? Won't this work?" Jackson asked.

"Jackson, if he is Cherokee, he must be buried by tomorrow. We cannot delay that, it is what we believe," said Sasa, concern in her voice.

"Uh, I am sorry, I wasn't thinking. Of course, I knew that. Let's get him back, get a better look at him first, then we can decide what to do. Maybe we could take his decorated shirt off and put something clean on him for his burial. Then possibly Medicine Man could identify him by that and from Sasa's description. We can bury him up the meadow from the house if we need to," said Jackson.

Without speaking further, Arch and Sasa nodded their agreement, then Arch took off at a fast trot. Wheezer sat at Sasa's feet watching and listening. After Arch left, Wheezer crept closer to the body to get a good sniff of the man's clothes. Sasa walked up behind him, knelt down and

stroked Wheezer's back. When Wheezer became more fo-
cused on the man's outstretched hand, nudging it this way
and that, she gently pulled him back while she turned the
lifeless hand over. Within its cold, stiff grasp was a piece of
dark cloth, its edges frayed as if it had been ripped from
something or someone. Not knowing why, nor stopping
to consider the reason, she pulled the piece of cloth from
his hand and quickly put it into her side pocket. This must
mean something.

Watching every move she made, Wheezer looked
puzzled by her actions.

"This may be important. Once we get back to the
house, we can look at it under the lamplight. Wheezer,
how did you know there was something out here?" she
said as if Wheezer could give her an answer.

Wheezer looked up at her, then turned his head in
the direction that the coyote had run through the grass
when he left. Sasa looked too, and following the sight line
of where Wheezer was gazing, she walked the few yards to
the beginning of the tall grass. Glancing back at Wheezer,
she knew he was telling her something, for he was now
standing stiff, his short tail straight up and quivering in the
fading moonlight, his ears perked and his mouth in an open
smile. She turned around to look closer at the area. It was
harder to see in the shadows of the moon on the grass, but
finally she saw where the grass had been parted.

Turning back to Wheezer she said, "I see. You have a
helper. I have never heard of the Creator sending a helper
for the helper, but who am I to argue. *Wado* (Thank you)
my dear friend."

Sasa walked back to Jackson where he stood over
the body.

"The light is beginning to fade, Jackson, the moon
will set soon," she said.

She bent over the body, looking closer at his hair, his facial features and his hands, too. Then she startled Jackson with her quick gasp.

"What is it Sasa, do you know him?" said Jackson.

Sasa thought of the piece of cloth she held in her pocket. It had been almost impossible to see what color it was, but the feel of the material made her think of a uniform.

"I do not know him, Jackson, but I see something important. He has light eyes. I can't say in this fading light what color the eyes are, but they are not dark like mine. That means that this man is not all Indian. And, this material, I would almost bet you that when we get back, we will see it is that same dark blue the soldiers wear at the fort," said Sasa, as she then moved to the feet. After a moment, she stood and faced Jackson.

"Jackson, this Indian may not be Cherokee, but I am not sure. He has a Cherokee hunting shirt that is true, but his moccasins are of the Osage, which is very strange. As you already know, the Cherokee and the Osage are more at war with each other than in peace, no matter how many treaties the government makes them sign. This is a great puzzle," said Sasa.

"You know, Sasa, I have lived around the Cherokee all my life, my best friend and partner is a full-blood Cherokee, but I still have trouble telling one tribe from another when it comes to clothing. Are you sure about what you are seeing?" asked Jackson.

"Yes, I am very sure. I cannot tell you if the man is part Osage, part Cherokee, or maybe of some other tribe that the government has moved into Indian Territory. He could have gotten these clothes anywhere. I hate to ask you to do this, Jackson, but would you please raise his shirt and lower his leggings for me? His breech clout will cover where I don't want to see," said Sasa.

"I am not sure this is the type of thing that a young lady should look at, Sasa," said Jackson. He could feel the warmth creeping up his cheeks at the thoughts he was thinking.

"Don't worry, Jackson, I have seen the bodies of men and boys. I helped to bury them on the Trail whenever they would let us. Plus, there are several ceremonies I have been to where it is necessary. And anyway, we don't swim in our deer skins. The boys just strip off and jump in while the women are bathing. We Cherokee do not look at our bodies the way the White Man does. We do not look at them as dirty things to be hidden," answered Sasa.

Totally embarrassed now, Jackson could not accomplish an answer, and quietly did as she asked. He watched as she took her time looking, however, the lowering moon would only allow so much. When she nodded to him that she was done, Jackson redressed the man, his hands moving quickly, but as he adjusted the man's shirt, Jackson discovered a pouch hanging around his neck. He quickly removed the pouch, but did not try to open it until he had more light. Just as he finished, Arch had arrived with the wagon and one of the hands.

"I did not see any other scars or tattooing. I thought if he had a clan symbol tattooed on him somewhere, I could tell you more. But, I did find this folded piece of paper. I was in a small pouch trapped around his waist underneath his clothes. I can't read it, the light is not strong enough for that, but other than that, I can't tell you anymore. I am sorry I could not help you, Jackson," said Sasa.

Jackson took the folded paper and tucked it into his shirt pocket to read later.

"You have already helped, although I shiver to think about the things you have seen. I think you may be more adult than child; I am sorry you had to grow up so fast,

69

Sasa. At any rate, it's going to be a long night, I'm afraid, and you still have school tomorrow," said Jackson, as they loaded the dead man into the wagon.

Sasa stood back as the wagon pulled away with the men walking along side, quietly talking about who it might be. In a few moments, she and Wheezer were alone.

Looking down at Wheezer she said, "Show me where your friend went, Wheezer."

Wheezer dutifully turned and lead down the path of broken grass that Sasa had seen earlier. She walked at a slow pace, looking at the grass for anything that would give her a clue to Wheezer's helper. She needed to know if she were looking for a man or an animal. As they passed by a dead leafless bush, Sasa happened to notice something on a branch, white in the moonlight. She bent and retrieved it, "This is a tuft of fur, Wheezer. But, I don't think this is rabbit fur. No! This is undeniably something much bigger."

Sasa stuffed the fur into the small pouch she carried around her neck and headed back to the house with Wheezer following along. Wheezer occasionally turned to gaze behind them, but there was nothing there to see. At one point Wheezer stopped to look, and the hair down his back began to stand up as he emitted his low warning growl.

Sasa crouched to the ground quickly and waited silently while Wheezer made sure there was no danger. It must have passed because Wheezer again turned and lead the way home. Later, Sasa would remember that episode, and considered that it had been her first warning.

When she arrived back at the ranch, Jackson was sitting on the front porch waiting for her.

"Ah, Sasa. I wanted to talk to you a moment," said Jackson, as he patted the seat next to him.

Sasa took a leap onto the porch and settled herself on the wooden chair, turned to Jackson with expectant eyes, which he could see now from the lighted lamp sitting next to him on a table.

"Arch and I discussed it, and we want you to go on to bed. You have school in the morning, and there is not much more you can tell us tonight. We plan on checking with some of the Indians that work near the fort tomorrow before we send for Medicine Man. He is getting on up in years; I hate to drag him over here if we don't have to. In the meantime, I don't want you to worry. This was probably the result of a fight. It could have been another Indian, as well as, a white man, so we won't make any assumptions until we know who he is."

"That is fine, Jackson, I am a little tired anyway. I will go to bed now if you will say a prayer to the Creator to help us find out who this man is. The Creator already knows, so he can guide us. Do not worry, Jackson, I will be fine," said Sasa.

With that, Sasa went to her room with Wheezer at her heels, to sleep the few hours left to her before dawn.

Chapter 7

Many hundreds of miles away in Massachusetts and many months earlier in a place called the Boston Harrison Club, wealthy and influential men sat to read or doze, even play a game of billiards. People of the female persuasion, where expressly not allowed in beyond the receiving room at the front. Past those stately and large solid oak doors, no woman had even had a glimpse. If any woman had been able to get past those formidable barriers of masculinity, she would first be aware of an unusual aroma, something of oiled wood, cigars, the dark redolence of aged leather, and a preponderance of men's cologne. Then she would notice the dark atmosphere, the rooms purposely shaded with heavy drapes, only allowing the smallest amount of light to invade. Upon arriving fully into the innermost chambers, she would at once notice the majority of chairs occupied by mostly aging men, paper in their laps, heads bowed, and snoring softly (or not so softly as the case may be). Next to their chair would be the remnant of some excellent brandy or the best whiskey money could buy, waiting for him to awaken and finish off the last dram.

The members would gather at most any time of the day, in fact, they could even spend the night in stately rooms kept just for this purpose. Or they might take a respite from their activities of their day just to sit, read their newspapers, doze quietly in their chairs or discuss politics. This was no small thing since it was an election year. Martin Van Buren, a democrat, had presided as President of the United States during the most alarming depression of the economy in the history of the young republic, beginning in 1837. President Van Buren, although having his hands full trying to help the country get back on its feet and deal with the relocation of the Indians, a task that President Andrew Jackson happily set into motion, was faced with a particularly virile opponent in the person of William Henry Harrison of the Whig party. The club was immensely devoted to their Whig Party, and so Harrison had become "their man". This was going to be such a close race that the younger members of the club had taken to inventing campaign songs. Even now a group of young men were gathered around the piano in the music room of the club singing the newest of the little ditties. This one being set to the melody of Yankee Doodle, they sang in lusty voices:

Wheezer and the Shy Coyote

The Hero Farmer is the man
The Buckeye boys delight in;
He'll renovate our State affairs,
And be the man for fighting.

Hero Farmer, boys hurrah,
Log cabins and hard cider;
We'll sing and vote for Harrison,
And make our circle wider.

Vans call him Granny Petticoats;
We do not care for this, sir;
He'll rid the nation of such rogues,
A Granny then he is, sir.

Hero Farmer, boys hurrah,
Log cabins and hard cider;
We'll sing and vote for Harrison,
And make our circle wider.

Let Matty come with all his host,
And office holding crew, sir;
We'll march up to the ballot-box,
And show that we are true, sir.

Hero Farmer, boys hurrah,
Log cabins and hard cider;
We'll sing and vote for Harrison,
And make our circle wider.

We'll wager now a cider cup,
And bring it on the table;
Since Yankee boys have started up,
To beat them we are able.

Hero Farmer, boys hurrah,
Log cabins and hard cider;
We'll sing and vote for Harrison,
And make our circle wider.

Columbia's freedom is assailed;
The people still are brothers;
The Government has nearly failed,
It must be worked by others.

Hero Farmer, boys hurrah,
Log cabins and hard cider;
We'll sing and vote for Harrison,
And make our circle wider.

Let's work and sing and vote like men,
By industry we thrive, sir;
And thus the drones at Washington,
We'll scout quite from the hive, sir.

Hero Farmer, boys hurrah,
Log cabins and hard cider;
We'll sing and vote for Harrison,
And make our circle wider.

Eventually another group of singers would form for yet another new song, and commandeer the piano seat to deliver their song to all those within ear shot while laughing most heartily.

It was here that Mr. Andrew Halley sat, hoping to have a few quiet moments before going back to his Boston financial office, but no such quiet was to be had. He replaced his reading glasses into their case, absently combed his middle-aged fingers through his graying hair, and softly sighed.

Andrew had had more than a difficult time in the last couple of years. Not only did he have to contend with the worst economy ever in United State history, but he had lost a sizable fortune when Andrew Jackson decided to throw caution to the winds and force the Cherokee to be removed off of their rightful lands. Halley's Financial had backed many Cherokee businesses and agricultural ventures for many years. Many had been able to pay their loans off and were making an increasingly sizable profit. At the time of the forced removal, those businesses had been producing much more corn, cotton, wheat, wool and beef than their white neighbors did. Andrew was beginning to show an extremely nice profit himself with new ventures being taken up by the various Cherokee families every year. However, his business had almost folded, so great were his losses. The Cherokee were driven from their farms and businesses, and not allowed to take anything of value with them. As far as the government was concerned, his legal investments meant nothing and he had no claim to anything from the sale of those improved properties. Land that had been worked cleared and farmed by the industrious Cherokee.

It was only by his quick thinking that he was able to save his company. He had closed several offices and now operated out of only a few, two of which were still doing well. One in Boston, where his wife and family still lived, and then one in St. Louis, which he had opened two years ago, spending much of his time personally guiding them to financial health. The sad part that Andrew regretted most keenly was the fact that his son, Jackson Halley had had to part with the company in order to lift the burden of his salary and set off on his own. Jackson seemed to be doing remarkably well so far. He partnered with his best friend Archibald Flint, and many of Flint's family joined the company, agreeing to make a new life in Arkansas, just a few miles from Indian Territory. He missed Jackson sorely.

Andrew folded his paper, giving up on trying to read it. Taking out his pipe and tobacco pouch he sadly shook his head as he stuffed his pipe full of the aromatic shag tobacco he favored from the South.

"They certainly are loud, sir. I could not hear myself think and gave up trying to read as well," said Mr. Henry Neugent sitting next to Andrew, each in a comfy tufted leather chair.

It was well that they sat in close proximity to each other for they still had to speak with raised voices to be heard by the other.

Mr. Neugent, or rather Neugent Brothers are builders of public buildings and bridges, and a few extravagantly large homes. His brothers had branched off into other ventures, leaving the building company to Henry. It was a fortuitous thing that he had made his fortune before the depression hit the market and happily he had made uncommonly wise investments or he would be in dire straits now.

"The noise is bothersome, but I suppose that the young must have their fun. But I don't find so much delight in this election. I am not enthused enough to bother voting," said Andrew.

Mr. Neugent was horrified. His short, stubby legs stiffened and his short stubby fingers flexed into fat balled fists, but he sat speechless since he had never met a free white man who did not want to vote. It was sacrilege not to vote, after all it was what the country was founded for.

Finally, he was able to moderate his temper some. "Sir, I am quite taken aback by your sentiment. It is our duty to choose a President, sir," said Mr. Neugent.

"Oh, I am afraid that I am a bit tainted. I spent many years loaning money to any number of ventures throughout the new republic, it is what my family and business have been devoted to since before the Revolution. All of it almost came for naught last year when I almost lost everything I owned, simply for some agenda concocted by the person occupying the Presidential seat. Are you aware, sir, that some of the oldest settlers of this continent are without any rights whatsoever?" asked Andrew.

"Of what people are you referring to, sir? I know of no such group. We are all free men here, the best country in the world," said Mr. Neugent.

"No, I would not say that, sir, not all of our country's citizens are free, and a large portion of them are not given the right to vote. It hardly seems fair to me if a group of people are not allowed to choose the person who would make the laws that they must live by," said Andrew as he lit and puffed on his pipe until he saw a neat red glow coming from the bowl.

"You have me intrigued sir, pray tell me of this group you say can't vote, although I hope you are not talking about the vote for women issue. I can't bear to think what would happen to the country should they get the vote. I also am aware of the desire to free the Negroes, which might not be a bad idea, but they would have a lot of catching up to do before they could vote. Most are terribly uneducated, actually on purpose. In the South, it is against the law to teach a Negro to read and write. Oh do pardon my going on like that, do continue," said Mr. Neugent.

"No, sir, I am speaking of the peoples who had occupied this entire continent before we came. I am speaking of the Native Indians. Especially the civilized tribes," said Andrew as he watched the color rise in his acquaintance's face and his bushy brown eyebrows shooting high on his forehead.

"I am at a loss, sir, to understand your position. The Indians can't read or write so how can they participate in our government?" replied Mr. Neugent, thinking his answer an exceedingly clever one indeed.

"Mr. Neugent, are you aware that many states have huge numbers of voters who cannot read or write, and yet they are allowed to vote? That is not a good excuse. As for this particular group I am speaking of, that of the Cherokee sir, the majority of them can read and write in their own language, and many in English, which is better than some of the immigrants coming over on ships every day can do. They have their own democratic government, that is, before the government swept them all away into Indian Territory, out of sight and out of mind," said Andrew, a bit despondently.

"I was not aware of this, sir. It seems you have a valid point. What a different idea that is, it just never had occurred to me. Are there other things these people are being denied? I mean, they should have reaped some reward for their land when they sold it to the government," said Mr. Neugent.

Andrew chuckled most unkindly, then said, "The government did not buy their land. That is a great myth the public wants to believe. Their land was stolen from them by a government who went against their own highest court in the land. Andrew Jackson thumbed his nose at the Supreme Court and removed them by force at the cost of the lives of over four thousand of them as they walked to a land nobody wants. Then last year they lost another thousand or so because the government's right hand doesn't know what its left hand is doing."

"Why, that is horrendous!," shouted Mr. Neugent while the startled other club members looked on with disdain and the singers at the piano momentarily stopped their caterwauling. He then continued more quietly, "I had no idea, why I thought the Cherokee had gotten a pretty fair shake. And here all along it was exactly the opposite."

"I'm a bit confused, Mr. Neugent. Have you not noticed the news articles about that ungodly march? It has been the talk of the east for some time. I am extremely surprised you were not aware of it," replied Andrew.

"I must admit, sir, that I lack a certain amount of interest in the goings on of politics and such with the exception of one subject. I have had my hands somewhat full these days with trying to help any candidate vying for the Presidency who will support abolition. I am totally against slavery, and I'm looking to form some type of association of like-minded men. It will take a mighty load of pressure to bring a political hot potato of a subject like freeing the slaves to bear upon the public. For that, we need a man who believes in it heart and soul. That is what I am about, sir," said Mr. Neugent.

"That truly is a noble cause Mr. Neugent, but I am afraid that my business, my family and my feelings are all tied up with trying to help the Cherokee. In fact, I plan on going out there to visit some of the new towns they have formed and see if my financial assets can be used to help some of my former good clients restart. I am not in a position to put as much in as I once did since the economy went to Hades in a hand basket, but I'm sure I can do some good. My son has a ranch not too far from where I am headed, he lives in Van Buren, Arkansas. He supplies mules to the Army posts on the frontier," said Andrew.

Andrew watched as Mr. Neugent sat with his eyes wide open, gazing off into the distance even though he was in a room with no windows. Obviously, something Andrew had said was now chiming a far off bell within Mr. Neugent's soul.

Andrew knew only a few men who had the funds to do whatever they pleased, for whomever they pleased and he guessed Mr. Neugent was one of those men. The depression had no hold on him, so vast was his fortune, but he was not a man who would twitter away his money on pleasure. No, Mr. Henry Neugent was a man who enjoyed making things happen, watching things grow, knowing he had a part in making it come to pass. So, it was logical that Andrew would make his next suggestion to this wealthy philanthropic.

"Mr. Neugent, would you like to make that trip with me? That way you can see it with your own eyes and not have to depend on what the newspapers have to say, which is often slanted at best and totally fabricated at worst. I would not mind the company, although we will first need to divert to St. Louis, then we can make our way dow...." Andrew was stopped in mid speech by the astounded look on Mr. Neugent's face. "Sir, are you well? Is something the matter?"

It took a moment or two for Mr. Neugent to recover from his astonishment. "Mr. Halley, sir, I would deem it a privilege to attend you on this trip of yours. I.....I have never been west, and it has always been a bit of a dream of mine, to see the frontier before I die. And here you are offering me the trip of my lifetime. Certainly, sir, I will come and maybe during the trip we can further discuss the ills of the world and its remedies." Neugent said with a hearty laugh.

"I must say, however, that the majority of the trip will be on horseback. Are you able to ride? I mean ride, all day, every day and then sleep on the ground in a bedroll?" asked Andrew.

"You see before you a middle-aged man, sir, but I am fit as a fiddle. I have been this same stocky size the whole of my adult life and what you see that looks like an old man's fat is actually bulk muscle. I was raised by strict Calvinists, and although we were not poor, they believed that a body could not please God well unless that body worked hard and sacrificed the sweat of one's brow. I may be built like a proverbial stump, sir, but I am solid as one as well," replied Neugent while hitting his abdomen with his fists to the exasperation of the other men in the room trying to read their papers.

"Then it is settled. We will need to go over what you should bring in your kit, as well as what items for defense you will need. No one ventures onto the frontier without a gun and a good skinning knife. Part of the trip will be an easy travel on riverboat and some on a flatboat going up the Missouri. However, we will be traveling down through parts of Missouri, Kansas and Indian Territory on horseback before we arrive at my son's ranch in Arkansas. And there is no telling who or what we will run into. There are any number of problems we might encounter. I will be most happy to have you. On the way, I will tell you more about my son's extraordinary experiences on the frontier, just in the last year," said Andrew. "Oh, and, by the way, we will be picking up a travel companion in St. Louis. I am expected to deliver her to my son in Van Buren, safe and sound."

"A female? On a trip like this? Why, sir, it is just not appropriate for a lady to travel with two men. I am sure we will be the talk of the country before long," said Mr. Neugent.

"Oh, don't worry. I have not actually met her yet, but I am told she is amazing. She is used to the, uh, "hunting life" back in England, and I shall deliver her myself. Now, Mr. Neugent, sir, please do calm yourself. I shan't tell you who she is or why I am taking her down, but suffice it to say that she will be a welcome addition to my son's household. I absolutely promise you that nary a person will give it a second thought. You will meet her at the same time that I do. I am going to let this be a pleasant surprise for us both," answered Andrew.

Mr. Neugent thought for a moment and then his springy eyebrows shot up in complete consternation.

"For your son's household? He has not bought a wife, has he? Why that is slavery just the same Mr. Halley. I would not be caught dead helping such a transaction," said Mr. Neugent.

While Mr. Neugent was loudly tut tutting, while Andrew was beginning to enjoy himself immensely, and soon was pulling his crumpled white hanky from the breast pocket of his coat to wipe away the tears from the high laughter flushing his face.

"Please, please, Mr. Neugent. It is nothing of the kind. I assure you that this is quite proper and above board. You will laugh when you look back on the words of your diatribe this day sir. I promise you, you will be happy to be entrusted with this important delivery. In fact, I will volunteer this; it will be a small moment in the history of the United States. Now, how is that for a puzzle. Come on, man! You are headed west, to the frontier. The possibilities are endless," replied Andrew.

The mention of the trip west seemed to assuage Mr. Neugent's fears. He smiled, making crinkle lines fold along the sides of his bumpy nose and on his white forehead.

"Very well, sir. I will place my trust with you. Everything I know about you is that you have the reputation of being a supremely upright individual, so I shall keep my counsel until you prove otherwise," said Mr. Neugent.

"You may not know this Mr. Neugent, but I am not a betting man, but I will make a wager with you. If you don't have the most exciting time of your life going to the frontier, I'll shave my head. Even though my hair is silver, I really don't relish losing any of it. Ha, ha," chuckled Andrew. "If I win, then I will have you kiss the young miss we are escorting."

They shook hands on the bet as Mr. Neugent bloomed a deep red.

Chapter 8

Mornings were always a blessing to Sasa. From the moment she opened her eyes, she found comfort and love. This morning was no different, except today Sasa did not wake on her own. She had been dreaming of the drums her people were playing. There they were, dancing in the setting sun, just warming up for a dance that would last late into the night. She could see across the circle from her was her father at the big drum, beating a steady rhythm, just one of several drummers for the dance. In the circle were the women of the village slowly stepping to the beat, their bodies swaying, the fringes on their shawls and dresses swayed with them too. And there, also in the circle, but doing his own dance, was her little brother, Usti Yansa. How proud she was of her family, and how handsome her people were. There was a strangeness to it, though, she could not understand. No matter how hard she tried she could not see her family clearly, as if there were some gauzy mesh between them.

Something kept tickling her nose. She rubbed it, but the tickle would not stop and the more she rubbed her nose, the dimmer the sight of her family became until finally the dance, the drums, the people and her family vanished. She opened her eyes and met another set of deep brown eyes staring back at her. Her nose was being tickled by Wheezer's whiskers, the same whiskers that were so unusual. Wheezer's face was divided somewhat, mostly brown on one side and mostly white on the other. The side that was brown had all white whiskers growing out, and the side of his muzzle that was white had black whiskers growing out. They were perfect whiskers in every way, long and shiny. That was why she named him a secret name, only meant for them. She called him White Black Whiskers, but only at important, confidential times.

He was so close to her face, she could feel his hot breath on her skin.

"Oh, it is you. Thank you for waking me, today is going to be a special day," she said still lying there stroking Wheezer's head.

Seeing that she was awake, Wheezer smiled and gave Sasa a morning face cleaning.

After her morning wash from Wheezer, which she would have to wash off later, she sat up in bed which triggered Wheezer's pee pee dance. That is what Sasa called his jumping to the floor and turning in circles until she got up to let him out; she had closed her window when they returned the night before.

She set about her morning toilet. It would take longer today as she wanted to look just right for Anna. There is so much more to being a white woman, *she thought.* It takes much more time to get ready in the morning. They seem to have different clothes for different times of day and these people will sometimes change their clothes before they will eat their evening meal, even if it is just the family.

Sasa had thought she knew how to eat with a fork and knife, but she soon learned that she only knew the most rudimentary customs the whites used before, during and after their meals. Thinking about the day Miss Edwards showed her the order in which the eating utensils must be laid on the table and then which fork must be used first and so on. It was all fascinating to her, almost like trying to learn a new language. She would have to master it all if she were going to be able to be accepted among the whites, at least the ones that mattered to the fate of her people. Well, today she would put some of what she had already learned to the test.

"Jackson, may I speak with you?" asked Sasa after she had knocked softly on Jackson's study door.

Jackson sat at his desk next to the south facing window. This day he was dressed in his skins, handmade for him by Mrs. Flint, Arch's mother. Mrs. Flint agreed to come and live in Arkansas when her son asked her to move with him before the forced march happened but only on one condition. She refused to live off of her son, so she asked for a job to do. Jackson had known Mrs. Flint for many years because Arch was his best friend from boyhood, and he knew that she was well known for her skill at tanning and making deerskin shirts, leggings and moccasins. He gladly gave her the job of making those items they would need as time went on and as garments wore out. Arch and Jackson would hunt for deer, providing meat for the entire company. They would slaughter it carefully so Mrs. Flint could have the full benefit of the hides with as few holes as possible. He also paid her a wage, which she never spent, but squirreled away for some unknown emergency, and if anybody said anything about it, she would always say, "Remember The Trail Where They Cried", and that would be the end of the discussion. Arch had said that his mother probably did that after seeing the pitiful state her people were in by the time they arrived in Indian Territory. The prominent, wealthy Cherokee did not suffer the same fate, since they had the funds to make their trip more comfortable. She did not want to be caught as the Cherokee Nation had, decimated, starving and depressed.

Jackson wore the skins when he hunted and sometimes when he went into town. When he worked in the barns, mucking out stalls or breaking a young mule to saddle, he wore his stiff and indestructible dungarees.

"Sure, I am not doing anything in particular at the moment. I have just been trying to write down all the facts as we know them, about the man we found last night in the field. I plan on informing Captain Stuart at the fort and see what he thinks we ought to do before we bury the poor soul. Since we are not sure what tribe he is from, I think it might be important that we do some investigating about him first. I think he might have family around that could shed some light on what happened to him," replied Jackson. "I have him down in the root cellar, laying on top of the big covered blocks of pond ice we have stored down there."

The image in Sasa's mind made her shiver. Today she was due in town at Anna's for another class, this time on reading. She was a little apprehensive, first because of

87

what they had discovered last night and second because today she would wear an outfit that Miss Anna sent over for her. It was special to Sasa because it was the outfit of an adult white woman. It was practical, not fancy, but still of extremely nice cloth and cut. Sasa was amazed at her image in the mirror once she tried it on. The skirt was smooth from waist to floor in a very good twill, dyed lavender with a small pocket on the right side. The blouse was white and felt soft, it slid through her fingers when she fondled it. Never had she felt anything so smooth. She also wore the accepted undergarments of a white woman, complete with petticoat, bloomers, stockings and the high button shoes with heels. The shoes were a bit trying to get used to. Miss Anna said that a corset was not yet needed, whatever that meant. After putting on the clothes, she did her best imitation of Miss Anna's pulled-back hair. Sasa decided that Miss Anna would have to show her the secret, for hers looked nothing like Anna's. The last thing she did was to put the scrap of cloth they found in the dead man's hand, in the small pocket of her new skirt.

Sasa stepped through the door so that Jackson would be able to see the new look for his Cherokee ward.

"What's this? Is this the same young Cherokee girl I saw this morning at breakfast? Goodness what a shock. Sasa, I must confess, I have always thought of you as a young girl and here you are before me, a grown woman," said Jackson.

"Miss Anna sent them to me. I can change if you don't approve of them," said Sasa.

"No, no. They are fine, really fine. You look, oh I don't know, so grown up and proper. How do you feel in them?" asked Jackson.

"I am honored that Miss Anna would send me such expensive gifts. I am not sure I am a woman yet, but I suppose that if I am going to learn the way of the whites, I should try to dress like a white woman. However, in my heart I will always be Cherokee," said Sasa.

"Of course, Sasa. I would not have it any other way. But, I know Miss Anna has a reason for having you wear these white woman's things. I'll bet she will explain it to you when you go. Is that what you will be wearing today for school?" asked Jackson.

"Yes, and that is why I am here. I need to ask your permission to allow Wheezer to accompany me when I go over to Miss Anna's for school," said Sasa as she twisted the handkerchief she held in her hand.

Jackson noticed the tension in her and thought there was a hidden meaning in the request. He said, "Sasa, you have been going over all this time without him tagging along, why do you need him now?"

"Oh, Jackson. I have not wanted to worry you. After what happened last night, I think I might need him. Sometimes, the men from the fort yell things at me. Sometimes they are mean things, but lately they have been yelling things they want to do with me. I am beginning to sense that I am in danger somehow. I would just feel better, if Wheezer was along. He will mind me, I know he will, and Miss Anna loves him so she won't mind for him to lie down inside her front door.

Sasa was unsure how much she should say to Jackson. Regardless of the fact that he had come to her rescue more times than she could count, there was something that told her there were parts of her life, as a woman and a Cherokee, which Jackson would never understand. It would not be for the lack of trying on his part, she was sure he would do anything within his power to help her, but this was something he would never be able to accomplish completely; for she had the weight of centuries of countless generations in her blood that determined her place in the world, among her own people, and among the whites. She could not put it into words, it was something she just knew. Still, she needed to learn to trust him with some of her life. After all, he was her guardian and a committed friend, who would undoubtedly encounter problems within his own race for the choices he made concerning making her his ward.

Jackson looked ready to explode; she could see it plain on his face.

"Now Sasa, you tell me the truth, has any of those men touched you, Sasa? You must tell me. Has anyone threatened you?" an overwrought Jackson asked.

Jackson's face was suffused with concern and fear. Something, it seemed to Sasa, brought out a dread within his soul and now threatened to choke him. She had not expected this violent of a reaction.

"Not exactly, Jackson. Just some, you know, suggestions. It was the way they said it, plus the whistles. But, it was not like the way they yell at the fancy women of the town when they walk around. The men admire those women, for some reason I don't understand. When they call to me, there is menace in it that makes me afraid. I would feel much better if Wheezer came with me on my trips," said Sasa.

"Now that you have told me, I insist on it, of course, Sasa," said Jackson, a more than a little bit shaken. "I will write a note to Miss Anna and make sure she is aware of the problem. Maybe, she should come to meet you at the dock from now on. It never occurred to me that those men might be rude to you and I think your idea is a very good one, Sasa," Jackson agreed, but she could see he still worried.

Then a second thought occurred to him, "In fact

Sasa, I am going to invite her over for Sunday dinner this week. I am planning on going into town later today and I will deliver the invitation. But Sasa, I need to ask you not to say anything about the dead man for a while. Not even to Miss Edwards, until we know what we are dealing with."

"Yes, Jackson. I will say nothing," said Sasa. Then, with her new school attire on, she wandered outside to call for Wheezer.

Chapter 9

Coyote had managed so far, to avoid meeting anyone on his journey. Taking his flute along to serenade the sky with the songs his mother taught him, he was able to keep himself company. Even in this early spring weather, the further south he traveled, the dryer and warmer it became. Some days, instead of riding his beautiful horse, he trotted at a goodly pace, since he could see no one for a great distance in all directions. Other days he had to be more cautions; if he saw a hunting party of some plains tribe just over the knoll, he skillfully retreated and navigated around the unwanted meeting. He seldom saw anyone and he had yet to see any white people at all.

The plains seemed to stretch on forever, and Coyote wondered if maybe there were actually no end to it, but gradually, the landscape finally began to change. First, rocky outcrops appeared more numerous and then the land began rolling away like some enormous river sending swell after swell, pushing the earth's crust up as it flowed. Coyote smiled to himself thinking how funny it was watching a sea of grass rolling along as fluid as the Big River, the one the whites called "Missouri".

On a cloudless day, the sky was a brilliant robin's egg blue and the swaying of the green, tall grass underneath it made him sleepy as he rode. Spring was growing warmer, so summer would not be far off, but it was hard to tell on this endless prairie. Coyote had been born and raised on the grasslands of the northern plains, but at least he had the Big River and its tributaries to break up the monotony of the scenery. Along the river, there were all sorts of plant and animal life to observe, so one never felt bored.

Alternating riding and walking, day after long day, the journey lost the flavor of adventure and soon enough it became hard to remember just how many days it had been since he left his mother's camp behind. Most nights he was able to build a small fire using dried buffalo dung for fuel and green willow sticks to roast one of the rabbits that were so plentiful on the prairie this time of year. In this spring season, water was not a problem. The rains came frequently in short bursts, and left quite enough water for Coyote and his horse to quench their thirsts.

He would sometimes find a small stream that was practically invisible, barely making a path through the tall grass, and Coyote would take the polished gourd, tucked into the parfleche that hung across the back and sides of the horse, and filled it with the clear water. Most of these streams were fed by springs which erupted on the vast prairie, seemingly coming from nowhere and then disappearing just as stealthily. Since the lid of the gourd had been cut from its own top at a slant, the water rarely spilled out.

It had been an excellent day, and Coyote felt that the prairie sparkled. It had rained the day before which made the morning dew especially heavy. When the sun came up over the horizon that day, the dew drops on each blade of grass sparkled as if dancing with delight. It had turned out to be a soft, peaceful evening, as well. He looked up to gaze at the expanse of the indigo blue sky above. The stars were just beginning to sparkle and show their positions. Forgets Things had spent much time showing Coyote how to tell the direction on the prairie by the location of the stars, it was one of the ways he depended to guide him upon on this journey. The Shaman also said that the stars contained the spirits of their ancestors, looking down on their families and either being pleased or not pleased. But Coyote's logical mind was sure that the stars were something else entirely. Someday, he would find out what their purpose actually was.

For now, his eyes traced the location of the now friendly companions in the sky, and as his gaze dropped further south to the horizon he saw what, at first, looked like a star, but flickering in a way he had never seen before. The longer he looked, the more he felt he was not looking at a star at all. Realization that he was seeing another encampment some way south of him made him feel exposed, for there is little on the prairie to hide behind. He had not started a fire of his own yet and now would not do so. Instead, he decided to make his way closer to that camp and investigate what sort of people these were.

He led his horse slowly across the prairie, then found a shrub to tie the beast to while he crept closer. He could not afford to bring the horse closer to the camp. Horses are highly social creatures, and if the other camp also had horses, it was possible his might whinny in greeting, thereby alerting the other camp of his presence. Having all the training of a warrior he knew that there might be a sentry further out from the camp, so he looked for a grassy knoll near the camp, for that would be the most likely place for the lookout to position himself. Thankfully there were three small hills, but only one on which a lookout perched. He chose the hill furthest from the sentry, and crawled through the grass to reach it unnoticed. From this vantage point, he could look down on the camp to see what sort of people these were.

It looked like a hunting party, but Coyote could not identify their tribe from their clothing. From his place of concealment on the grassy hill, he could barely hear their conversation. As soon as he quieted himself, he was able to concentrate. However, it was all in vain because their language was different, much different from his. He watched for some time and noticed when one of the warriors stood, that he was fairly tall, well-built and clean. Yes, clean, which struck him as odd. His experience with his own people made him wonder because, in his village, it was hard to keep clothes, skin and hair well-kept and clean. For one thing, the winds that never stopped blowing on the endless prairie carried dust, bits of sand, twigs, leaves and sometimes seeds, bits and pieces from the surrounding grass. By the end of a day, he could not remember ever looking clean.

Engaged in thought, he was late in becoming aware of a slight rustle of the tall grass behind him, and before he could turn, he heard the whir of a club coming down swiftly against the back of his head, and the world went dark. But oddly enough, for a little bit of time he could still hear the sounds going on around him and then that too faded into nothingness.

The first time he awoke, he could barely make out the sounds around him. He was lying on his back, that he did know, but whether he was prisoner or not, he could not tell. Sounds of laughter, the crackling of the nearby fire and a woman's voice saying something low and soothing even though he could not understand her, were swirling around him. Soon his vision faded to black again, and when next he came to, things were a little clearer. He could see he was now in the camp of those he had been spying on, and he had been rolled on to his side while someone was applying a compress to the back of his head. As soon as his captors saw that he was awake, the leader was notified. Rough hands grabbed him and sat him up which brought about a pounding in his head that was almost so loud he could not hear anything else. He ducked his head to get away from the pounding pain, but to no avail. A horn cup of willow bark tea was given him, and he drank greedily.

The leader, for Coyote assumed him to be just that, came and sat in front of him. He had that look when a man has the authority and confidence. The man wore no shirt, but his arms and chest were painted with thin red stripes. His head was shaved except for a topknot, and that was covered with a headdress called a roach, made of long porcupine quills that stood on end, that then draped down the back of his head. Coyote had worn such a headdress himself during dances and festive occasions. The roach the warrior wore was dyed red, and the sharp, pointed tips were black. Coyote could not help but stare at this man. He wore much jewelry including earrings—something unknown in his village— made of a shiny white metal he had never seen before. A red woolen blanket was worn around

96

his waist and over one arm. His muscular arms wore several armbands made of the same shiny white metal. At his waist hung a hatchet and as he approached Coyote he carried a spear, but did not threaten him with it. Instead, he just sat, waiting for Coyote to speak, he supposed.

The man spoke, and Coyote thought he recognized some of the words, or at least some of the leader's words had a similar sound to his own language, however, he still had no idea what the man had said. Fortunately, Coyote knew the trade side language that all tribes in the North American Continent knew how to use. The words were limited, but adequate to get a point across.

"My name is Coyote, and I come from many moons north from this land. I am only a traveler," Coyote signed.

Recognition bloomed on the man's face. He immediately began to reply in sign, but spoke the words in unison.

"My name is Satta Wapoke (Five Owls) of the Wazhazhe (Osage). We are a hunting party. Why were you hiding and looking down on us?" said Five Owls.

Coyote began to realize he might be in serious danger if he answered in the wrong way. Five Owls was peering at him with narrowed eyes, watching for an untruth.

"I was only curious. My journey has been long and lonely. I am on a quest, but do not know of what. I saw your fire and only wanted to see who was close to me on the prairie. As you see, I carry no weapon," said Coyote.

Five Owls breathed a sigh of relief and made a quick sign to his men. They quickly cut his bonds. Five Owls motioned and a woman appeared with a bowl with fresh buffalo hump meat in a broth with edible plants from the prairie. It smelled wonderful. The men were patient while he ate. Then they settled down around the fire for some conversation.

"You are lucky my warriors did not kill you right off. You are not from any of the tribes in Indian Territory, I can see that. What is your tribe?" said Five Owls.

Coyote visibly stiffened while fear crept into his face, but there was no way to deceive these men. He had never been a skilled liar.

"I was born of two warring tribes. I am Blackfoot and Lakota Sioux. My village could not accept me, so the Shaman prepared me to make a quest to see what the Creator has in mind for me. I am traveling south until I find what the Creator wishes me to learn," said Coyote.

Five Owls smiled for the first time, nodded his head once and continued.

"You are the first Lakota Sioux or Blackfoot I have met. Our people call the plains people the "Wild Indians". It might be interesting for you to travel with us as we continue our journey home into Indian Territory," said Five Owls.

"Indian Territory? You said that before, but I really don't understand what that is. Is it a town?" said Coyote.

All of the men laughed at him and he sat there waiting for an answer.

"The government of the white man has conquered many tribes, including ours. They have made the tribes live in certain areas with very little room between us. We are right next to enemies of ours, and they are next to their enemies on their other sides, as well. We are trying to learn the white man's way, but it is most difficult. The land they sold to us is almost worthless for growing anything on. Even though we are not farmers, we would try it, but the ground is extremely dry and hard with lots of rocks. They call this land Indian Territory, and it is a place of great sorrow.

"Many in our tribe are dying. There is nothing for them to eat. The white man government is supposed to give us food, but there are greedy men who keep what they are supposed to give to us. We have lost a great many warriors and their families. That is why we are here on this prairie. This is not Indian Territory, but here is where we might find some buffalo to take back to our families. This trip we killed two and we are bringing the meat back to our town. If we were found doing this thing, we would be killed. But we cannot stand by and watch as our wives and children grow weak and sickly," said Five Owls.

"This thing you speak of is very strange to me. I cannot believe that all of the tribes have fallen victim and are pushed out of their homelands. I would like to see this place you call Indian Territory," said Coyote.

"I would be happy to have you come with us. My scouts found your horse back on the prairie, so we will be able to go in the morning," said Five Owls.

Coyote did not know if he were a prisoner or a guest, but the opportunity to go and see this "Indian Territory" Five Owls mentioned was too interesting to pass up. Still, he could not imagine the conquering of so many tribes. Why did they not all band together and fight the white men off? It was a complete puzzle to him. He would ask Five Owls more questions as they traveled.

It was strange to Coyote that his fear of Five Owls had vanished. They seemed to have a common interest. Five Owls took on the position of teacher and Coyote gladly bowed to his authority. Because Five Owls always spoke the words he was signing, Coyote was able to learn some of the basics of the Osage tongue. Soon he was able to slip a word here and there into his speech, which gave Five Owls occasion to grin. Later, when Coyote looked back at this part of his journey, he would wonder how he escaped being killed by the fierce men of the Wazhazhe, but was also glad that he had made a friend of the powerful leader, Satta Wapoke. When and if he rode back to his people in the north, he would make the opportunity to visit Five Owls' village, even if he had to divert many suns to do so.

Chapter 10

Wheezer found an unexpected pleasure on this magnificent early summer morning. Instead of having to stay at home, watching Sasa walk towards the river, then cross and not be back until late in the afternoon, he was being allowed to accompany her. He looked up at Sasa as they walked along, him with a huge grin on his face, eyes dancing and ears perked up with the tops flopped over, and Sasa in her new clothes, walking more like a lady than she ever had before. She occasionally stumbled, seemingly over nothing. Wheezer could see the new shoes but could not fathom the reason for them. That was one of the things he did not try to understand. It just was not important to him, and it did not affect his love for Sasa in the slightest. Humans just did strange things like putting on shoes and clothes.

They walked together, the sun up just a little way in the sky. Wheezer could smell the new grass and plants; also he picked up the scents of animals and people too. None were particularly recent, so there was no reason to be on alert. There was now a well-worn path that Sasa had made by her several times weekly treks to Fort Smith, so there was no need to worry about looking for a good way to get where they were going. Wheezer spotted a jackrabbit, its immense erect ears sticking up so high they almost protruded over the tips of the tall grasses. Wheezer gave chase, knowing he would not catch it, but the run was fun. Especially seeing the rump of the rabbit scurrying away. The rabbit did not run at full speed. He supposed that the rabbit was just as inclined to play as he was. Hearing Sasa's soft call brought him back beside her.

They reached a protected area where a sloping ridge blocked the view of the river, and it was here that Sasa had to stop to refasten one of the buttons on her shoes. Wheezer sat waiting for her to finish, but kept a vigilant eye on their surroundings. Wheezer's gaze raked across an area of last year's stand of dead grass and there, low to the ground, perfectly still, and unblinking, was the coyote. Wheezer's tail stopped its incessant wagging but stood straight up and quivered. Sasa saw the change immediately and even though she was in her white woman's clothes she spontaneously went into a crouch.

Coyote did not move, did not react in any way.

"Woof, woof," said Wheezer in an undertone.

Sasa followed Wheezer's gaze. She knew by the almost silent woof that the danger was minimal and that he wanted her to stand still and look, the same way that he was doing. She lifted her head to peer into the grasses that surrounded them and there against the small ridge, in the dead grasses was Wheezer's helper, the coyote, staring back at them with his luminous yellow eyes. Oddly enough, she felt no fear at seeing the wild coyote so close, only a friendly encouragement emanated from his eyes.

"Ahhhh," said Sasa, "I see now. This is your animal helper Wheezer. So, I finally get to meet you Mr. Coyote. You have been a good friend to Wheezer who is also my friend."

Sasa purposely put her hand on the top of Wheezer's head while speaking to send the message of their relationship. The coyote quickly absorbed the intent and lowered his head to his paws. Something no coyote would do if on the alert against a threat.

Wheezer casually walked over to the coyote, and he rose and stepped forward, partially revealing his beautiful tan with black tips coat. He made the usual greeting, and once they both were satisfied with each other's scent, Wheezer came to the coyote's head, stuck his long snout into the coyote's ear and gave it a thorough cleaning. The coyote stood perfectly still, its eyes on Sasa while Wheezer did the other ear and then trotted back to where Sasa waited.

"Oh, you are well acquainted. Thank you for being Wheezer's friend and helper. But I can't just go around calling you the coyote. There are lots of them around. So I will give you a Cherokee name. You are now Dalonige Digatoli, or Yellow Eyes, brother of Wheezer. You are welcome to come to our house when you want to, and I will tell Jackson of my promise to you and of your naming. *Wado*, Yellow Eyes for introducing yourself. I hope we will be friends, too, said Sasa as she looked deep into Yellow Eyes' return gaze. We must hurry, or we will be late for school, *donadagohái*, that is Cherokee for goodbye.

Wheezer wagged his tail, gave Sasa a wet kiss on her cheek before continuing along the worn path. He had been this way a few times, just to see where Sasa went walking so often. She did not go this way every day, but often enough to make him curious. Soon, the path began to descend gradually, and after rounding a rocky outcrop, there stood the Arkansas River directly ahead. Wheezer had never been across it and did not understand how it was done. He saw the ferry go across several times, but the concept escaped his abilities. He did not have any experiences to draw from, so it remained a mystery to him. It looked like today he would go with Sasa and for the first time see how the humans managed to get across this wide river.

They came to the water's edge, but the ferry was not yet moored at the dock. Wheezer was pacing, yapping and panting. His excitement was building so Sasa told him to sit. He obliged her, but it was darn hard to do. While they waited, some men in blue army uniforms were sitting on barrels near the loading ramp of the dock. They had noticed her, and Wheezer also noticed them.

"Well, what have we here boys? Ain't that the squaw girl that comes over ta Fort Smith ta get schooled by that Miss Edwards a-waitin' over there? Let's say we just mosey on over there an' see if she is the friendly sort," said one of the soldiers.

Sasa stiffened and looked behind her to check her avenue of retreat, but the men were at her side before she had a moment to react.

"We been a-waitin' fur ya. We knowd you be comin' this way most days. Now little squaw, I reckon ya might like to have us some fun a-fore ya go over tah other side. Bruce here is new to the fort, but me, I'm Tom, and this here's Johnny, we been here a long time and we seen ya coming over reg'lar enough," said Tom.

Sasa's jaw clenched she stoically looked at the river, hoping for the ferry to hurry. She refused to look at the men, and when one touched her shoulder, she jerked her body away.

"Seems to me boys, this little squaw don't know her place. See, she's dressed in white woman's clothes. Well, I guess that Mr. Halley has been training her for more n just a maid," Tom said, then hawked up a brown mass of chewing tobacco and spit it at Sasa's new shoes hitting one of them on the toe.

"Please, leave me alone. I haven't done anything to you. Let me be on my way, and there won't be any trouble," pleaded Sasa.

Wheezer stood between the men and Sasa curiously unnoticed but emitting a low growl. He could smell the grimy sweat on the soldier's clothes, the mule excrement on his boots, and one other scent that only male animals exuded during courtship.

"Naw, I think we arta have some fun first, now ya just come on over here behind the barrels and... " said Tom, who had placed his grimy hand on Sasa's arm, but was interrupted by the lightning quick flash of white fur and teeth that bit into Tom's arm and ripped away part of his blue uniform sleeve as Tom threw him off. Wheezer did not lunge again but stood firm emitting a fierce growl and bark.

The men jumped back some but did not leave. Wheezer placed himself in front of Sasa and gave the men the full view of his alligator-like canines, ears flat against the head and tail sticking straight back. He lifted his front paw in preparation for another lunge and waited.

"What in tar-nation? Ya can't do that to the United State Army, and missy, ya shouldn't be goin' around town with a mean animal like that," said Tom as he rubbed his wrist where Wheezer's teeth marks showed but had not broken through the skin.

"Look Tom, why don't we get on over tah the fort and forget about this squaw. That dog could-a ripped your arm clean off," said Bruce.

Sasa took the chance of giving a warning, "Yes he could, and maybe he might succeed if you don't leave me alone. I do not want your company and Wheezer has taken an extreme dislike to you. So I think you better back off. If you try to bother me again, I will let Wheezer have at you, besides talking to the commander at the fort," said Sasa.

The men just stood there, not liking being bested by a dog and a redskin, but at the moment there was no options open to them. Wheezer began to smell the fear on them.

"Well, missy, you just bought yourself a whole heap of trouble. If'n ya think the commander is goin' to listen to a good for nothin' squaw, ya got a surprise a-commin'. One of these days or nights, you mightn't be so cocky. You just keep that in mind, an' next time, be a little friendlier," said Tom.

"I have no intention of being friendly with you men. It is not proper behavior, and I am not one of them Fancy women like in town," answered Sasa.

"No? You're just a dirty injun. Ya have no business telling a white man what he can or can't do. The sooner ya figger that out the better. You're just an animal, not even human, so ya better learn how things go around here," shouted Tom as Bruce and Johnny were backing away from the situation, trying to get as far from the trouble as possible.

Tom was still standing his ground and made another grab at Sasa while kicking Wheezer in the ribs. Wheezer rolled and clearly had a hard time getting his breath. Tom had gained Sasa's arm and was dragging her over to the big barrels. "I should'a never bothered a-talkin' to her," he mumbled as he kept pulling Sasa closer and closer to the barrels.

Sasa was frantic. She knew if he got her concealed behind all the shipping crates and barrels, there would be no one to see what they would do to her.

"Let go of me. You've hurt Wheezer. Let go or I'll...," cried Sasa.

"Or you'll what?" growled Tom.

The soldier had Sasa almost to the barrels, a sickening grin on his unshaven face. He was so sure of his quarry that he forgot to look back past Sasa when he was grabbed by clenching teeth at the elbow and another at the knee. First Tom howled at the pain, letting go of Sasa, and then noticed he had Wheezer at his leg, but what looked like a full grown coyote hanging off his arm, his mouth full of teeth looking like the gates of doom itself.

The coyote's eyes looked straight into Tom's and gave him the message of his deadly intent. Tom screamed in utter terror as blood dripped to the ground. The man flopped and turned, but no matter which way he gyrated, the coyote and the dog still hung on. He tried lifting his leg, and Wheezer dangled in midair, his jaw locked, his teeth firmly fastened on the pants and the flesh underneath. Tom could feel the skin tearing as he squirmed. The coyote's jaws were like a steel vice, grinding the cartilage of his elbow into mush, and he was sure that a demon had him.

"Okay Wheezer and Yellow Eyes, let go, let go now boys," commanded Sasa.

In unison, the two canines let go of the soldier and the momentum from him pulling to get free sent him tumbling backwards off the dock and plopping into the water of the Arkansas.

"This ain't over, squaw. One of these times I'm gonna' teach you real good," threatened Tom from the river.

Sasa bent down and stroked Wheezer, and for the first time in her life, she placed her hand on top of the head of a real coyote, Yellow Eyes, then she patted lightly and said, "*Wado*". Satisfied with the acknowledgment from Sasa, Yellow Eyes turned and ran back into the grass and vanished. It was a little while before Wheezer could respond for he never took his eyes off of the soldier until he was utterly out of sight. Sniffing around the dock, he picked something up in his mouth and brought it over to her. It was part of the soldier's shirt cuff, but Sasa knew that it was also something else. She quickly pulled out the piece of cloth in her pocket to compare them. Finding them exactly the same, she now knew that the dead man was trying to tell them something. He was trying to tell them that his attacker was wearing an army uniform. This time she would show both pieces of cloth to Jackson before dinner.

She worried about Tom telling about Yellow Eyes and getting a bunch of men to hunt him down. After thinking about it, she realized no one would believe him. The chances of a coyote coming to the rescue of a human or even just coming into the open where humans were was next to zero. By the time she had dusted off her dress and straightened her hair, the ferry arrived at the dock. She also thought that these white woman's clothes were decidedly inconvenient. There was no place to carry her Green River knife. If she had had the knife, the men would not have gotten so far. Sasa and Wheezer boarded the ferry. The man minding the tiller had not seemed to hear the fight on the dock before he reached it with his flatboat. Sasa began to wonder. Would anyone have done anything to help her, if they had seen what was happening? The question thought unsettled her.

Wheezer now knew why he was to accompany Sasa to school, and he also knew he had help. His helper would not cower in the bushes when his friend was in peril, and that drew him closer to Yellow Eyes.

Chapter 11

"I swear Sergeant. It was a real live coyote. See, it ripped my sleeve an' coulda' kilt me. We need to get a huntin' party up an' kill it. Bruce and Johnny saw it, I think," said Tom.

Tom had made his way to the infirmary to get his arm stitched up and his knee bandaged. He had never had that much damage done to him, all in just a few seconds, in his whole life. He was clearly scared of the animal that caused all the mess, but he had a hard time explaining just where the coyote had come from.

"Private, I have no intention of do'n any such a thing. If'n I go to the captain with this story, he would laugh me outa the Army. And I want you men to keep clear from that squaw girl from the Halley's. That man has some pretty high connections and I know for a fact that he rooted out that bad Indian Agent over at one of the last camps in Indian Territory. That kind of man is a snooper. If'n he gets a whiff of anything going on over here, especially when it comes to that Indian girl, he would be over here right quick, like a fly on stink, making himself down right worrisome," replied Sergeant Willis. "And Tom, you gonna' have to pay out from you month's pay for a new Army issue shirt."

"But Sergeant, ain't you upset that she treated a white man like she done?" asked Tom, as he fumed at having to pay for the damage the squaw caused.

"Normally, we would have had a right good time of teach'n her a lesson she wouldn't forget, but I got bigger fish to fry right now. So you boys just simmer down, or I will clap you in irons and throw the key in the Arkansas," said Sergeant Willis.

Tom reluctantly agreed, but the desire to do some damage to that snooty redskin still burned like a raging fire in him. He had no intention of forgetting it, but he could wait. The day would come when he would have the upper hand and then that squaw would be fixed for sure. He had had his eye on her for a while now, times when she wasn't lookin', even private times. But the way she had acted when he was being real nice, well, a squaw shouldn't get away with it, and he knew a couple of great ways to change her mind right fast. Before he did anything, though, he would have to do some plannin' so that her mutt would be out of the way.

I just don't know. Maybe I didn't see a coyote. Maybe it was just that one dog, he thought. And if that was true, then he could handle that.

* * * * *

109

Sergeant Willis busied himself with camp business, what there was of it. These days he and his men were relegated as "go-fetchers" for the contracted help the Captain hired back east. None of his men had any skills that would allow them to do any real building onto the fort, but even so, it rankled the men to have to fetch and carry for a bunch of Yankees they didn't even know and could hardly understand.

There was a contingent of troops of about thirty men at the fort right now. They had had more, but Captain Belknap, over at Fort Gibson, requisitioned a squad of about ten to relocate over the line of Indian Territory, about seventy miles to the northwest. That just made his job even harder. By the time his boys were finished for the day helping the builders, they almost had no gumption left to haul whiskey across the river. But, Willis made sure it was worth their while since their Army pay for a Private was only about twenty-two dollars a month and smuggling for Willis made them almost that in a week. So his men had the incentives, and he didn't worry about any malcontents among them either, because when he got one that didn't want to play along with his "distribution" efforts, he made sure they knew that their lives would be in danger if they told anyone about the arrangements at Fort Smith.

But, I am worried, *he thought*. The Captain has been makin' it his business to try and stop the trafficking of whiskey to the redskins and even though I know them orders have come down from the higher command, but that don't mean he has to be so darn religious about it. Heck, the government arta be given us a commendation for the fine work we're a-doin'. The drunker those fool redskins stay, the better to control them, and if they just happen to drink themselves to death or get caught in a knife fight with one of their own over a jug, why that should be extra gravy. But that Captain Stuart is just a low down boot-licker. He'd do anything a-tall to get a promotion, and this here building project is the only thing a-keepin' him assigned here. If'n we had Captain Belknap back here instead of him having to go on to Fort Gibson, this Whiskey thing would be even easier since that man was always so busy, he rarely noticed what his men did on their off hours.

But Sergeant Willis knew he was not the last step on this gravy boat ladder. There was one more step up, and Willis wanted to keep relations with that man at an even keel. Nothing frightened Willis except possibly being found out, but one thing petrified him, and that was making the man at the top mad. He could lose his Army career, and that was not such a bad problem., because Willis had enough saved back from this venture he could retire in comfort in Mexico. But, he knew he could lose his life if the man at the top so deemed it necessary and that is what Willis was determined to not let happen. He was careful to keep his nose out of the man's business. The less Willis knew about him the better.

It was hard, though, *he thought,* seein' the man almost every other day around town. No one knows him like they think they do, and Willis knew the man was considered one of the founding fathers of the newly named town of Fort Smith, so it was not too likely anyone would discover what kind of a man they actually had in their company. Willis had seen him kill a redskin without blinking an eye and just left him lying on the ground just the other night. Cold-hearted and mean as a rattle snake.

Yes, Willis would do his best not to cross this man, ever.

Chapter 12

"Captain Belknap, I am at your disposal," said Captain John Stuart when Captain William Goldsmith Belknap entered his office.

"I'm not here for long Toby, I have to get back to Fort Gibson by tomorrow. You know it sure is darned inconvenient to be the Commandant over two forts seventy miles apart. But, I guess they could not find a Major willing to come out to the frontier, just to supervise a building project," said Captain Belknap as he sat down in the Captain Wall burg's chair.

112

The Captain's comment made Stuart grimace at the slight of his usefulness at Fort Smith, plus using his given name instead of his rank, which was the same as Belknap's, was a way of demoting him.

"Army Headquarters told me, they had to have someone familiar with building things and hiring labor, supervising their work and able to read plans and such," replied Captain Stuart.

"Well, I don't know. This project must be done, I understand that, but I am spread too thin. I have a lot of things on my plate what with keeping the Cherokee and the Osages from tearing each other up. I also have the Creeks, the Choctaws, Chickasaw and the Seminole that we are responsible to resupply. Not to mention the problem with the whiskey trade. I can't seem to get a handle on it. Just when I think I have corked the bottle, we spring another leak. There are endless ways to slip away from our troops and dragoons, and these whiskey peddlers seem to know every back trail in the district. We have tried to blockade the Arkansas River, but the way the laws are written, our Army has no jurisdiction over anything going up and down on our waterways. So that means we have to catch them before they get to the river or when they are disembarking. I am here now to try to coordinate our efforts to stop this illegal trade. I hope I can have your cooperation," said Captain Belknap.

Captain Stuart was not prepared to talk about whiskey right now. He had stone mason's waiting for his instructions on laying the foundation of one of the buildings. And then he had the woodcutters ready to grab logs out of the Arkansas River, which was a slow and dangerous job. Once on shore, the logs would be taken to their new saw mill to be cut into lumber for the buildings. There was so much happening here, there just was no time to sit and listen to Belknap. True, Belknap had jurisdiction over everything that transpired at Fort Smith, even though he was, the majority of the time, over at Fort Gibson, so he had every right to be here and Stuart was forced to sit and listen because his assignment was to build the new fort. Stuart had tried to stop the sale of whiskey. And it chapped his hide to have to admit that he had failed miserably.

Fort Smith actually backed up against Indian Territory, so an Indian could actually buy whiskey and step over the line and there was absolutely nothing Stuart could do about it. And who did he have to thank for that? Congress, of course. The real problem was that there were several self-serving congressmen and their cronies who had their own ideas about how to deal with the Indians. It did not take a genius to see that even though the Army was taxed with the enforcement of preventing the sale of whiskey to the Indians, Congress made laws that hamstrung them from doing their job. Most of congress did not have an inkling of what was going on in Indian Territory. They had other, more important worries. First was the current presidential election heating up in Washington City and added to that was the controversy over slavery. So most of them could not wrap their minds around something going on so far away. But, that left the road wide open for some scheming, greedy bounders to get their way with the votes in congress.

"Toby, are you listing to me? I swear, I travel all this way, and I can't seem to get your undivided attention," complained Captain Belknap.

"I apologize, Captain Belknap, I am a little preoccupied with all the activities I have going on just now. I truly beg your pardon. Uh, you were saying?" said Stuart.

"I was saying that we need to devise a plan to stop this illicit trade. It seems to me that before the whiskey runners can get over to me, they have got to go through your defenses. Now I know you have filed reports of your efforts, but something is very wrong here Toby. Your men should be catching somebody, and so far they just seem to be marching around, watching the sales as they happen. Do you have any explanation for the lack of arrests at Fort Smith?" asked Captain Belknap.

"Truthfully no. I have no idea how it is happening. The sellers just seem to always give my boys the slip. I have a very competent sergeant by the name of Willis. I'll send for him, and we can discuss why his efforts have not been satisfactory," said Stuart who then turned to an orderly with the order.

Stuart had often wondered the same thing. Unfortunately, his days were so busy trying to build this fort there was just not much time to devote to the whiskey problem. His commission was to build the fort. He had been brought straight from Washington to accomplish just that, and even this task came with its own set of problems with Congress. All of his appropriations had to come from Congress. Those congressmen had no idea how hard it was to get tradesmen from the east to come out here on the frontier. Once, Congress tabled his budget until the next session, and he lost his tradesmen because he could not pay them. Then a few months later, in came the funds and he had no one to build the fort. And they wondered why the construction was going so slow. Each time he lost his tradesmen, he had to make a trip east to advertise for workers and journeymen. That all took time. Then getting them to the frontier took some weeks, too. Add to that the weather and illness among his men, the list of his problems went on and on.

Willis arrived, saluted smartly and waited.

"Sergeant Willis, I understand that you have been placed in charge of organizing your men to stop the trade of whiskey to the Indians," said Captain Belknap.

Willis had a loss for words. This was one of his worst nightmares. He was hoping the commanders would not look his way, but no such luck. He needed to show progress, but he had effectively kept the sellers from getting arrested. Heck, he did business with them on a daily bases, plus he and his men were the biggest venders on the Arkansas. How could he dare show even one arrest without getting found out?

"Well, sir, it's like this, see. We all have been tryin' our very best, but them wily rascals keep givin' us the slip. Why, they seem to knowd the best roads in and outa here pretty well. We just can't seem to get a handle on 'em," replied Sergeant Willis.

"Then, maybe while I am here tonight, we all can sit down and hammer out a plan. I want some progress on this here problem, Sergeant Willis, and something is not right about it," said Belknap.

Captain Stuart stood aside while Captain Belknap discussed things with Sergeant Willis. At first, he paid no attention to their discussion, his thoughts strayed to the things that needed doing on the construction site that day. Eventually, Stuart began to notice the sly way Sergeant Willis evaded Belknap's questions and his indecisive way of not coming to any solid conclusions. Minute by minute, the conversation between the Sergeant and Captain Belknap became more interesting, especially the way that Willis avoided nailing down any course of action. Captain Belknap may not have noticed it, but Willis was manipulating him. He doubted that anything of any solid nature would be decided and that Belknap would leave having failed to put any course into action.

Why would that be? *he wondered.* I have never seen Willis dance around a subject so much since he was caught racing the mules along the Arkansas last year. I can't imagine what has gotten into Willis' head. What is so hard about doubling patrols, catching and arresting some of the whis-key sellers or beginning an investigation as to where the nasty stuff is being brewed? Our stockade should have at least a few unseemly vagabonds resting on its bunks, but in the few months since I have been here, I have yet to see so much as one arrest. Why had I not noticed this before?

As Captain Stuart was thus engaged, there came a rap on the heavy plank door of the captain's office. He looked up from his musings to see a vision of loveliness standing in the doorway.

"Captain Stuart, ah and Captain Belknap, so nice to see you again," said Anna. "If I am interrupting anything, I can come back another time."

"No, no problem," both captains replied in unison.

"Truly, Miss Edwards, we can always spare a moment to greet one of the finest ladies at Fort Smith. Please, please come in, take my chair," said Captain Stuart, "and I will have Willis here order us a spot of tea and some biscuits for a mid-morning repast. Uh, Sergeant Willis, please make your-self available to Captain Belknap as soon as he calls for you, and please ask my orderly to bring in some refreshments on your way out. You are dismissed, Sergeant Willis."

"Yes, sir, Captain," said Sergeant Willis, saluting be-fore he exited through the door, wondering what he was missing in this meeting with the Edwards woman.

"This is a very nice surprise Miss Edwards. What brings you to the fort this morning?" asked Captain Stuart.

Anna took her seat and straightened out her full-length pale, pink batiste skirt with horizontal rows of pleats. The day had not yet warmed uncomfortably, so Anna had worn a matching pink velvet short-wasted jacket with a full epaulette collar over puff sleeves and pink pearl buttons down the front and on the sleeves. She carried a gauzy pink linen parasol with pink fringe and when opened it was only big enough to shade her head. Her translucent taupe blond hair was pulled away from her face, but allowed to fall down her back in soft ringlets. Her bonnet was a white muslin with pink trim, and she wore white gloves. The only jewelry she allowed herself were matching pink pearls at her dainty ears. When she entered, the room had filled with the scent of vanilla and ginger. The men seemed to enjoy the interruption.

"I am on an errand of concern gentlemen. I had hoped you could spare a small amount of your time so that I might impart those concerns to you," said Anna with a sincere smile.

"Why, Miss Edwards, you have our utmost attention. Any concern of yours is naturally important to us," said Captain Stuart.

"Gentlemen, as you are probably already aware, I have been engaged by Mr. Jackson Halley of Van Buren, Arkansas to educate his ward, Sasa Halley," said Anna.

However, at the mention of Sasa's name a puzzled look came over Captain Belknap's face. Possibly, he was unaware of the arrangement.

"Captain Belknap, you may not be aware that Mr. Jackson Halley the muleteer, has adopted a young girl named Sasa who has lost her entire family last year. I am to educate her so that she might be sent to a proper finishing school for further education," said Anna.

There still appeared some doubt in Captain Belknap's face, so Captain Stuart felt more information was in order.

"Uh, Captain Belknap, Sasa is the young Cherokee girl who Jackson helped last year when Miss Edward's father conspired to rob the food allotments. Mr. Edwards was one of those responsible for a young boy's murder. Sasa was his sister," said Captain Stuart.

When the information finally sunk in, Captain Belknap's face began to look a little feverish.

"Ah, Miss Edwards, I am very sure your teaching abilities are more than adequate for this task, however, don't you think that your time could better be spent with teaching some of our white children in Fort Smith, leaving the teaching of the Indians to the missionaries? Mr. Halley should be encouraged to send the young squaw packing back to her own people across the line. I am sure you will agree that these people cannot hope to attain to the same high standards of scholarship as our white children and therefore, your efforts are being wasted. You were right to come to us for advice," said Captain Belknap.

Anna was nonplussed, but only for the count of three, as long as it took for her to regain her temper.

"Oh, my dear Captains," she began sweetly, "I am so sorry to have worried you in any way. I believe that you have not actually given me time to state my concern for which I came to speak to you. Before, I go on to explain these very serious concerns I would like to make a few things clear," said Anna. At that very moment, the men began to witness an unearthly transformation unfolding before them in the person of Miss Anna Edwards. Where, not five minutes before, a demure sweet and lovely young woman sat across from them, pleading for their help in some way, where now sat a taller, upright woman with a stiff back, a firm line to her lips, a flush on her checks, and steel in her eyes, no not steal, sparks.

"My I begin by saying, sirs, that Sasa would not be without a family now if the War Department and the United States Army had done their jobs adequately in the first place. I happen to know from reports I receive from back east, that the stealing of the food allotments has continued, and at this very moment, the Osage Nation has lost almost half of their number for want of food, and that within the last six months, the Cherokee have lost over one thousand of their number, from starvation alone. Am I wrong, sirs, in the assumption that the United States agreed by treaty to feed these people you have trapped in Indian Territory, and that, by law, you should be holding up your side of the bargain?

"So before you expound on your own petty prejudices of what you think I should or should not be doing, I suggest that you get control of your own people and pay attention to your own duty," Anna replied.

"My dear Miss Edwards, I believe you have overstepped your bounds, ma'am. You can have no knowledge of what is or is not in our treaties with the Indians, and even if you did, it is not your place to counsel us," said an upset Captain Belknap while Captain Stuart sat stunned into silence.

"Gentlemen, you underestimate me, and I daresay women in general. I can and do know of what I speak. Women may not have any say-so in government affairs including the right to vote, but I have a close cousin who is secretary to the Governor of Massachusetts, sir. Of course, nothing he has told me is a secret and can be read in the papers by any literate person who desires to know the facts of our governmental agreements. Is it possible, captains, that the army is hoping for our Native Nations to fade away by starvation? Is this a policy of genocide?" accused Anna.

Captain Belknap began to splutter, and Captain Stuart became scarlet faced just thinking about the accusations, but both were afraid to say another word, for it seemed no matter what they said, the woman was able to turn the tables on them.

"Now, if you gentlemen are through telling me what I should be doing with my time and who I should teach, I will now discuss what it is I came here for," said Anna calmly.

Captain Belknap coughed a few times, then cleared his throat while Captain Stuart struggled with something other than anger. When Anna took a second look at him, she could plainly see that he had begun to laugh. First a chuckle under his breath and then he became unable to control it.

"I surrender, dear lady, I capitulate entirely. Please forgive our transgressions, we should have never ventured to discuss your own private affairs without your consent. But, on the matter of genocide, I would like to say that I am totally unaware of any such mandate by the United States Army or any other branch of our government. That said, please do us the favor of telling us, what can we do for you Miss Edwards," said Captain Stuart with the leftover glow of a smile on his handsome face.

"Very well, I shall continue. This morning while Sasa was coming to the river to cross over on the ferry for our study, she was accosted by two of your men. They very nearly dragged her behind some barrels for God know what. I want to stipulate here, sirs, that Sasa is a very good and upright Cherokee girl. She was instrumental in solving the conspiracy that my father was sadly a part of, and she also was responsible for the return of a large sum of money stolen from the United States Government. She and her dog Wheezer should be getting your heartfelt thanks and your protection as well," said Anna.

"What, you say? This happened here, at this fort? I – I am stunned, ma'am. I can say that I am familiar with this young girl's deeds, although I confess I have not ever met her, but she certainly does not deserve ill treatment. Who were these soldiers and how, might I ask, did she get away from them?" asked Captain Stuart.

"She did not know their names except what they called each other. The main culprit's name was Tom, but that may not have been his real name. Thankfully she had Wheezer, Jackson Halley's Jack Russell Terrier with her. He made it very clear he would not hesitate to take a good bit of flesh off of anyone trying to hurt her. In fact, Wheezer managed to succeed in that, to the sorrow of one of the soldiers. But, she should not have to go through this sort of thing. I am telling you now, I expect you to get a handle on those men, if you ever expect our little town to be a safe place to raise a family in the future. I have no intention of stopping my teaching of Sasa. Someday she will be a help to her people and to the United States Government," said Anna.

"But, Miss Edwards, we can't watch our men every moment. We live on the frontier. The men are used to... you know... getting their way with the squaws," said Captain Belknap.

"Do you honestly expect me to believe that every Indian woman they have relations with has gone willingly? Because if that is what you believe, you are sadly mistaken and blind to boot. Rape, sirs, rape, pure and simple, is what your men are used to. The army has the upper hand and the men take what they want, when they want. Even on the removal march, the army's men were guilty of murder, killing babies and old people that could not keep up, and rape, as well. You know it happened, and I know it happened. Just because, you did not catch them in the act because you were looking the other way, does not mean it did not happen. There were too many witnesses, even white ones.

"Captains, let me make myself clear. Either you stop your men from doing anything to harm Sasa, or any other Indian girl who comes to town, or I will personally send a report to my cousin who will in turn give it to the governor. At the same time, I will also send the report to the newspapers back East. My father may have been a scoundrel, gentlemen, but my mother's family are very highly placed in society and there is no telling where that report might go," finished Anna.

Captain Stuart pondered a moment, trying to think of ways to curtail his soldiers from this very common activity. Serving at an outpost on the frontier was a lonely job for an enlisted soldier. However, he had never stopped to consider if the squaws participated willingly. In fact, he had never thought of a squaw as having morals of any kind, even though many claimed to be Christians.

"Well... I suppose all we can do is comply, ma'am. I will call a meeting with all the company as well as the builders and lay out a proper punishment. I hope it will put a stop to it," said Captain Stuart, while Captain Belknap sat sullen faced and insulted.

Temporarily mollified, Anna took her leave, leaving the Captains to decide how to best accomplish her request. Earlier that morning, Sasa had arrived visibly shaken, with Wheezer at her heels. The narrow escape with the soldiers was going to make it difficult for her to come to Fort Smith for her lessons. Anna did not have any faith in the command at the fort to be able to control its men. So, maybe now would be the time for Anna and Jackson to put their heads together and rethink how Sasa would continue to get her lessons.

There were only a few short streets between her and her cabin. Anna leisurely walked while considering her conversation with the Captains, analyzing every word they had uttered. She wanted to be able to describe the complete scene to Jackson when they met to discuss it.

Rounding a corner of the dusty dirt street she came up short, a man blocking her path. It had not occurred to her to be weary of the criminal element while in broad daylight. The man did not have on a uniform, but for some reason, she thought of the army personnel the moment she looked at him. There was nothing about him that was unusual except that he was clean shaven under a trimmed mustachio. That alone said that this man was not one of the town's inhabitants. Many of them had not had a bath in six months if ever. No, this man must be a soldier in civilian clothes.

"Excuse me, sir," said Anna as she tried to pass, however, the man refused to turn aside.

"I said excuse me, sir. Please allow me to pass," she repeated, but the man continued to stand in her way and stare.

Then with a smirk on his otherwise featureless face, he said, "I believe, I got Miss Anna Edwards a-fore me. You don't need to know my name, but I got a message for you."

"And what would that message be, sir?" said Anna.

The man stepped forward and took hold of Anna's arm in an iron grip.

"The message is that you need to stay outa' the goins on of the soldiers and that high-falutin' squaw you're a-teachin'. Them captains don't need any information 'bout that, ya hear?" he said.

Anna knew she had only one chance to get the upper hand. She was being warned to look the other way, and allow Sasa to be molested, however that was something she would never do willingly. In the year that she had lived near Indian Territory, if she had learned nothing else, she did learn to carry protection. Not for protection from the Indians, but from the white men who considered themselves past the reach of law here on the frontier.

"I assume you mean Jackson Halley's ward?" she asked stalling for a little time while she reached into the fold of her skirt where a secret pocket lay, concealing her little Pepper Box hand gun.

Anna looked him in the eye and stepped even closer to him, so close that his breath could be felt on her eyelashes. She said, "Why, sir, I don't believe I know your name. Have we met?"

All the while Anna had brought her little gun out and placed it gently up against the man's midriff. "Oh, now I seem to know who you are, sir. You are the man who is going to get out of my way and leave me alone, or you will have your intestines laying all over the street in about two seconds," she said with her own brand of smirk.

The man looked down quickly and paled at the sight. A Pepper Box hand gun was a lethal thing at close range. The man knew that if she shot, all four of its barrels could explode into his gut, and there would be no putting him back together again. So without further ado he placed both hands in the air and slowly backed away. When he got a few yards away, he turned and ran like his pants were on fire. Anna would have liked to have laughed at the retreating sight, but she was too much aware that this was not the end of the matter.

Just as the man made it out of sight, another man ran up to her side and uttered, "Miss Edwards, are you all right, lassie?" Anna was pleasantly pleased to see Lucius O'Malley, puffing as if he had run extremely hard.

"Dear lady, I saw him grab your arm, but I was too far away to do much. Then, as I ran, I saw the man take himself away, saints preserve us. Are ya all right then? Did the eejit hurt you? Did he threaten you? Did he rob you?" a frantic O'Malley said.

"Why, no Mr. O'Malley. He did not hurt me. I think he had a change of heart once I showed him the friend I carry in my pocket," said Anna as she showed Lucius her petite Allen and Thurber Pepper Box 4 barrel hand gun.

"Well glory be, I never would've guessed it. I am most happy. Why that's grand, that is. Might I be walking you home then?" said Lucius.

"That would be most welcome Mr. O'Malley. I am very glad that you were there, just in case he decided to test my mettle. But, he would have been very sorry. I would not have hesitated if he had taken another step towards me. I do need to go home so that I may write a note to a friend and get it out to him by tonight," said Anna.

"To him? Who might that be, may I ask?" said Lucius.

"Oh, how rude of me, I don't know if you have never met him. He is Mr. Jackson Halley, and he is the guardian of the young Cherokee girl I teach at my home. She also had a near miss of trouble today, and I need to discuss it with him as soon as possible," said Anna.

It was then that Lucius noticed the way Anna was dressed, how the light played on the curls hanging down from her bonnet and the lovely overall pink of her attire. Her perfume had wafted past his nose briefly, and the scent reminded him of Ireland. While she spoke, he tried to listen to her account of what had happened to Sasa, the Cherokee girl, but his emotions were reeling wildly. He thought he had not seen a lovelier lass in all his born days. And yet, he had no idea how to win her affections.

"I see, Miss, that you have a spark to you, and your last name is Edwards. Would you be Irish then?" asked Lucius.

"I suppose it is so, but it would be many generations back to the beginning of colonization when the Edwards fam-

126

ily first came to this continent. I apologize if I seem bold, but being on the frontier has made me so. There is nothing timid about the west, sir, and timid people die here. It is definitely a challenge to change from all the things I was taught about being a lady. There is very little opportunity to use those things here. Although, someday this frontier will be settled and we again will need those gentle, civil and social skills that are needed among a settled people," said Anna.

Lucius and Anna were nearing her house, and he hated for this moment to end. Then a thought came to him.

"Miss Edwards, am I correct that you intend to go to see Mr. Halley sometime soon?" said Lucius.

"Why yes. As soon as he can make time, although it is usually for dinner. If I get my note off today then it may be as early as tomorrow evening when I will head over on the ferry," answered Anna.

"In view of the two incidents, Miss Edwards, might I be escorting you over to Mr. Halley's ranch. It would give me great pleasure, that it would," said Lucius.

Anna did not need any time to think for she was glad of the protection he offered her.

"Yes Mr. O'Malley, I would be honored if you could. I will inform Jackson of your coming so that Masey can have enough food prepared and a room for you. Since the ferry quits running before we have dinner, I usually stay the night. He has plenty of extra rooms in that big house he built. I should know for sure by morning," said Anna.

Lucius took his leave and walked back to his shop on cloud nine, but as soon as he reached his door and turned the key in the lock, he remembered the secret merchants meeting being called for tonight. After such a glorious morning, the thought of that meeting brought him down to earth hard. He knew beyond the shadow of the doubt that a woman like Anna would never want a man who would be involved in breaking the law. Especially after what he had found out about her father and what she thought of him. But, how could he get free from this group of no-gooders? He had to find a way, and there was no two ways about it either.

*****

Anna had finished penning her note to Jackson Halley. She had tried extremely hard not to alarm him concerning Sasa's welfare. Hopefully, they could come to some agreement as to a safer way to proceed.

It was now later in the afternoon, and she knew she must hurry to get the note over to the ferryman before he made his last run. There was no particular schedule Mr. Lancaster, the ferryman at the fort crossing kept, but generally he would stop before nightfall. The river could be treacherous in the dark. There was another to the north going across the river to Van Buren. Since it was more likely that someone would be on the other side from the fort that could deliver her note, she decided to head over there.

After replacing her pink bonnet and she grabbed her parasol and opened her door just in time to see Jackson Halley with his arm upraised to knock. They both jumped back a step and then laughed at the surprise.

"Anna, I am so glad I could catch you before you went out. I need to catch the ferry at the fort before they close up for the day. Would it be an imposition if I asked you to delay your trip for a few minutes so that we can have a chat?" said Jackson with a blissful smile across his face.

"No it wouldn't and yes, you may," chuckled Anna. "I was actually going to the ferry so that I might send a note to you. Now I don't need to go. Here is the note and won't you please come in?"

Anna quickly removed her bonnet, tidied her hair and led Jackson into her small parlor.

"Well, it seems we both had need to speak to the other. My news is rather lengthy so why don't you begin first?" said Jackson.

"I am afraid that mine is as well," said Anna.

They both laughed, breaking the tension of the uncertain moment.

"Well, first I was coming to invite you over for dinner on Sunday after church," said Jackson.

Anna forgot the unpleasantness of the day, sitting here with Jackson. *Why doesn't he come over more often? Am I not attractive to him?* she thought.

Chapter 13

Lucius O'Malley sat at the back of the room at the livery stable, his chair leaning on the rear two legs and his shoulders resting against the log wall. He was bored and unhappy. The smell of the place got in to your nose and stayed, even when you left for fresher air. It clung to a person's clothes and hair. Then add to that, the smell of cheap cigars and a corncob pipe or two and you had a smell that would wake the dead. Why they chose to have these meetings in this godawful place was beyond him.

He hated being there. All the townspeople ever seemed to do was scheme to go against the law. Even

130

though Fort Smith was new as a fresh born babe, there were still rules to abide by. Some of those rules were made by Captain Stuart at the Fort. Lucius knew that many of the town's people didn't put much stock in the man because he had been sent by Congress to build a new fort just a few hundred yards from the old one, but they felt he was building it as slow as molasses, not to mention that he was mandated to stop the sale of Whiskey to the Indians. Relations with the commander and the townspeople were rubbing raw. It was a cat and mouse game with the mouse usually winning, but Lucius was concerned that, once again, he had chosen to be on the wrong side of the battle.

All he wanted to do when he came to America was to start over with a clean slate, and he had almost achieved it until Reardon wheedled the story of his past out of him, claiming to be his friend, but all the while planning on roping him into this hellish unpleasant business. He looked around the room, usually filled with the townspeople whose greed had persuaded them to participate in Whiskey smuggling, but tonight there were only about ten. But for a few of the occupants, the townspeople were utterly lawless; some came to elude the law in the States, and when Arkansas finally became a state, they stayed on, figuring there was not enough law to catch them anyway. Others were here to homestead, but quickly abandoned their allotted land, finding the effort it took to farm was too much of a bother; it was easier to make money by breaking the law, and to lie, cheat or steal, whatever was the quickest.

However, Lucius imagined that there had to be a few that were like him. He hadn't seen the harm in it until he found out what it was doing to the Indian people. There was something in their makeup that made liquor almost like a poison to them. It did not just make them drunk, it made some of them crazy, and most became dependent on it. He could see it was killing those people. It was then that he realized the darker side of their activity. Now, he just wanted out, but Reardon kept making threats to expose his past to the authorities if he didn't play along.

"All right now you B'hoys, settle yourselves down, ya here? We've got a lot of palaverin' ta do tonight so just quieten down," said Private Mathews. "Sergeant Willis and I don't have much time 'fore we gotta' get back 'fore we missed. Now that's a heap better. I been asked to pass on to you'ins that we got us a problem here, and we gotta' make sure this next load of squeezins makes it 'cross the border quick-like this time. Captain Stuart is settin' out patrols on this side of the river most nights, and those patrols are mostly our own boys, so we gotta' be careful."

"Well, them soldiers can't be everywhere all the time, now, can they? Especially when the Captain has them working all day laying stone, chopping down trees and making bricks. How much sleep can they lose anyway?" said Bill Feldon who came from the Ohio River Valley. He ran a saloon down the street.

"Now Bill, we can't get lazy or careless if'in we don't want to get caught. As long as I am a Sergeant on the post, I can work things around some. But, I can't prevent you bein' caught if'in you do somethin' stupid. So we are here tonight to warn you about that, but also we needs to talk about helpin' me keep the old codgers from comin' around and preventin' their tribesmen from buying. I had to show one of 'em what was what the other day. I don't always have time for that. Fact is, I'm surprised the old man lived through it. We just gotta' be more careful cause I don't want no Indian man from the government snooping around here," said Sergeant Willis.

Lucius had decided not to say much of anything, but the subject piqued his interest.

"What's the harm in the old ones coming around might I ask? As sure as I'm in America, I thought they had a great say-so in what happens on their side of the line, do they not? If the whiskey is causing all that much trouble, then I'm say'n that maybe they should be able to say "No" if they are a-wanting to," said Lucius.

Sergeant Willis looked over at Lucius with a cold as steel stare. Lucius felt like the barrel of a cold revolver was pointing straight at his gut.

"Naw, all them Indians deserve to be drunk. In fact, that is the only way the settlers are going to get their land back from across that line. Anyway, all this here land should be for the taking is what I say. Why give it to those red devils in the first place? I had plans of homesteadin', a place all marked out when all of a sudden the government up and decides to move the Arkansas border east and then to give everything west of that line to them redskins. It just ain't right. Gettin'em and keepin'em drunk most of the time will convince those pencil pushers in Washington City that it was a big mistake they made, give'n that land to those redskins. You'll see. We keep going on like we been doin' and low and behold, we will have our country back," said Willis.

So that was it, thought Lucius, it's not just about money, but by the saints they want to take the Indian's land. Lucius knew there had to be more to it than just getting rich. So far though, Willis had not mentioned how they would accomplish the gargantuan task of gaining the land given to them by the United States government by treaty. He knew that Willis was a conniver, but he didn't think he had the brains to pull anything complicated off, and this would be very complicated. The Irish knew all about complicated plans. They'd been fighting the British since before he was

133

born and any headway they had made came from complex planning. There had to be someone else giving the orders.

As Lucius continued to listen, he noticed the gleam in the eyes of all those involved. Greed had gotten hold of them. Lucius' mom had always said greed was a sickness and hard to get cured of. Most times, people never got cured, nor did they much want to. However, he knew that greed was dangerous. It caused a man to do risky things that often got them caught. Lucius pondered the web of lies he had fallen into. None of these people knew the real Lucius O'Malley, the freedom fighter.

These people were not fighting for freedom, though. They were scheming to take what rightfully belonged to the tribes in Indian Territory. They were all forced to give up their own homelands in trade for this barren piece of dry prairie. They had not only paid for it with their homes, they had paid for it with their lives. Every tribe now jammed into Indian Territory had needlessly paid with the blood of their people. Not just the Cherokee, but all of the tribes paid this high price. The land they now were on had been paid for many times over and Lucius thought there was no justice in what he was helping these people do.

He was becoming sick of himself, but he could not work out how to change the course he was on without destroying himself. And after meeting Anna Edwards, he had to face the question, could a gentle woman like Anna fall in love with a man that could do this kind of damage to a helpless people? He already knew the answer to that.

Chapter 14

"Ahh, Andrew my friend. There you are. Did you have a good night?" asked Henry Neugent as he sat on the upper deck of the steamboat.

The trip to St. Louis had been stimulating, at least up to this point. Andrew wondered if Henry was sorry he came, what with the first part of their tedious voyage aboard the cargo ship Timoleon. Generally, it was not all that hard to find passage these days to New Orleans. Western expansion had fired up trade, and New Orleans was sitting in the catbird seat, at the mouth of the Mississippi. However, they had some time constraints that made it necessary to take the first ship going to that southern city. A cargo ship was the first ship ready to set sail, so they bought passage and prepared for a boring voyage. If a person loved sailing, the Timoleon was a marvelous experience with all her sails unfurled while braving the gusty Atlantic winds. But, since it was a cargo ship, its amenities were Spartan with little to break the monotony of the almost three month voyage with stops at various ports along the eastern seaboard. They were welcomed to eat what was provided. Thankfully, they were given time to disembark and buy fresh fruits and vegetables for their own consumption since the galley cook planned the most basic meals for the crew.

Now, though, they were aboard the J.M. White, captained by her namesake, Captain J.M White. One of the first of a new class of steamboat meant to ply the inland waters for passengers. She was fairly new and considered to be one of the fastest ships in existence. The promise was that they would land at the St. Louis levee within ten days. This same steamboat had once been clocked at only four days, but that was with extremely few stops along the way and no passengers.

The ship ran on steam, and it ate wood like candy. The constant sound of steam escaping out of the escarpments, or long oversized pipes standing straight up on both sides of the ship, and the sizzle and popping sounds became the constant background noise. Occasionally, they would stop at a place out in the middle of nowhere to load wood where some enterprising men had traveled into the wilds and staked out a few acres of wooded forest along the great Mississippi and proceeded to cut down the trees, cutting them into five foot long logs, the size needed for the furnace which kept a roaring blaze. At those times, they would power down the boilers, and it was then that a person remembered what life was like without the constant cacophony of sounds. The wood was fed into the huge below decks boilers to keep bringing up the steam pressure again, and the boat would move forward. Without the wood, there would be no travel at all because steamboats had no oars or sails. The captain would bargain with the woodcutters for a good price and then continue on. Usually, they only had to stop for wood once a day.

The difference between the sailing ship and the steamship was absolute. Now they could relax on the upper deck, or engage in a card or billiard game, in the game room. They were treated to excellent food, prepared by chefs, eating in a well-appointed dining room, and the cabins were opulent affairs with high ceilings of molded tin, woodwork of mahogany and the finest of linen on the beds. They chose a cabin with two bedrooms, and it was still large enough to accept a couple people more. Both men were used to fine dining and excellent accommodations on land, but not while traveling on a steamboat. The steamboat passage up the Mississippi to St. Louis would be as relaxing as traveling on a train from Boston to New York.

"Andrew, did you notice the brochure that was left in our cabin? Most unusual. In fact, I cannot put it into words so I will have to read it to you. Ah... Here, it says:

Wooding

A passenger can reduce his fare by wooding on a trip. For instance: A trip from Pittsburgh to St. Louis may only cost two dollars; from St. Louis to Galena, only a dollar. The job of cutting and carrying wood is a hard one. It should be attempted by only those used to hard work. The crew will also need help in scooping animal manure off the deck. Most captains try to clean the deck once each day.

"As a young man, I did my share of cutting wood, and I dare say, I could probably help. What do you think, are you up for a bit of chopping wood?" chuckled Henry.

"Actually, I had planned on it. I frequently use steamboats to travel the rivers after you get out and away from the cities. It is the only mode of travel faster than a flat boat or horse. I have been asked to help cut wood on numerous occasions. I'm not as fast as some of those young whelps, but I can contribute," said Andrew with a grin.

"I have to confess, I am more used to sailing ships and trains than steamboats. This new steamboat ship seems to provide for their first class passengers. See here, this says:

Toilet Facilities
The toilet facilities are vastly improved on the new craft. Some have a washstand and basin in each of the staterooms. However, on the older craft, the two washrooms, one each for ladies and gentlemen, are located near the wheelhouses. Sometimes there are only two washbasins, with one hair brush, a comb, a community toothbrush, and a roller type towel. However, on the better steamers more washroom facilities are provided. The crew keeps the pitchers filled with river water. The toilets are like the outdoor variety. Sometimes they are placed over the paddle wheel, other times they are built next to the wheel."

"Well, that is a first for me. I usually have to bring my own brush and comb. I guess Henry, we can say we traveled in style this trip," said Andrew, "but, that will end when we set out for Indian Territory. Then you will think we are a couple of mountain men. At least this way, you will truly see what the western frontier is all about."

"I am curious, what will St. Louis be like? I have heard so many stories. Some say it's a lawless town, full of fur traders, harlots and gaming saloons. Others say that it is fast becoming a jewel of economic growth for America. I am not sure what to expect," said Henry.

"St. Louis is all of those things and more. I don't mean to scare you, but you will need to watch your step when you are there. I have not been there for a year, and that last time I had been shot and I almost died. Of course, the man that shot me was no ruffian, but a born gentlemen who schemed to defraud the government. I had been gathering clues to the disappearance of the funds for the food allotments given to the Indian nations we relocated, but I had no idea who was behind it. He lured me to a warehouse and shot me point blank, fortunately I had my pocket gun with me and I evened the score.

"Then some of the mountain men, come in with their furs for Pierre Chouteau, the leading fur merchant in the whole of America, are an honorable lot. Many of them are famous in their own right. But, I am sure you will see your share of degradation that comes with a frontier stronghold. There is refinement as well, but most of all, St. Louis is an exciting place. More business is done in one day than you can imagine. It is also where Lewis and Clark set out from in 1804 for their Corp of Discovery for Thomas Jefferson. In fact, General Clark is still there. He is in charge of all of the Indian Territories west of the Mississippi. He says what can and cannot go into that province beyond this great dividing line of water," said Andrew, "and right now one of his biggest problems in the smuggling of whiskey into the west, destined for the fur trading posts. The traders use it two get every last skin and buffalo robe from the Indians. Even in the dead of winter, those traders don't care if a drunk Indian gives his only means of keeping warm and alive through the winter in trade for one cup of his watered down and doctored whiskey. And no matter how tight he makes the net, a goodly supply always gets through. It is sad to see it."

"But, don't the tribes catch on to what the traders are doing?" asked Henry.

"Some do, but a Chief does not have complete control over his people. He can't stop them if they won't listen. There have been losses of whole villages, all frozen to death, after a party with the traders' whiskey. Some are killed by the elements, others die of alcohol poisoning. Some of the fur traders put stuff in the whiskey that will clean out an entire village. They do it on purpose, not just for the robes, but to kill them ruthlessly," said Andrew shaking his head sadly.

"I can't fathom it, Andrew. Has our country lost its mind? Does no one in the east care about the tribes?" asked Henry.

"Some do, but they are grossly outnumbered. Last year, just as the Cherokee removal was at its end, the newspapers that had been writing stories about the cruelties of the forced march and the deaths along the way received so many letters of reproach from their readership that they all pulled out. The people back east just did not want to hear about it. It made their consciences sting, I think, they just don't want to know," replied Andrew.

"I can't imagine it. I think one day, people will be sorry for what they did to all the native tribes. Someday, there will be a price to pay. Maybe we won't see it; however, I am certain it will happen. That last story reminds me of a bunch of ostriches that stick their heads down in holes so they won't see the danger coming. I think that is what this country is doing. It doesn't matter if they refuse to see it, it will still come," warned Henry.

"You may be right Henry, you may be right. All I know to do is to help people like my boy in Van Buren. He does all he can to help his friends, the Cherokee, and he doesn't care who it makes mad either," said Andrew.

Just then, a tall black man in ships uniform strolled by ringing a bell and announcing, "Baton Rouge up ahead. Dock side in one hour. Shore leave of two hours. Last stop befo' Vicksburg."

Andrew wondered at that because he had been told they would have a stop in Natchez. Quickly, he caught up with the porter.

"Aren't we going to stop at Natchez? I was told that Natchez was a regular stop," said Andrew as Henry came up beside him.

"No suh, no suh, we can't dock there. A few days ago, a huge mile wide tornada' come right up dis here riva' and plumb knocked down everythin' in its path for twenty miles or so. Yes, suhree. They says dat hundreds of people has died. Natchez almos' wiped out, an' Vadalia across the riva' too. Hundreds of slaves upriva' on them plantations, all dead. Buildings flat, almos' nothin left. Dat was May 7, 'bout more dan three week now, an dey still don't got no dock fo us to pull up to," said the porter.

"We didn't hear about it. We were at sea on a sailing vessel. This is the first we heard of it. But, won't they need help? Food, blankets, medicines?" asked Andrew truly alarmed at the thought of all the devastation.

"Cap'n say we gonna' bring dat stuff on the way back, an' maybe by den, day have someplace fo' a steamboat to pull up to. Right now, if'n weeks to try dat, we get stuck on all of da sand dat done floated in on dat storm.

141

Cap'n say we gonna' pick up even more den dat. We's gonna' bring back doctors an' nurses, plus a crew ta help bury da dead. If'n ya wants ta reads about it, here is a piece I cut out of the New Orleans Picayune," said the porter as he walked on with his message of the next stop.

The article was a reprint from the Natchez Courier of May 8.

HORRIBLE STORM!—NATCHES IN RUINS!

Our devoted city is in ruins, and we have a heart of stone to detail while the dead remain unburied, and the wounded groan for help. Yesterday, at 1 o'clock while all was peace, and most of our population were at the dining table, a storm burst upon our city and raged for half an hour with most destructive and dreadful power. We look around and see Natchez, yesterday lovely and cheerful Natchez, in ruins, and hundreds of our citizens without a shelter or a pillow. Genius cannot imagine, poetry itself cannot fill up a picture that would match the ruin and distress which everywhere meet the eye.

Twas the voice of the almighty that spoke, and prudence should dictate reverence rather than execration. All have suffered, and all should display the feelings of humanity and the benevolence of religion!

Under the Hill presents a scene of desolation and ruin which sickens the heart and beggars description--all, all, is swept away, and beneath the ruins still lie crushed the bodies of many strangers. It would fill volumes to depict the many escapes and heart rending scenes; one of the most interesting was the rescue of Mrs. Alexander from the ruins of the Steamboat Hotel; she was found greatly injured, with two children in her arms, and they were both dead!

Andrew could not bear to read the rest of the article, and Henry stood open mouthed, thinking about all the things that would be needed to help these people. The article was already a week old, and still a ship could not dock to bring in supplies.

"Andrew, if that is the true size of it, then when we get up to St. Louis, I'm going to get with our ship's captain and see what might be needed in terms of funds. I can help pay for some of the supplies if nothing else. I mean, what else is money for anyway?" said Henry.

"Well Henry, I think that would be a noble gesture. I think I can make some arrangements once we get to my offices in St. Louis. I can order some supplies sent down the river to them, and then maybe on our way back, we can stop at Natchez. I want to see what the businesses there need in the way of loans to get them back on their feet. If the businesses can't begin again, then the whole of the area will suffer the loss. In fact, if the captain will give me enough time, I can make some arrangements right away at any of the banks of Baton Rouge," said Andrew.

They waited on deck so they could see the city of Baton Rouge from the river. Already, they had the experience of coming in the mouth of the Mississippi before they got to New Orleans. Both men had not known that the city was surrounded by dense swampland, but as the boat carefully floated in the center of the river, they were treated to an amazing variety of sight and sound. The sheer enormity of the creatures that made this river their home was astounding and the plant life was so lush and green it was like nothing either one had ever seen. From the colorful birds to the flowers in every imaginable color, and the smell redolent of water, fish, floral perfume and rotting vegetation, they traveled speechless through a fantasy land.

Now the magnificent city was coming into focus as they slowly plied the muddy water. Henry had thought there might be a fanfare for the new vessel that was by far the fastest ever made, but what greeted them was anything but that. The city was alive with activity, and from their distance the people looked like ants scurrying around, too busy to notice another ship readying to dock. One amongst so many, since the wharf for Baton Rouge was crowded with steamboats, keel boats, flatboats and even smaller craft.

The ship pulled into a berth made available by a departing ship. They pulled in smooth and slow, then a long ramp was flung across the void between the ship and the dock and a deck hand jumped to shore to anchor the boat with the huge hawser, attaching it to one of the great pilings sunk into the deep Mississippi mud.

The captain was happy to help, but urged haste and directed Andrew to the largest of the banks, the Bank of Louisiana. After making some arrangements for funds to be sent to the City of Natchez, he went to the Post Office for any mail waiting for him there. Before his trip, Andrew had informed all of his business offices and his son Jackson in Van Buren, Arkansas, of the stops the ship would be making and that he would make a point of checking at each Post Office for anything waiting for his collection. So he was not surprised when there had been a couple of notes from his offices and a letter from his son waiting for his arrival. The notes were only progress reports on projects being funded by his financial company, but the one from Jackson worried him a little. He decided not to open it until he was back on the ship and again plying the muddy waters.

Now in his comfortable cabin and Henry in his room changing for dinner, he sat down by the light of an oil lamp bolted to the wall above the writing desk and opened his son's letter.

Dear Father:

I hope the second part of your trip is going well, and you are in good health after your sea journey. We are all fine and healthy, awaiting your visit most eagerly. We are all happy that you will finally come to Van Buren and see what I have done with my business. I hope you will be pleased with what I have done with my savings thus far.

This letter is not meant to worry you in any way; however, I wanted to inform you of some events that have caused considerable consternation here at the ranch. In late spring, we have noticed a large increase of problems in the town of Fort Smith concerning the sale of illegal spirits to the Indians in Indian Territory. The Captain at the fort, a Captain Stuart, has tried to run down the culprits, but to no avail. It seems that no matter how many of his men he sends out to patrol, they are never able to catch anyone in the act.

In addition, there has just been a murder, perpetrated at the edge of my acreage, and we have yet to understand why or even the identity of the man. As usual, Sasa and Wheezer have been much help in our investigation; in fact, it was Wheezer who found the corpse. I am checking with the only physician available, the one at the fort, but since we can see very well the cause of death, he may not need to check it out.

We believe that the murder has something to do with the illegal sale of whiskey, but we have no way to confirm that suspicion. At the writing of this letter, there have been no new developments.

We read in the paper about the great tornado that destroyed Natchez, Mississippi and so we did not try to leave any messages at their Post Office. If there is anything newsworthy, we will send word to your offices in St. Louis since messages get there fairly fast, sometimes just a week to ten days.

I am not sure why you have chosen to ride down from St. Louis when you could very well take a steamboat from St. Louis on the Mississippi, then take a flatboat up the Arkansas River to the fort. Since I know you to be an exceptionally intelligent man, I am assuming you have your reasons for taking the longer route. With that said, I would ask you to keep your eyes and ears open to anything having to do with the whiskey trade. You will be going through Indian Territory, so you may be able to see things I might not.

On a personal note, I would like to spend a little time speaking with you about Miss Anna Edwards. You may have guessed that I am quite taken with her, but I am unsure if I would be doing her a disservice by making her choose between civilization with its society and gaiety, and life on the frontier, full of hard work and harsh weather. So far, I have not voiced any of these worries with Miss Edwards. I am not even sure if she knows of my feelings towards her. I do not want to do anything that would cause her any grief whatsoever.

One last thing. As you know, Wheezer, or Jack as you knew him, is an exceptional dog. He has an intuitive nature, and if I were not sure, I would believe that he can understand English. He has developed a friendship with another animal, however, we are not sure what. He spends part of his day away from the ranch, playing. I also believe that Sasa is aware of who or what Wheezer has made friends with. What she tells me is hard to believe. She says that she and Wheezer have made friends with a wild coyote which is next to impossible. Arch tells me that Indians, including the Cherokee, have a different view of animals and that Sasa will reveal the identity of Wheezer's playmate when she is sure that Wheezer wishes us to know it. It is my belief that it is this playmate who led Wheezer to find the corpse. I overheard Sasa call it the helper's helper, whatever that means.

Hopefully, many of these things will be resolved before your arrival. Please, take every care while you make your way down to us.

Your loving son.
Jackson

Andrew was subdued during dinner. He knew his son exceedingly well. Jackson would not write unless he was truly troubled. *There must be things happening that he is not telling me, which makes me worry even more,* he thought. Then a smile crept over his face as he reread the portion of the letter concerning Anna Edwards. If he had been there, he would have told Jackson that he was in love with her. It was obvious that she felt the same way as well, for why else would she be living in that horrible town out on the frontier. But Andrew knew that some things are better left alone. Jackson, if he was the man he raised him to be, would find his way eventually.

Chapter 15

In a remote cabin in the backwoods of Fort Smith, the man contemplated his next moves. So far his plan had proceeded well. Each day another Indian was succumbing to the wiles of whiskey, leaving off working on his farm and stealing from his neighbors to pay for more. Sooner or later, the government will rethink their own strategy and take the land away from the dirty redskins. And even though that fop Samuel Edwards, Miss Anna's dead father, was caught with his hand in the cookie jar, and they discovered the man behind him, the skimming of the allotments was still alive and well.

His thing was whiskey, but the starving of the Indians was helping his plan to succeed, because when the braves drank and there was no food coming in from the allotments, then the families starved. The two things worked hand in hand. His goal was to get his land back that was taken to be part of the new Indian Territory. *I don't mind if I get rich while I do it,* he thought.

He knew that his plans could not go on forever. The chance that someone would find out his identity was becoming greater by the day. So far, no one here knew his true identity and he planned on continuing the charade as long as he could. Even that pretend wife he hired had no idea who he actually was. He could not allow anyone to know that he was a high born aristocrat from Ireland and that several countries half a world away were looking for him. The hardest part was trying to speak like an illiterate, uneducated ruffian, but it had to be that way if the disguise were to work.

His next in charge, Sergeant Willis, was not half as smart as he thought he was, but he was willing to do the job and be discreet. The problem now was that Willis had informed him that Captain Stuart and Captain Belknap were both getting tired of not catching anyone selling the whiskey when they knew darn good and well that the Indians weren't getting drunk on thin air. Eventually, they would catch on, and the first person they would look at would be Sergeant Willis. *I am not so sure he would keep my secret if his own neck were on the line,* he mused. Therefore, he needed to think up a new plan to direct suspicion elsewhere. All it would take would be a little gossip and maybe a letter directed to the proper person in Washington and the fat would be in the fire, but was there time. Things seemed to be moving too fast for him to think it through.

Willis is the only one who knows who is in charge, however, even he does not know who he is truly dealing with. All the rest of Fort Smith just looks at him as another struggling merchant with a decidedly unpleasant wife. *Down deep he knew that his only protection was to illuminate any person who got too close to the truth. Thank goodness he had underlings who were willing to kill for money.*

*****

Poison Woman lay on her pallet, looking up through the cracks in the roof of their shack, listening to her brother, Medicine Man, snore. She could see a few twinkling stars glinting down at her and wondered which of her ancestors was signaling her if that was what they were. She wondered when she would be walking the death road. That was something that she and her brother differed on, although they never argued about it. Each accepted the others right to believe in their own way. Medicine Man was a spiritual leader of the People and so, believed in the traditional Cherokee beliefs about death. It was odd how closely the Cherokee teaching about the soul and death resembled the teachings of the missionaries that taught them to be Christians -- only the number of souls a person had was different.

Medicine Man believed that humans have four souls. The first is the soul of conscious life. It is human, not physical and is our thoughts, desires, memory and our conscience and resides in the top of the head. That is why they used to scalp their enemies. It was an attack on their first soul. The Cherokee believe that this first soul animates all the other souls and that when it dies, it stays around for a while.

The second soul is in the liver and when its secretions are black, it can mean death is near. The third soul is in the heart and creates blood; it is circulation itself and is

150

something that all humans and animals have. The fourth and last soul is in the bones and is the last soul to die. Medicine Man had lived by these things all of his life.

Poison Woman, though, listened to the missionaries back in their homeland, and they also talked about the soul, but in a different way. She was not sure if any of it was true, because many of the church people were mean and pressured people to get baptized, sometimes beating them. No, where she got her own ideas were from reading in the Cherokee Holy Bible.

Some of the People believed that when you die that the first soul goes to the Land of the Dead in the West. Some say that it walks down the middle of the river until it goes underground. But which one is true? In all her long life, no one had ever come back to say where they went. And what about other peoples and tribes who believed in different places for the dead? Why would the Creator of all things make so many different places for the dead anyway? She knew she believed in the Creator, for only a stupid person would think all the things in the world were not created.

She never asked her brother to explain about the souls, because he did not know for sure either. She supposed that she would find out eventually. *Logically*, she decided, *if all those souls could come back and tell us, they would have already.*

She was sure evil existed too and that some of the People practiced witchcraft, but she did not think that the evil things people called ghosts were the ancestors. Why would they want to come back and scare everyone? That led her to the conclusion that ghosts were evil spirits.

Now, as she looked at the blinking stars, she made a quiet prayer to the Creator that someday he would reveal to her the truth. In some way, that comforted her. She and her brother were extremely old and could remember back when there were few white people in their land in the East. The Cherokee people never had anything like whiskey before the white man came. That, too, she believed was evil and very bad for her people.

In every camp, in every tribe in Indian Territory, people were starving. The men begin to drink and what is the family supposed to do about it? They have only been in this new land for one year, and the Cherokee still have much to learn about what the land will grow what kinds of animals they can keep on the sparse grasses. Heat was a huge factor. They had already seen one full summer. The People watched as the land dried and cracked, the grass became brown and lifeless. The creeks dried up, and even the Arkansas River dropped so low that boats could not go up or down it. *She wanted to live a little while longer so that she could be of use to her people. So many of the old ones died on the Trail Where They Cried. So much knowledge was gone forever, leaving a big gap in their oral histories.*

Her thoughts turned to Medicine Man, who had been greatly changed after the day he came back from his ordeal. He has been so quiet and depressed. Today, Jackson Halley sent a runner to come to ask Medicine Man to come and try to identify a murdered Indian. But, her brother refused and said he had seen enough of death and then walked away. It was she who had sent a message back so that they would look for a Chief to come and that Medicine Man did not want to come. She was sad that her brother was rude to Jackson. That white man was one of the good ones, and she and her brother had promised to be available to help if Jackson needed it. This is the first time Jackson had ever asked Medicine Man to do anything. *She was beginning to think that an evil spirit had gotten into her brother. If so, there was nothing that she and all her herbal remedies could do about it. And, if he continued in having this bad mind, she feared she would find him dead on his pallet some morning soon.*

Tomorrow would be another day. Another day to try to stay alive, try to help the People, try to fight against the evil all around them and try to keep her brother from crossing over, wherever the dead go.

*****

Coyote had left the camp of the Osage some time ago, but he kept thinking about the things they had told him. About how the tribes were being squeezed into this small part of the land and having to live so close to their life long enemies. Five Owls invited Coyote to stay a few days, and so Coyote took the opportunity to learn all he could, like how all these tribes were able to live in one small place.

With friendly goodbyes, Coyote left the Osage village and continued on his journey. He had been traveling farther South, and as he went, he began to notice unfinished homes made of logs. A curious way to make a lodge although he did see a tipi here and there. He began to notice heavily traveled unusually wide trails and sometimes saw wagons drawn by mules, or a strange, furless buffalo pulling massive loads. His people had never thought to make a buffalo pull anything. They might kill you if you tried.

He began meeting Indians on the trail. They nodded their heads, but never tried to talk to him. He was glad they did not try, for he would not have been able to understand them and they might think he was an enemy.

Then one day he was riding along and around a bend of the trail came a wagon with white men driving it. There was no place for Coyote to run and hide. The land was flat, and the tall trees were too far away to get to in time. The men saw him right away and motioned him to come close. Coyote did not want to do it, but he was close enough to know that they could kill him with their firesticks if he did not. He pulled up alongside the driver of the wagon and waited.

"Hey, redskin. We got some fine whiskey here. You want a drinkie?" they said.

Coyote did not understand a word. He tried to make the sign language, but the men just kept repeating the words they said before only louder. A big man on a funny looking horse, with long ears and a dumb look, said something even louder, but he still could not fathom what they wanted.

"Well boys, I thinks we got here a stubborn injun. You know fellas. If'n we let him get away with this, then all them others will think they can just walk away when we are offering them something fine to drink. What say we show him the error of his ways?" said the big man.

Suddenly, Coyote was jumped from behind, knocked off his horse and wrestled to the ground. Coyote tried to protect himself, but the punches came so quickly and from many directions. Just as suddenly as they started his beating, they stopped, jumped into their wagon and slapped the reins to make their strange beasts go. Coyote was too hurt to lift his head to see why they were leaving. His vision dimmed as he watched several Indian men approach. He lay there, helpless, pulling his arms up shield himself from the next round of abuse.

But, the abuse did not happen, for the last thing he remembered was being lifted by many hands, gentle hands, and hearing their voices discussing something in angry tones. Coyote seemed to know that the anger was not directed toward him. With that realization, he allowed himself to close his eyes and let dreams to take over.

Coyote woke on the floor of a mean shack made of sticks. An old Indian man was sitting on his own pallet staring at him with dull, lifeless eyes, while an Indian woman with abundant wrinkles was putting herbs on his wounds. He only had a vague memory of what had happened to him, but every time he tried to speak, the woman would shush him. Finally, when she was finished with the wounds on his face, she allowed him to talk, which turned out to be a futile endeavor. She could not understand his language any better than he could understand hers. Again the trader's sign language came to the rescue and before long he was able to make Poison Woman understand who he was and why he was in Indian Territory.

"I am Sunkmanitu," said Coyote as he made the sign for the animal.

As he signed while speaking in Lakota Sioux, the woman began to tend some of his other wounds. There was a deep gash on his ribs she had not seen at first.

"Well now," she signed and said in English when she was done dressing his wounds, "I think this will make you better. I am made to believe this is a bad time for Coyote to come to the new home of the Cherokee."

Coyote's eyes immediately reflected the wonder and puzzlement at her words that sounded like no other language he had ever heard. Poison Woman instantly understood what had caused such a look.

"The sounds that you hear are the white man's language called English. We Cherokee have known the white man for many generations. At one time, the white man was our friend, and we even helped to fight his battles. That was when there were not so many white men here. Now there are more than you could count in your lifetime," she said.

He signed, "I have not seen this thing. It is hard to believe. Where I come from, we seldom see the white man and then only for trade. We see them on the Big River on their way to the mountains to trap the Beaver. I have seen

155

them coming back with all of their skins, their boats so heavy they could barely guide them. They say their people like to use the fur for hats. I think this is very strange, how could there be so many people wanting to wear Beaver on their heads?"

Poison Woman had made a cup of willow bark tea which she had poured into a wooden cup. She handed it to Coyote and gave the sign for him to drink. However, he was unsure if he could trust her and looked at the brew with skeptical eyes.

"This is made with the bark of the river willow tree," she signed.

Coyote quickly became animated with smiles and gestures. Finally, he pulled himself together and signed, "I know the willow bark tea. My shaman from my village taught me all about the herbs and how to use them. He had much knowledge."

Coyote drank the brew eagerly. He lay back against the wall next to the pallet she had for made him on the floor and, between sips, he continued to ask questions. "If the white man was your friend, what happened that your friends then sent you so far away from them?"

Poison Woman was surprised and pleased that this young man wanted to know more about her tribe's history.

"At that time, the white man's chief was far across the big waters where the sun comes up in the morning. After a time, other white men with other white chiefs came to claim the land, so the Cherokee fought with the English against the ones they called 'The French'. After a long time, the white men who made our land their home got tired of their chief, so they fought a war, white man against white man. We had to take sides, so we chose to fight on the white chief's side. It turned out to be the wrong side. When the war was over, we had to give up much of our lands, but we stayed on the land they let us have. But, white people are mostly a greedy people. They could not stand it that we had this small portion of our rightful homeland. We had made the land desirable to look at and good for hunting and growing food. We were pushed off of our land and marched many moons across the earth in winter to get here. Now the white men are filling all the places we left behind, and still more come on boats, more filling up the land. I know, someday they will forget the treaty they made with us for this new land and want to take it away."

"Can you not fight them? Why do you not join with all of these other tribes and go against them?" Coyote asked.

At that moment, Medicine Man decided to join in the conversation. Coyote was fearful that he had offended him.

"Why? You ask why? Because the People do not all agree. They fight among themselves like children fighting in a stickball game. Then a new and bad enemy comes that destroys us from within and ruins our resolve to protect ourselves. That enemy is 'Whiskey'" said Medicine Man vehemently, spitting the word out, his hands moving fiercely.

Coyote was not sure what stickball was, but he did know what whiskey was.

"I have seen this thing. The drink that makes men crazy. When our people are given this drink, we don't care if we are stolen blind. It is a sad thing. I have not tasted this bad drink, but I have seen when some of our people do, and it makes me want to pour it on the ground." said Coyote.

"That is what those men wanted you to do today. When you did not understand what they wanted to sell to you, they thought you were not listening on purpose. That is why they tried to kill you. If they had killed you, there would be no one to mourn you or to get revenge. White men are not punished for killing Indians," she said, sadness filling her face. "Enough is said tonight. Tomorrow is soon

157

enough to learn what type of place you have walked into," she said as she motioned for him to lay his head down.

As Coyote lay back, he had the feeling that this was his stopping place. He did not know why he should not walk any further south, but he was sure beyond doubt. It was obvious that this place was dangerous, especially for someone like him that did not speak anyone's language. While listening to Poison Woman speak as she signed to him, he felt a desire to learn this new language. Before he closed his eyes, he hummed a prayer to Wakan Tanka. He prayed for wisdom to know what it was Wakan Tanka wished him to learn.

As Coyote hummed his prayer, Medicine Man sat on his pallet, now in deep shadow, and listened to the young man. Light from the low fire glinted off of the few hairs on his head. He did not have to speak the Lakota language to know that he was praying to the Creator. A gleam began to take hold in his heart, and the depression of the last few days began to drift away from him, like water on the skin disappears unseen. Then slowly, faintly, Medicine Man began his own prayer to Creator and it oddly meshed with Coyote's. Together, the young man and the old serenaded the night and found comfort between strangers.

Poison Woman listened to the two as she put away the cups and herbs she had used to help Coyote. She wore a faint smile on her wrinkled face and her old eyes sparked with knowing relief, because life had come back into her brother's heart again and she would not find him dead on his pallet in the morning. This must be an answer to her own prayer. She decided that she would do all she could to help Coyote while he was with them.

Chapter 16

Jackson wondered if something was happening to Medicine Man. It was not like him to not want to help, but it was good that he sent Joseph Deerslayer, one of the sub-chiefs, to try and help. Joseph was not nearly as old as Medicine Man, however, it was obvious from his bearing, he was a trusted and serious elder to his people. He wore denim dungarees, a calico shirt with flat red ribbon sewn across the chest and at the cuffs. His hair was pulled back and tied with a rawhide strip. He wore no feathers and no jewelry. Jackson thought he looked a confident and sober man. A good choice for this task.

Jackson explained the circumstances of finding the body and explained what it was they needed. Joseph made a slight bow in acquiescence and followed Jackson to the ice house.

Arch joined them at the door to the ice house, and they each took a lamp inside with them. Wordlessly, Arch removed the sheet over the body to reveal the face of the dead man and then looked up at Joseph to see any signs of recognition. What he saw was a look of complete horror. Nothing could have prepared Jackson or Arch for the anguish they now witnessed in Joseph. Joseph motioned for them to cover the body again as he wearily stepped out of the cold environs of the ice house.

"Mr. Halley, may we go to a private place where we three can talk, but not here?" said Joseph.

"Yes, we can go to my office in the house. And please call me Jackson."

They next found themselves in Jackson's office. As requested, Masey brought them iced tea to drink. They had seated themselves silently and thus it stayed until finally Joseph broke the silence and explained.

"I am very sorry to say that I know who the man is," said Joseph as he took another sip of his tea to steady his trembling voice. "His name is James Koni, it means Skunk in Choctaw. He was a close friend of mine.

Just outside in the yard, Sasa was walking in from the river, coming back from her class with Anna. Wheezer trotted at her side, happy to be with her and going somewhere, anywhere. She sat herself down on a bench in the side yard, not too terribly far from the open window of Jackson's office where the men had only begun to speak of the dead man. She was not afraid to go and knock on the door to be included in the discussion, however, Cherokee manners forbade it without being invited by the Cherokee elder present at that meeting. So she satisfied herself with sitting quietly and listening. Occasionally, she would throw a stick for Wheezer to chase to give him something to do, because he was not patient enough to sit for any length of time, and he had just spent the day sitting at Anna's, which was more than any Jack Russell could take in one day.

"Mr. Halley, uh... Jackson, I was at the camp last year when you helped my people, and I know you have a good and kind heart for the Cherokee and hopefully for the Choctaw as well, so I feel I can tell you something that was not known by anyone outside of the government.

"James Koni was a brave Choctaw Frenchman who wanted to help his Choctaw people. The Army has been seeing so much drunkenness among the Cherokee and Choctaw, and they complained to Washington about the whiskey sellers. The captain at Fort Smith was command-ed to find these men and stop them from selling whiskey to our peoples. That, so far, has been unsuccessful, so the government asked us to choose someone who would pretend to be a buyer of whiskey and see if he could not find out who was the leader. If possible, James was to try and become one of them, helping them to sell it, in order for him to gain information which would help them catch whoever is doing it.

"The last time I saw James was last week. He reported that he was sure the main man directing the whiskey sellers was in Fort Smith and was one of the merchants. He must have gotten too close, and they found him out. Now he is dead and can't tell us anything," said Joseph, bowing his head and turning his face away so his face might not be seen.

He softly pounded the chair arm rests to get con-trol over his emotions. Jackson waited patiently and then proceeded.

"Joseph, can you put me in touch with the person in the government who asked James to do this?" said Jackson.

"No. They only talked to him, but I don't think they know anything more. I was the assistant, helping James to find out things, and I reported everything to him," said Joseph.

Jackson thought the arrangement strange. Why was Joseph kept in the dark?

"There are many merchants in Fort Smith and most of them are far from upstanding citizens, and the Army contingent are tight lipped besides being rough around the edges, as well. However, we did find a piece of paper he kept in a special place. We found it when we were searching for his identity," said Jackson.

Joseph's eyes opened wide and looked confused, but quickly brought his attention back to Jackson.

"I had forgotten that I even had it until you showed up. It looks like some kind of poem, but I am not sure what it means. Was this some type of code to help to identify the right person?" said Jackson.

Joseph thought for a moment, looking down at the soiled piece of paper, reading it to the end. He handed it back to Jackson, looking like he was trying to remember.

"It mystifies me. So if I don't understand what he wrote, how could it help. He never told me he had written anything down," Joseph finally said.

"It is another piece of the puzzle," said an ethereal voice from the open window.

The men all looked in unison at the window, but saw nothing there. Jackson arose from his chair, knowing who made the abrupt comment, he walked around his desk and looked out of the window to find Sasa and Wheezer standing underneath. He gave her a sly smile, and waved his arm to come in to the office if she wanted to participate.

In spite of the trappings of white civilization she had worn that day, Sasa took very little time indeed getting around the side of the house, taking two steps at a time by pulling up her skirt to her knees, through the front door and finally into Jackson's office, Wheezer close at her heels, happy to be running.

After taking a seat, Sasa pulled from her pocket the two pieces of cloth, one from the dead man and one from the man that attacked her that day.

"Jackson, I have two more pieces to the puzzle as well," said Sasa.

Joseph's eyes grew large at the discovery. Then Jackson spoke to Sasa.

"Ah Sasa, I have been watching for you to come home, I want to tell you that I am so sorry about what happened this morning at the Van Buren dock. I was told that Wheezer came to your rescue. I hate to think what would have happened if you had not asked me this morning for permission for Wheezer to go with you," said Jackson.

He could see the shock in her face, for Sasa was not one to whine and cry about close calls and danger. Joseph looked down at the happy dog sitting beside Sasa, looking as if it understood everything that was being said. It gave him the shivers.

"I was in town today, and I went to see Anna. She is the one that told me of your ordeal, and she told me something that you may not be aware of. She went to the fort, and it just so happened that both Captains were there, Captain Stuart and Captain Belknap from Fort Gibson. She had a time with them, so I don't think they can be of much use to stopping this from happening again, but she is coming over tomorrow night so that we can discuss it further," said Jackson.

Feeling guilty about interrupting Jackson's private meeting, she said, "I am very sorry, Jackson. I did not mean to interfere, and I did not mean to listen in at your meeting, but I also have some evidence for you," said Sasa.

Joseph edged closer to see what Sasa had.

As she held out the pieces of cloth to Jackson, she proceeded to tell them the entire story of what had happened, including the actions of Yellow Eyes in coming to her rescue. Joseph's eyes widened when she explained how Yellow Eyes attacked in unison with her dog, and how it was Yellow Eyes that lead Wheezer to the dead body. As she spoke, Joseph looked at Wheezer then at Sasa and back again, clearly stunned by the story of the coyote she had named Yellow Eyes. He stroked his chin in thought.

"I did not understand the importance of this piece of cloth last night when I pulled it out of the dead man's hand, but today, Yellow Eyes managed to rip another piece of cloth from the soldier who attacked me. I saw right away that both pieces were important. See, Jackson," Sasa said as she held up both pieces of cloth, " they are the same. Exactly the same material."

The realization of this new evidence was mind boggling. Somehow, the Army was involved in the highly illegal actions they were supposed to investigate. No wonder they never put anybody in jail. Finding out who would be much more difficult to accomplish.

"You say James had this cloth in his hand when he died?" asked Joseph, sounding a little condescending.

"Yes," she answered matter-of-factly, "I hope you will forgive me, Jackson, for keeping the cloth and not telling you. I am not sure why I did," said Sasa.

Finally, Arch spoke up.

"That also means that if they ever find out that we

have come this close to finding out who is behind this, our lives would be in danger. It is clear, they will stop at nothing, not even killing," said Arch.

"We must make sure that does not happen until we can actually do something about it. From here on out, we say nothing to anyone at the fort except Captain Stuart and even then, we will need to be careful," said Jackson.

"Jackson, would you like me to hold on to those pieces and the note for safekeeping?" asked Joseph.

Jackson was not sure why Joseph might think they were not safe with him.

"No, I think I have a very secure place to keep them. Don't worry Joseph, they are safe with me," said Jackson.

Sasa looked to the men in the room, wondering if one of her new family could be hurt by all that was happening.

"Excuse me for my rudeness in interrupting you again, but did you not say you found some clue that you were about to read? Please continue. I will be silent," said Sasa.

That will be the day, thought Jackson, with a grin on his face. "Oh, er...yes. Well, like I said, it really makes no sense to me. It seems to be a poem," he said, as all in the room looked puzzled. "Joseph, are you acquainted with poetry? Do you know what it is?"

"Yes, I am. You see, the government chose us because both James and I were well educated. We have been taught reading, writing, speaking in the white man's way most of our lives. James even went to university back east for a while. So, yes, James liked poetry. It does not look as if it has anything to do with his death, though," said Joseph.

"It seems like a message within a riddle. Here, let me read it out loud and see if you can understand anything in it," said Jackson.

"But Jackson, it's gibberish. How can I possibly know what it means?" answered Joseph.

"Just try to listen. You never know, it might jog a memory about something.

The rapier swirled down, he was deaf to her plea,
her heart blood he did smite.
Down the coast he dashed by the dark angry sea
the Royal Bard did run from his plight.

Off to the far West the Royal Bard did go
his unreasoning hatred consumed him.
He may run fast and deep, but how far can he go
when he is running away from his sin?

Tis fitting the emblem his family does carry
two lions, two rapiers, mighty and true.
Alas, he murdered the one he would marry
from his family in Kerry he withdrew.

Flee, yes flee, but your rapier follows thee
Royal Bard run to the setting sun,
You may have some repast, then still you must flee
For the foul deed was yours - -

"See, I told you it was gibberish. Why James thought we would get anything out of this, I will never know. It does not even have the last two words. I could rack my brain trying to figure it out, but I just don't understand what he means. He must have known something that he assumed others would know too. I am so sorry, I can't help any more than this," said Joseph looking sad.

Joseph shoved the folded piece of paper the poem was written on, over to Jackson. He determined it was meaningless and nothing to worry about. He was better at tangible things, like his revolver and his horse.

"At least we have a small clue. The name of the person must rhyme with sun, and we have the army cloth. Maybe I should go over to the fort and see if any of the enlisted men have had to get their shirts repaired. I can talk to Captain Stuart and see if anyone has turned in any uniforms with chunks missing," said Jackson.

"Jackson," Arch spoke up again, "I think we need to send a runner down to the Choctaw Nation. They need to know that James has been found. The funeral rites of the Choctaw are long and varied, so the sooner they know the better."

Jackson stepped out of the room to arrange for the runner.

Sasa had not actually known very many Choctaw people since they came from a different part of the country.

"Do their customs at death differ from ours?" she asked.

"Have you ever heard of the 'Bone Pickers'?" asked Joseph. "Long ago, the Choctaw would place their dead on a scaffold, which is not so rare. However, it was built next to their home. You can imagine the stench it created. They wrapped the dead in skins and bark, but after some months the Bone Pickers would climb up to the body and pull all the flesh from the bones. The people that did this grew their nails long just for this purpose. Once the bones were picked clean they were handed down to the family. The flesh they had picked off was then burned, scaffold and all.

"When they buried the bones, the people would scream and cry out. It is nothing like you have ever heard before, and once you do, you can never forget it. The screaming and crying can go on for months, sporadically, like on special occasions or after church and before a big feast.

"That is not something they normally do today, but there still is much ritual involved in the burial. It is best if we hurry so they can begin the whole process," explained Joseph.

Sasa shuddered at the thought of having to pick her brother's bones. She was glad that the Cherokee just buried their dead the next day and sang a death song for them.

Jackson entered the room, interrupting the chilling story, "Sasa, we have a long day tomorrow. We have company coming for dinner, but you won't be going in to town until Anna and I discuss it. We want you to be safe. You are family now, and I don't think I could bear it if something happened to you. So, before you have time to ask Joseph for another story, please go in to Masey and tell her, we will be having an extra one for dinner. And, apparently, Anna is bringing someone with her as well tomorrow. I am assuming Joseph will at least stay the night and get an early start in the morning?" asked Jackson turning to Joseph.

Joseph, surprised to be asked, but said he needed to be getting back.

"So go on tell Masey about tomorrow's dinner and ask her to pack something to eat for Joseph on his trip. Anna and her guest will be spending at least one night as well, so maybe you could help Masey get the rooms ready. I very much appreciate it. *Wado*, Sasa," said Jackson.

After Sasa left the room, Jackson sat down behind his writing desk and reached for a sheet of paper, ink and a pen nub. Attaching the nub to the pen, he settled himself, ready to take notes of their discussion.

"All right, let's see if we can try to get somewhere with what we already know of this poem," said Jackson. "We know what a rapier is."

"I think it is a type of sword?" ventured Arch.

"A very old type of sword, but there are many descriptions," said Joseph

"Yes, I think I remember this from school. I had to take lessons in sword play, and the fencing master taught me about different types of them," said Jackson.

"They are usually slender and can be short or long, but with a very sharp point. They are always straight, not curved, and they can be sharpened on one or both sides. The fencing master showed me some, and they all had fancy complex hilts that went over the hand. He said they were designed to protect the hand during battle. What puzzles me is that they are not much in use these days. Most of the swords used by our Army officers, as well as the Navy, are curved. So the term gives this a feeling of either an antique being used or a family heirloom. That is something to think about," said Jackson as he made a note of it.

"It is obvious the person struck a woman and that she had been fatally stabbed in the heart," said Arch, happy to be able to contribute in some small way since he had not the formal education of the other two men.

"But, the mention of the coast and the dark, angry sea does not help much. That could mean any coast. And the mention of the Royal Bard could place it somewhere in Europe. Europe is a mighty big place," said Joseph. "I don't understand why he used the term 'Royal Bard'. Have you thought that this might just be a poem he enjoyed?" said Joseph.

"Yes I have, Joseph, but let's see if there is a reason for him going to the trouble of writing it down. I assume since we can't place a particular country attached to that name, the term must be specific to the person. Without more knowledge, it is useless to try." added Jackson as the dinner bell rang.

"Well gentlemen, we will have to ponder over this later, but we won't give up," stated Jackson.

"It is probably useless information, but if you need my help any further, please send a runner. I am over at the new capital of the Cherokee Nation they named Tahlequah. Everyone knows me, so I won't be hard to find," said Joseph

"Yes, I heard they named that place last September. 1839 sure turned out to be a momentous year. The Trail Where They Cried ended that spring and then in the fall they set to build a capitol city. Now that's progress," said Jackson with wonderment in his eyes.

"Did you know that the Choctaw call it, The Trail of Tears? I did not know that they lost quite a few people on their march as well. James told me, they lost over 6,000. I think we should all just call it that. I mean, it says it all, doesn't it?" said Joseph shaking his head as they entered the dining room.

"Yes Joseph, Trail of Tears says it all," said Jackson with true sorrow in his eyes. "It says it all for all of Indian Territory's tribes."

Chapter 17

All of Wheezer's humans were having dinner. He had already scarfed down his own, then ran out to hunt for whatever he could scare up. Nose to the ground and not paying attention to how far he was going from the house, he came to the tall prairie grass. He heard a rustle of grass blade against grass blade. Looking up quickly, he saw Yellow Eyes standing between parted layers of new tall grass. Yellow Eyes put his muzzle down, turned in a circle and then pointed his nose toward the Arkansas River. Turning back into the grass, Yellow Eyes made a path in that same direction, but under the cover of the grass. Wheezer knew he was being asked to follow, so right behind Yellow Eyes' bushy tail he trotted. He vaguely knew his position, so getting lost was not a problem. At least it was not the forest to the west which could swallow up a small dog, he was proof of it. Wheezer had almost died last year when he got lost in that forest.

They emerged close to the ferry docks across from the fort. This was not the main Van Buren dock which was closer to the town of Van Buren, however, it was the same dock where they had saved Sasa. Yellow Eyes spotted men, so he quickly concealed both himself and Wheezer in the tall grass and lay down, facing out so they could see everything, and being extremely quiet. They both laid there to watch.

The sun was already over the horizon when a man they had not seen before came from a small boat. It had been rowing along the shore, concealing itself in the shadows of the trees during dusk. The man, who wore a plain shirt and worn work pants was now close enough they both could hear him talk with the other men, who all wore the same dark clothes, like the men that Wheezer and Yellow Eyes attacked the other day to protect Sasa.

They began carrying big round wooden things that sloshed as they moved them from the small boat to the dock. Then the same things were concealed behind several large wooden boxes.

Yellow Eyes felt uneasy. He was not sure what alarmed him. He remained still as stone. He had been coming here almost nightly to see the same thing, but tonight felt different in some way. He turned to look at Wheezer, who was caught up in watching, seemingly not feeling the same tension he felt.

After the loading was done, the men wearing the same clothes got on a raft and went across, missing the fort dock and silently floating down from the fort a-ways. The man in the plain clothes was preparing to get back in his boat when a lone figure approached. He appeared in traditional Indian clothes, deer skin shirt, breach clout, leggings and tall moccasins. His shortish black hair was shot with gray, and he wore something that looked like red patterned cloth wrapped around his head and a fluffy feather stuck in it. He was upset about something and Wheezer, who knew much more English than Yellow Eyes listened very carefully.

"I am Sam Bushyhead, I live down by the new capital of our Cherokee Nation, Tahlequah. I have come to ask you to stop selling this drink 'whiskey' to my brothers. They are getting very sick from it. And they are falling under its spell. It is like witchcraft in the way that it holds a man captive. I have come to ask politely for you to stop selling this drink to the Cherokee," said Sam.

"Ha, who do you think you are, old man?" said the white man.

"I have told you, Sam Bushyhead from the Cherokee Nation," said Sam.

"Boy, you beat all, don't ya know? Ya think I kin just give up and go away? Well, not hardly, no how. Now, why don't ya just have ya a free drink on me and we'll just call it a day? Okay? I have some fresh from the still," said the white man.

"No, I do not want this. I want you to stop. I know you white men think the Cherokee seem tame Indians to you, but deep within us is a warrior spirit and we will not let you destroy our nation," said Sam.

"Look old man, I'm tired of talking to ya," said the white man. Then he took another approach. "Anyway, I can't do nothin' about it. I'm just the delivery man, I have nothing to do with running the business, see?"

"No, those are all lies. We know who you are. I am not the only one who knows that you are not who you say you are in town. We know you are the one who runs this whiskey business. And we know that you are running from some other bad deeds you have done somewhere else. Here is what we say, either stop selling the whiskey, or we will go to the fort and tell the captain who you really are," said Sam, with a stony stare set to his brown eyes.

But Sam Bushyhead's last words seemed to stop the white man in stride. He placed his hand in his pocket and turned to face Sam.

Cocking his head, the white man said, "Well now, that sorta' changes things. Now, I might be willin' to stop... I would need to have a talk with the other folks you mentioned. Bring 'em here an' then we can all talk together."

Wheezer and Yellow Eyes saw the Cherokee stiffen and then he said, "No. They have sent me to speak to you. You will do or not do, but I will not reveal who else knows all these things about you. We are not without thinking ability."

The white man crept closer, his head tilted as if he were trying to hear better. Then without warning, the white man pulled from his pocket, or maybe some type of holder, a knife. Bushyhead expected this response, so he feinted to the right, pulled his own knife and shot his arm out with it to slash the white man's arm. The white man fell back against some crates, fire leaped into his eyes as he quickly rolled, keeping the knife from striking his heart. Sam took a defensive stance. Arms open wide, both feet planted with the knees bent slightly. It seemed that Sam would prevail when suddenly, from out of the darkness a man appeared who ran up behind Sam, plunging a knife into his back. Sam crumpled to the ground, not moving.

"Thanks for the help, Willis, I was losin' ground there for a minute. So glad you showed up," said the white man.

"Well, I was visitin' one of my 'lady friends' over ta Van Buren and got back late. Maybe you could row me over ta other shore 'fore the commander knows I am not there," said Sergeant Willis.

"Don't mind if I do, happy to oblige you," said the white man as he bent to pick up his knife from the ground.

"What was he so all-fired upset about anyways, was the man out to kill ya?" said Willis.

"I don't rightly know, he just up and came at me with is knife. Probably drunk if'n you ask me," the white man replied.

"Do ya want me to do somethin' with the body?" asked Willis.

"Naw, just leave it there, let the buzzards clean it up for us. There is no one around to investigate anyway, so we is free and clear. Since he was knifed, they will just think it was a fight betwixt Indians. Let's get us on over ta the other side, quick-like afore anyone comes snooping around," said the man.

The two men spoke softly as they made their way down to the white man's small boat, then all was quiet.

Wheezer and Yellow Eyes looked at each other. They both wondered if they should have done something, but it was too hard to know who the enemy was and whom to protect. Wheezer hated violence of any kind, but he had waited for Yellow Eyes to take the lead, when together, they were a pack and Yellow Eyes was the leader. However, both would not forget the face of the man who struck down the other man. Now, again, Wheezer would have to go and get his people and alert them that a bad thing happened.

They both had risen from their hiding place. Wheezer inadvertently stepped out from among the tall grass just when the man who stabbed the dead man on the ground, came back up onto the landing. He bent down to pick something up off of the ground, and that is when he caught sight of Wheezer. Somehow Wheezer knew he had been spotted and turned to look into the intense, dark eyes staring back at him. It seemed the man realized the dog had been there the entire time.

"Hey, dog. Come here, boy! Come on, boy, come here, I say!" screamed the man as Wheezer trotted back into the tall grass quickly.

Yellow Eyes accompanied Wheezer as far as the end of the tall grass close to Wheezer's home, and then went back to his den. As Yellow Eyes walked, he felt something was going to happen soon. Not so much a bad thing, but something that would affect him. He had been feeling this way for days now. Every day he looked for it, he sniffed the breeze for it and even tasted the new sprouts of grass for it, but nothing revealed itself. He did not understand many things, like the strange sounds that the humans made, or the reason why Wheezer went to live with them instead of coming with him as a pack brother should do.

He was so lonely in his den, but he had no desire to seek out a mate. That was done at a younger age. Now all the female coyotes would already be spoken for. And even if he fought another male and won a mate, she might not accept him. Did that mean he would have to spend the rest of his life alone? What puzzled him more was that Wheezer did not have a mate and he seemed to be happy, but then Wheezer was not a coyote, was he? Wheezer was something different, but still the same. Coyote could not figure it out, and it didn't figure in the overall shape of things anyway. As long as Wheezer saw Yellow Eyes as a friend, then he would continue to consider him as part of his pack. The thing coming would make itself known, eventually.

Wheezer, for his part, went straight home to alert Jackson and Sasa about this new bad thing.

The man watched the dog disappear into the grass. He recognized the dog. It belonged to that muleteer Jackson Halley. He thought, had it been standing there when I dispatched the Indian? Maybe so, but dogs can't talk. Most dogs are usually too dumb to recognize what is going on around them anyway. Just the same, I will keep my eyes open. If that dog causes me any trouble, then that will be the end for him, but I can't think of any scenario where that dog could tell anyone what he saw, so it's silly to worry about it.

*****

After gathering Jackson and Sasa with his "it is an emergency" bark, they mounted the horses for the trek and followed Wheezer to the docks where it had happened. Wheezer slowed his trot as he got close to the dock. It was almost night, but not quite. Sam Bushyhead still lay in the same position he had from the time he fell. Jackson dismounted and rushed over to the fallen man, noting the stab wound in his back. First he checked for a pulse and with hope dawning he gently turned Sam over.

Sasa realized Jackson would not have turned him over immediately if the man were dead, so she reached into her pocket for the cloth she carried and went down to the dock to wet it. Sam was just opening his eyes when she got there, and she quickly bent to put the cooling cloth to his brow.

"He has been mumbling in Cherokee, but I am not able to understand what he is saying," said Jackson. "Do you recognize him?"

"Yes, I do know him. He is one of our elders, Sam Bushyhead," she said as she bent closer and whispered to Sam, "Grandfather, it is Sasa. I am here to help you. Who did this thing to you, Grandfather?" asked Sasa.

Sam made an effort to grunt out a few words. Sasa

bent lower so she could put her ear close to his mouth to hear him better.

"My daughter, please tell my family at Tahlequah so that they can sing my death song for me. I am too weak to sing it now," whispered Sam.

"Yes Grandfather, I will. Please help us to catch who did this to you. Who was it?" Sasa asked again.

With great effort, Sam put all his last remaining energy into his last few words. It would have to suffice.

"My daughter, there are demons in our midst. They sell the whiskey to our people. One man gives orders to soldiers and the other runs from himself and is a merchant, an Irishman behind a mask, a murderer in disguise. Yet one more wears the skin of a Cherokee, but is worse than any white man. You must be careful, daughter, life means nothing to them. Ugh..." said Sam, then his body relaxed and Sam Bushyhead was no more with the People.

Stoically, Sasa stood to allow Jackson to check Sam again, but she knew it was over for him. What a puzzle he gave to her. How could she unravel this tangled mess, but there were important clues in his last words and Sasa would remember them. Somehow she would figure this out.

*****

"Sir, I have a notion that maybe one of them there merchants in town may be headed up this whiskey sellin' business here abouts," said Sergeant Willis.

"The devil you say. Well, man, spit it out. Don't keep me waiting all night long," said Captain Stuart.

"Well, Sir, it's like this here: I overheard some gossip an' well, maybe some people are thinkin' it is that O'Malley fella. You know, that dry goods shop keeper. He is kinda' a loner, Sir, and he seems to be pals with some of the riff-raff in town. I'm thinkin' it's him all right. Want me to go and drag him in?" said Sergeant Willis.

"Heavens no! Where did you get a fool idea like that? I am not the Sheriff, nor any kind of lawman. I am only to report my findings and wait for orders. I have been accused before of meddling in the town's business. So let me think on this for a while," said Captain Stuart.

Captain Stuart was highly suspicious of the suggestion Sergeant Willis had just made. Something was just not right.

Chapter 18

Poison Woman had been able to get Coyote up and mobile. Strangely, Medicine Man had perked up. He no longer moped around the lodge, but spent hour, after hour talking with Coyote. Since it was all in sign, she did not have the time to sit and watch all the movements of their hands, but occasionally she would hear her brother speak an English word and Coyote would repeat it. It had only been a few days and already Coyote could speak in halting English. Poison Woman secretly admired the young man for his quick intelligence and desire to learn, something that seemed to be lacking in many of the young Cherokee these days.

She was fishing a fired pot out of the ashes of the cooling fire pit when she saw Joseph walking up the road to the Agency grounds. Then he turned to make his way to their lodge. She motioned to Medicine Man that he had a visitor coming, and she quickly began to prepare some tea for their visitor while Medicine Man directed Coyote where to sit and to keep still.

"*Osiyo*, Grandmother. I hope the Creator has smiled at you today. I would like to have a moment to speak with Medicine Man. Would you please, see if he will receive my visit today, Grandmother?" said Joseph as he waited patiently outside of the lodge.

Poison Woman returned, nodded her head and held the hide flap aside for him.

"*Wado*, Grandmother," he said to her as he passed into the lodge.

Upon entering the lodge, Medicine Man had only the floor to offer Joseph, but he motioned him to come and sit in the place of honor at the back of the lodge, furthest from the door.

"*Osiyo*, Joseph. We are honored to have you as our guest this day," said Medicine Man, who then pulled down his old medicine pipe and tobacco for the welcoming ceremony. Before he began, he signed to Coyote to occupy the other side, sitting across from Joseph.

There was no problem for Coyote in understanding the ceremony because he was delighted to find that it was much like the ceremony his own people observed. However, he still watched in case there was some fundamental nuance he should learn. After blowing smoke to the four directions plus heaven and earth, the pipe was passed from person to person until the bowl was ash. Medicine Man knocked the dottle out of the pipe before putting it back in its place.

Coyote noticed that Joseph was looking with curious eyes at him. Although Medicine Man had every intention of introducing the two, he enjoyed letting Joseph wonder who or what this newcomer was, since he did not look like a Cherokee, nor any of the woodland Indians made to live in Indian Territory. His manner of dress was simple, but exceedingly different, having everything made out of buffalo hide, trade beads and feathers, held together with sinew. Joseph was almost sure he was beholding a wild Indian, but propriety would have to be observed while he waited for Medicine Man to make the introductions.

Poison Woman brought in the tea. Today it was simply willow and mint. Willow for the help it gave to their old joints, and mint to give it a cooling taste for the hot day. She also waited for Medicine Man to finish having his fun. Finally, he deemed it time to get on with finding out the purpose of Joseph's visit.

"Joseph, you are welcome in my lodge. I have a visitor from far away. His name is Coyote, and he is on a journey to learn what he can while he is among us," said Medicine Man.

"Most Honored Elder, I am pleased to know your guest. Might I inquire what tribe you are from, Coyote?" asked Joseph, while Medicine Man's eyes glittered with humor.

Coyote for his part had only spoken English with Medicine Man. He began haltingly, "I am Coyote. I come far from north tribe," he replied. Joseph's eyebrow rose slightly.

"But, what tribe Coyote?" Joseph repeated.

Coyote was racking his brain for the right words, "Ah...Lakota," he said.

Joseph was somewhat taken aback for what he knew of the Lakota was of a fierce and bloodthirsty tribe who ruled their territories with an iron fist. When he finally noticed that Coyote did not even have a weapon nearby, he relaxed a bit.

"I am Joseph Deerslayer," he said while Medicine Man signed, as well. "Why are you here with us?" he asked.

"I Lakota, also Blackfoot. Village, not happy. I not like war. Shaman send on journey, find out what Wakan Tanka want me... uh... make," said Coyote.

At first Joseph was unsure of Coyote's meaning, then recognition dawned.

"I understand, you mean what the Creator wants you to make of yourself, wants you to be. Is that right?" he asked.

"Yes. Yes. Right," Coyote said smiling over the fact that he had just carried on a conversation with someone in a different language for the first time in his life. It was a sublime thrill.

"Welcome to Indian Territory. I hope what you learn will help you, but I must warn you, there is not much good news...uh... good things happening now for all the peoples here. Some is our own fault, some from the white man and maybe some as a punishment from Creator who you call Wakan Tanka and we call more than one name. Some say Unelanahi and some say Yahweh, but all mean the one God, the Creator.

"The only advice I can give is to be careful who you talk to. Try not to get involved with the whites. Some will not wish you harm, but there are many who will and will want to know why an Indian from the plains has come here. Many of our young men might wish to demonstrate their bravery against you, since there is nothing else they can physically fight against now. We are not allowed to fight our enemies. Our young men are drinking too much of the white man's drink that makes men crazy, and they do not listen to wisdom after drinking it," said Joseph.

"I, Coyote, am honorable man. I do not come for trouble. I am trained as healer," said Coyote in mixed sign and English words.

Medicine Man seemed to be aglow with Coyote's

183

progress, but he knew that he was not up to the job of helping Coyote out among the People.

"Joseph, you are a man who goes and comes among the People and the whites. Could you not help Coyote? Could he be your guest for a while?" asked Medicine Man.

Joseph thought for a moment, he was not sure if he should take the risk. His job for the white government occupied much of his time, and he was asked to help find the killer of James, but he could not say these things because no one was to know this. At the same time, he had other, important things he had to take care of. Secret things. However, it would be ungracious for him to say no.

"Yes, Coyote, you can stay with me and my family. We will help you along your journey, and maybe I can teach you a few more English words. You will need them if you are to understand what is happening here," said Joseph as he gave a short bow to Coyote from across the small fire.

Poison Woman, standing at the back preparing to make tea for them all, grunted her satisfaction, but added in a low voice in her brother's ear, "Brother, may I ask you to favor me by asking that Coyote come to see me later. I would like to compare his herbs with what I have. He may know of the strange plants that grow in this dry place. The more I know of these plants, the more I can help the People."

Medicine Man nodded, then turning to Coyote asked for him to come and visit, explaining the reason. Coyote's eyes shone with excitement, and he nodded his head smiling broadly.

All in all, it had been an eventful day for Coyote. He believed that Wakan Tanka had led him here so he could open his eyes and drink in what life is like with the whites, should the same thing happen to them.

Chapter 19

Andrew Halley and Henry Neugent both heard the landing bell, which could only mean one thing, that they were about to dock at one of the St. Louis piers. This would be their stopping off place; from there they would continue on horseback, west on the Santa Fe Trail, then down the old Osage trails through Kansas Territory until they would, at last, pass over into Indian Territory. First, however, Andrew had a hot bath, a shave and haircut in mind before they went to dinner.

When they stepped off the boat, they immediately became aware of being hailed.

"Mr. Halley, sir, Mr. Halley. Over here, sir," the man screamed as he waved his beaver felt bowler hat to and fro until finally Andrew saw him and waved in return.

"That is my accountant, Mr. Horace Northrop. A fine chap, one of the very best and loyal to a fault. I don't know that I could run this office without him," said Andrew over his shoulder as they walked down the ramp that had been swung over to the quay.

"Ah, there you are Mr. Northrop. Punctual as always. I think I would have had a conniption fit I had not seen you here at the dock," said a laughing Andrew. "Mr. Northrop, sir, this gentleman is my traveling companion. His name is Mr. Henry Neugent. He has agreed to make this trip with me, so if you should get any messages for him, please forward them to the Army fort at Fort Smith."

"Yes, sir, how do you do, sir," said Mr. Northrop as they began walking toward Market and 4th street where the frontier office of Halley's Financial was located.

As buildings went on the frontier, Halley's was considered one of the most modern. A full three stories tall, and one of the first buildings with indoor plumbing, but that status would not last for much longer. St. Louis was bursting at the seams. When last Andrew was here, the streets were busy with mostly frontiersmen in their skin shirts and pants, wearing tall moccasins. Those frontiersmen where still there, but along with them now were families, settlers. Respectable women were going from shop to shop as fine carriages plied the streets for passengers who could afford to pay for the ride, and wagon loads of lumber for homes, or vegetables of all sorts offered their wares. Shops selling fabric in the latest colors and patterns and even a sweets shop were now firmly established for business. St. Louis was losing its mud streets as well, Andrew noticed since Market Street had been paved with cobbles. It looked magnificent, very impressive to Andrew. This was the sort of progress he reveled in.

"Sir, I beg your pardon, there is a man to see you at your office. He came here specifically to see you, sir, and he has visited your office every day now for a week. He is there now," said Mr. Northrop, then he added, "He does not dress like a businessman."

"Ah, Mr. Northrop, I was expecting someone. I suppose the bath and all will have to wait, Henry. Do you mind coming up for a few moments?" said Andrew.

"I would be happy to. In fact, I am as happy as I think I have ever been in my life," said Henry exuberantly. "I could not have imagined this in a million years, Andrew. None of the pictures and drawings in the papers do this frontier town justice. Why, this city is absolutely alive. Alive with dreams and hopes for tomorrow. I can feel it. Oh my, what an experience," said Henry.

Andrew turned to his accountant to confirm they would come, but Mr. Northrop looked a little sheepish.

"Yes, Northrop, what else?" said a curious Andrew.

"Uh... Sir, there was a delivery for you some days ago. I have... it... waiting for you at the office. I am not sure if you were expecting this particular delivery, but... uh, we have been taking very good care of it, or I should say, we have tried to protect the office from it," said a dubious Mr. Northrop.

A slow smile spread over Andrew's face. Pure pleasure sprang from his countenance.

"Very good, Northrop, very good indeed. I was expecting just such a delivery and knowing what I know of the... package...you have done very well to protect the office successfully," said Andrew chuckling.

"Sir, I am afraid that you misunderstood. I did not

say I was successful. Some things are broken, some things we can no longer find, and certain particular pieces of clothing will never be the same again, sir," said a singularly serious Mr. Northrop.

"Do not fret so, Mr. Northrop. If anything has been damaged that belongs to you or any of the staff, I am happy to replace it. Oh, what a joy this is going to be," Andrew said happily.

Henry was entirely in the dark. He could not imagine what kind of delivery would cause damage. So he said, "Andrew my friend, is this something I need fear? It sounds as if someone has sent explosives to your office."

"No, no. Do not fear, Henry. But, I think explosive is the correct description. You will see soon. No more questions now, I want to surprise you," said Andrew as they rounded the corner of 4th street onto Market, arriving at the front door of Halley's Financial.

Before Andrew could grab the door handle, Mr. Northrop again interrupted the proceedings.

"Sir, I really must first express my deepest apologies for not taking care of your interests here at the firm. And if you deem it necessary after you have greeted your guest and met your delivery, I will tender my resignation at once," said Mr. Northrop.

In response, Andrew only raised his eyebrows and assumed a wry grin before opening the door to his business.

The sight before them took a while to assimilate. Andrew stopped just in the short hall to the main business lobby. Henry peeked around him from behind, half expecting to be shot at on the spot. Mr. Northrop stayed to the back with his head down, hat in hand, almost ready to bolt back out of the door they just entered.

At one end of the room was an upright commanding, sturdy frontiersman, propped on a straight backed chair backwards, straddling the chair. He had dark unruly hair, a confident bearing and he laughed uproariously while throwing a small ball to the end of the room which bounced off the back wall, sailing high into the air. When the ball seemed to be heading back at the thrower, a small blur of white and black came bounding out from behind a desk, jumping as high as a man is tall, catching the ball in its mouth. Then a chase would ensue. The man in buckskins jumped from his chair, bounded across the tops of desks as papers went flying about like oversized snow until he jumped down in the path of the beast that had the ball, quickly seizing the ball and after a brief tug of war, gained possession of it. The man then went back to his chair, straddling it, to begin the exercise all over again.

"Huh Hem...," said Andrew. "Having fun are we Nathan, old boy?"

"Why I'll be a dog gone whippersnapper if it ain't Andrew Halley. What a pleasure to see you again, old friend," said the man.

"Henry, may I introduce you to Nathan Boone, son of the late Daniel Boone and none other," said Andrew proudly.

Henry was speechless. It took a moment for him to realize he should say something.

"Pardon me, please, I...I can't believe I am meeting such a famous personage. Why, everyone knows you and your father. I am indeed blessed this day. I am very pleased to meet you. Andrew forgot to say, my name is Henry Neugent, from Boston," said Henry.

"Well, I am plumb happy to make your acquaintance. You all must think I'm as crazy as a bed bug, a-runnin' around here, jumpin' off your desks. I hope I haven't damaged anything too important, Andrew. You see, I got to playin' with your little friend there and well, we just got carried away with the game. She sure is a feisty little thing, and... what?" Nathan Boone was stopped abruptly by the look of wonderment in the other gentleman's eyes as they looked at the floor.

Nathan followed their gazes to the small perky black and white dog, sitting next to Nathan's foot. Her ears were alert and perked up, but bent at the middle, the ends flopped over neatly. Her head was held at a tilted angle as if to ask a question. Her face was all dark with sparkling mischievous black eyes, and her body was almost all white with a few brown/black splotches across her shoulders and rump, which was compact and muscular. The tail, which had been cropped short, stood at attention, quivering. Her legs were short but not out of proportion to her compact body. As she sat waiting, she panted to cool down. Suddenly she gave a piercing bark, and it was then that they got a good look at her teeth. Formidable was the only word for them.

"Am I mistaken in thinkin' you have not met, yet?" asked Nathan.

Waking up from a daze, Andrew smiled broadly.

"No, not yet, but I have been expecting her," said Andrew.

"Then let me introduce you to Penny, second Jack Russell Terrier to bless American shores. She was shipped here by special courier, a gift as I understand it, for your son, Jackson. I was asked to accept delivery since it was known you were not yet in your offices. We have had quite a time getting to know one another, haven't we girl?" said Nathan Boone.

"Rrrrup... rrrrrup," answered Penny.

"She is not quite a year old, and of a different blood-line from the other Jack Russell the Reverend sent to your son a few of years ago, I gather. I believe he already wrote to you. Something about having a mated pair and not letting the male sire with any other breed. I gather it is serious stuff, Andrew. But, I am telling you here, and now, playin' with her is like three jerks of a cat's tail. She just don't wear out and smart, whooowe...smart as a whip. Well, I mean real smart. She can plum wear a fella' out, she is a real flutterbudget, she just can't stand still for no time a-tall. Uh... oh, I been caught," said Nathan as Penny tugged fiercely on his pant leg.

"I think she wants her ball back," said Andrew, smiling from ear to ear, "We are to accompany her to her new home down by Fort Smith. That new town called Van Buren, where my son raises and breaks mules for sale, mostly to the Army."

For the first time since they walked in the building, Henry realized something, "Why, you old scallywag. This is the female we are supposed to accompany to your son's place? You had me thinking we were about to take on a troublesome female."

"Whoa, now wait a gosh dern minute. You have not met a troublesome female until you have spent a day with Penny here. I am no young'un anymore, and you saw what she had me doin' just to keep her happy. She's no lap dog, I guarantee it," said Nathan.

As the three men talked and got acquainted, Andrew took them to his office on the second floor of the building. Every step taken was taken with Penny attached to Nathan's pant leg, tugging for all she was worth. Nathan just adjusted his gait, so she would not get hurt and proceeded up the stairs and into Andrew's office.

Andrew sat down in the chair behind his desk, Nathan and Henry both scooting chairs close to the side so they could talk in confidence. Andrew began petting the top of Penny's head while stroking his chin.

"I do believe, Henry, we may have to rethink our plans to ride down through Kansas Territory. If she is as mischievous as Nathan says, we two old fogies won't be able to keep track of her. We might just have to go on the steamboat just to get her, or us come to think of it, there safely," said Andrew.

"Now, that's the second reason why I am here to see you, Andrew," said Nathan. "You may already know, that since my last campaign in '34 with Gen. Henry Leavenworth when he tried to make a treaty with the Comanche, Kiowa and Wichita down on the Red River, I been doing various duty for the Army. You know that Leavenworth, along with 150 of our men, died out there, most of them from lack of water. I was a Captain in command of Company H of the First Dragoons.

"That sure was a memorable trip, though. We had that famous artist George Catlin with us, plus I had a dandy interpreter with me, man by the name of Jesse Chisholm, a Cherokee, and a right good man. I am back here and alive to tell the story partly because of him.

"Now, I've been requisitioned by the Army to do some surveying for them. I have already done some in Indian Territory, surveying the line between Fort Snelling and Fort Gibson and there is more to do yet.

"However, I think there are some troublesome things beginning to happen within Indian Territory. I may have to head up a dragoon company to keep the peace if I can. They have ordered me to come down, post haste to Fort Gibson, but first they wanted me to persuade you not to go the land route south. We are having a real time of it with the whiskey traders down yonder, and it is not safe, plus your son asked the commander at Fort Smith to request an escort. We are to take you down the ole Mississip if you're of a mind to comply," said Nathan respectfully.

Andrew looked at Henry who left the decision up to him.

"I am extremely sorry, Henry. I wanted to take you out on the trail where not many white men have ever been. It looks as though we are going to have to make the trip on a steamboat," said Andrew.

"Now, don't go an' get your drawers in a knot," said Nathan. "You can still do that after you get down there for the way back. The Captain at the fort can give you some good directions to keep you gents out of trouble on the trail. So just think of it as being postponed. Alrighty?"

"That sounds like an excellent idea, Nathan, as long as Andrew is happy with it," said Henry.

With Andrew's firm nod, they set about making arrangements to board the next steamboat available going south. They would have to think of a way to keep Penny from making too much mischief. It was obvious that she was going to be a handful for Jackson.

For Penny's part, she finally tired of playing and made it clear she needed to go outside. Once back in, she lay down at Nathan's feet for a nap. Nathan sighed, looking at her. She was a truly different type of dog than he had ever been around. She made him feel young. He made a note to himself to get a pup, possibly from Jackson from the first litter. Yes, Penny was remarkable.

Chapter 20

Medicine Man sat silently in front of the low smokeless fire, praying. It was late afternoon, and the sun was far in its decent. The light breeze came through the cracks in the lodge walls, but Medicine Man paid no attention, felt no joy in the beautiful day. Something was terribly wrong, and he needed the Creator's help. It had depressed him profoundly once he realized how easily those men could have killed him, and there was no one to stop them, no one who even cared if an Indian lived or died. His gut always felt like it had a knot in it these days, but sitting in his lodge moping would not change anything. An answer came to him, right to his very own door, in the form of Coyote, that young Lakota/Blackfoot brother. Looking into Coyote's eyes was like looking into the days when there were no white men. Pure innocence. Coyote had come there to learn, and it was Medicine Man's belief that Coyote would be the one to save his people from the fate of the Cherokee if his people would heed the warnings.

And then there were the problems here in Indian Territory. When Joseph was here, he had told him about the many lives the Choctaw had lost so far from lack of food. He also told him about the Osage losing half of their number. This was truly an unspeakable evil. How could they fight against men who never came to the Indian Territory from Washington, but always sent a man who hated them with his entire being? Were they afraid they might actually like us? Are they running away from finding out that we are the same? Earlier he had heard the phrase "Manifest Destiny" many times, but did not understand what it was. Now he knew. He wished he could forget. He wished he could be like Coyote, blissfully ignorant, and then maybe it would not hurt so much. They used that phrase as an excuse to take what did not belong to them, to salve their consciences. They invented a lie and then proceeded to believe their own lie.

Medicine Man did not know how long he could live with this pain tucked deep inside of him. He felt the many years of his life, heavy on his shoulders, yet inside he still felt like a young man. He was supposed to be a spiritual leader among his people, but his people were losing their way, dividing into different factions. The Cherokee nation may as well break up into different nations if it kept on like this. The white man had done an exceptionally good job of driving wedges between brothers and not just in the Cherokee nation, but also in every Indian nation they took hold of.

But, it was not like the Cherokee had been wild Indians. They were as civilized as their white neighbors and still it was not enough to secure their rights to their own lands. It seems, the white man will not tolerate any difference in the color of skin either ours, which they call red, or the African's black or the Mexican's brown. The thought made him pause and wonder a moment. Then he heard the hide at the door swish open. Poison Woman was back from picking herbs in the nearby fields and woods.

"*Osiyo*, my brother, I hope you are well, and the Creator is smiling at you. I see you have been praying. I have also," said Poison Woman.

"Has the Creator answered your prayer, my sister?" asked Medicine Man.

"I did not think he had until Coyote was brought to your door. Now I am made to believe that we should ask for a few days visit from Sasa and her special friend, Wheezer. I am not sure why this has come into my heart, but I think it is what we are supposed to do," said Poison Woman.

"Then, sister, instead of sending a message, I am made to think we should both go and personally make the invitation. I feel bad that I did not go when Jackson called for me as I promised I would. It is only right that we go to them for this request now," answered Medicine Man.

It would be an all day trip, so they decided they would prepare for their journey that evening and go first thing after the sun woke up.

*****

Anna sat back on the straight backed chair in the parlor, sipping her after dinner coffee and listening to the others talk. It seems so strange that she should be in love with the man responsible for exposing her father's duplicity, but she had to admit that she loved Jackson's values.

196

What other man would care for the Cherokee the way that he did, or any of the tribes for that matter. How was she to nudge him into proposing? Anna wanted to be married to Jackson for love, not just to be his friend. This time, though, she came to dinner with a plan.

Lucius O'Malley had taken time away from his business so that he could insure her safety traveling from Fort Smith to Van Buren. It was not a particularly long trip, but in view of the attack on her person a couple of days ago, she was gratefully happy to have the company. They had arrived at Jackson's mule breeding ranch in the afternoon. They planned on spending the night, and the next day. Maybe, on this occasion, she could show Jackson what kind of woman she was.

"Jackson, I was hoping that tomorrow you would show me around your breeding ranch. I am anxious to know how you raise the offspring; how you prepare them for the jobs they will do once they are of adult age. Maybe, you could even show me how a mule is made, you know, the scientific side of it," said Anna boldly.

Jackson flushed red first at his ears, then it spread down his cheeks and soon his entire head was a red as a beet.

"Well, I guess I can do that Anna. Uh... are you sure you want to be out in all that dust? I am not sure you want to hear about the full process, I mean, it is a bit graphic. Remember, I have quite a few stock. The smell alone can be difficult to handle, uh... for a lady," said Jackson.

Anna seethed inside but only smiled benignly on the outside.

"I will be fine, Jackson. Just think of me as one of the boys," said Anna.

"Wha... uh... sure. If that is what you want," said Jackson whose sweat was now popping out and dripping down his face. Anna just looked as if she had not seen his consternation.

Sasa sat across the room, quietly stroking Wheezer as he lay on the hearth, his head on her lap, his eyes closed. She watched Anna and Jackson with tender amusement. She smiled at the two of them. She could not understand why they didn't just speak plainly to one another. In her tribe, a woman knew a man was interested by the gifts he brought to her father and sometimes by his playing of his flute outside of her lodge. It was an old custom, but still in use and highly effective. If a girl were interested, she would come out of the lodge and comment on his playing then invite him in to sit with her family. There was no skirting around the subject as Jackson and Anna seem to do. Sasa had known for some time that Anna loved Jackson, but she was also a lady and was not about to go chasing off after a man. Even in Sasa's tribe that would be a dishonor to her family. The boy must show his interest first before anything else can happen. That was the way that Yahweh or God in the English, said it should be. She thought Anna and Jackson might benefit from that Cherokee teaching if they would stand still long enough to listen.

Then a thought popped into her head. Just before, they greeted their guests for the next couple of days, Sasa and Jackson had had the solemn duty to bring another slain Indian's body back to their ice house until a runner could bring the family back to claim him. The last words of Sam Bushyhead came back to her in a crushing blow. The comment about the masked Irishman in disguise made her think about Mr. O'Malley. He was a merchant, which fit Sam's puzzling description. He was Irish, also, but Sam had said he was masked and in disguise.

She looked down at Wheezer, and it was then that she realized that Mr. O'Malley was probably not the person.

If he had been a cold blooded killer, Wheezer would not have let him near her. So, that meant that the killer was disguising himself as someone else. She would need to look over the poem which had been found on James, who had been hot on the trail of a criminal. Maybe this person was one in the same man for both murders and the whiskey dealing, as well. It was another piece to the puzzle.

Lucius sat there with his plastered smile on his face, trying hard not to show his desperate feelings for Anna. He could see how she looked at Jackson. Could she not see that he also looked at her in that same way? This visit was going to be harder than he thought. He had been overjoyed to spend so much time with Anna, but he had not thought she had feelings for anyone else. Now he could see how much he lacked in comparison with Jackson Halley. And yet, Jackson was being extremely civil to him. *Could it be that Jackson was unaware of Anna's regard for him? If this was so, then there is hope for me after all*, he thought.

Chapter 21

The man bent forward, looking both ways before he slipped out of the remote shack where he had the finished kegs of whiskey stored just before delivery. No one had bothered to look in this out-of-the-way place. Why? From the outside, it only looked like a tumble down heap destined for a winter's supply of firewood from the outside. But, inside it was ingeniously expanded down underground through generous use of planking and sturdy posts to hold back the sandy soil found close to the Arkansas River. Even if one had opened the creaky door, they would not see anything of value. Down below in a small dug out room, dark and dank, were stored

keg after keg of whiskey. If whiskey production stopped today, they would still have an ample supply for many weeks.
However, that was not likely to happen.

Captain Stuart was his chief opponent; the one sad-
dled with the responsibility to stop him from getting his
whiskey into Indian Territory. The man was still formulat-
ing his plan to shift suspicion to a very small player in his
enterprise. But, so far, the captain had not been much of
a threat, so there was certainly no reason why the man
should be worried, but inexplicably he was worried. He felt
he was being watched, almost continually and the feeling
would not leave him no matter how much he looked for the
hidden threat. It was a bit uncanny, though he tried hard
not to fall back on his cultural heritage, believing in the 'little people' and feeling ominous omens in any chance thing
that happened. Still, he could not chase the feeling away.

More than anything, he wanted to escape exposure. Every day he pretended to be a lowly uneducated
merchant settler on the new frontier while his mind cried
out for the refined life he had led as a part of the ruling
lords of Ireland. There was no use in pining for that life
since he could never go back unless it was in a pine box.

There were advantages to his new persona. The opportunity for profit was limitless for a clever lad like him
and, if you did not mind leaving a few bodies behind you,
you could carve out a veritable empire under the very nose
of the Army Captain who had been ordered to find the
leader and bring him to justice. One such body was that
of that fool Indian, James. The one thing that made it easy
here on the frontier was that it was not against the law to
dispatch an Indian or even a half-breed. Virtually nothing
was said about it, and no one bothered to investigate. So,
the few bodies he had left strewn on the ground as he con-

ducted his lucrative commerce were just part of the business. However, it still gave him satisfaction since he felt any dead Indian was one less Indian that would have to be dealt with later.

The government had seriously erred when making these treaties in exchange for land. What kind of thinking was that when they could have made these people their slaves at the very least? At the most, they could have sold them down into Mexican territories, never to be heard from again. Then, instead of whiskey running, he would have become a land baron as his family had been for generations. That, he thought, would be his ultimate achievement as long as his true identity could remain unknown and buried for all time.

It was silly to think he suspected a little dog, but there was something accusing in the look of that dog the other night on the dock. He could not think of a scenario where a dog could expose him, but still the worry kept digging at his every waking thought. He knew the dog belonged to that Halley man over in Van Buren.

Tonight he had something to take care of. That ridiculous woman he had chosen to pretend to be his wife was becoming an extreme liability. Somehow she had gotten the notion in her head that they were man and wife. He had sent her to visit that Edwards woman to sniff out what Miss Edwards was doing with that young squaw coming over to her house in town every day and that was fine, however, she was beginning to make sounds as if she were a society matron of the town. He did not want attention brought unduly to his activities. Right now, he was a happy, congenial merchant of Fort Smith, and it was just the kind of blind he wished to project. So tonight, he would have to persuade the old cow physically to keep to the script. If he had wanted attention, he would have gotten a bit of fluff to play the part. Instead, he got this frump of a woman from a backwater in Tennessee.

And if he were unable to convince her of his sincerity, he would have to devise a method of removing the problem permanently. He also thought he might slip across the river to Van Buren and check out the Halley property, to see if anything important was going on over there.

*****

Coyote was getting restless living in the home of Joseph. It was not that they were not hospitable to him, in fact, they had welcomed him even though they knew of his tribe and their thirst for war. Joseph had had little time to spend with Coyote since Joseph said he was still trying to find some clue as to how his friend James met his end. Coyote had gotten up at dawn to greet the sun. He was surprised to see that Joseph and all his family did the same thing. It had never occurred to him that other tribes could be so similar in their habits. After a little soup, and something they called 'fry bread', Coyote was ready to learn more of his surroundings.

Joseph had left for a little while, but returned with a terribly sour look on his face.

"My brother Joseph, I see you are troubled. What has happened so early in the morning to ruin your day?" said Coyote in sign and some English words he had learned.

"I am sad and angry, Coyote. I have just returned from our council house and found that a very good friend was murdered. They just got word, so someone must to go to Van Buren and pick up his body so he can be buried on his family's place. I am sure that it is again about this whiskey selling. I cannot say his name, but his family are the Bushyheads. He was one of our esteemed elders, bent on stopping this bad trade with our people.

"Earlier this year a great prophet and Chief of the Cherokee died, and our elder was badly upset by it. The Chief was able to convince his whole town not to take the drink that makes men crazy. The whites call this drink by many names like rum or whiskey. Some taste different from others, but all are dangerous for the People. The Chief's name was Yonaguska, an Oconaluftee Cherokee, and he was almost ruined by this drink. For most of his life, he was like a crazy man, drinking until he fell down and slept wherever he was. He became sick and was not with us for many days. When he woke up, he said he had a vision and that no one of his band were to drink any more of the bad drink. We all looked up to this Chief because he was blessed with wisdom," said Joseph.

"This Yonaguska, was he a warrior? Did he win any battles against the whites?" asked Coyote, hoping that he might learn a strategy that could help his people.

Joseph sat for a moment on a tree stump of newly cleared forest area. He shook his head solemnly before he finally said, "I knew him and his family and his clan called him Drowning Bear, but to the whites he was only Yonaguska, a Cherokee who resisted the whites peaceably. When other Chiefs bargained with the white government to give up more of their land, Yonaguska refused even to go to the council meetings. He would not listen to such talk, and he told the whites that, too. But he was also a clever Chief. He had adopted a young white boy named Thomas, William Holland Thomas. He raised that boy and sent him to school so he could be a lawyer to represent the Oconaluftee Cherokee to the government. It was this move that actually saved him. His adopted son advised him to become a citizen of the United States. Then William bought some of the land that was most sacred to the Cherokee, over 640 acres, and held the deed for his father Yonaguska and his people. It is said that Yonaguska was rounded up and made to walk on the Trail Where They Cried, and he walked with the People for many miles. Then one night, he slipped away from the soldiers and walked all the way back to North Carolina. He was able to find several of the mountain Cherokee, and he brought them onto the land that William Thomas bought. They were protected there by the white man's own laws. He beat them at their own game.

"Our elder also knew Yonaguska and he wanted to help his clan that were here, but he knew that the whiskey had to stop, or our people were doomed. His family says that he went out yesterday and did not come back. He was found stabbed on the dock that crosses over to Fort Smith, which is a long walk for an elder. He may have ridden a horse, but none was found near him.

"A daughter of the People heard his last words, and she made sure we knew them, but the words do not mean anything to me. Now I must go to where our daughter lives to ask her new white father what he thinks we need to do and then bring our elder back to his family," said Joseph.

"How is this, that you have a daughter of your tribe claim a white man for a father. Can this really be true?" asked Coyote, very puzzled.

"I am hitching up the wagon to ride over to our daughter's house in Van Buren. Would you go with me and then I can tell you more about our tribe's daughter, Sasa. So please, come out and help me get ready to go, I will show you how to hook up a horse so that it will be happy to pull a wagon," said Joseph.

"Yes, this is good. In my tribe, we do not have such things. We use a travois as our fathers have done. A wagon in our camp would be considered a bad thing," cautioned Coyote.

"Do not worry my friend, the wagon is similar, but it can move more and heavier things. Many Indian tribes use these. On the Trail Where They Cried, there were a few wagons, but mostly for the old, sick and dying. Come, I will show you this. Then you can decide for yourself what is good for your own people," said Joseph as he hurried Coyote out of the lodge into the early morning dew.

Coyote lashed the reins of his horse to the back of the wagon, for he wanted to listen to Joseph as they went. Coyote was in awe of what this man Joseph was making his horses do for him. When he thought of the herds of ponies his tribe possessed, he could not think of any that would submit to pulling a wagon, not even his own pony. They would kill themselves bucking and thrashing around. However, he noticed that Joseph's horses did not seem to mind; in fact both horses seemed eager to go.

As they traveled, Joseph told Coyote the story of their long trek from their homeland, and how all the People's hearts were low to the ground. So many died, lost to them forever. So many of the young died on the way. Almost an entire generation of children were lost, so now his people were making as many babies as they could, but starvation still hovered over them and the whiskey was making many desperate families turn to stealing. When the man will not work to feed his wife and children, where could they go for help? Since it was mostly the government agents taking money from the food allotments, there was nowhere for his people to turn.

He told Coyote about last year when they arrived in Indian Territory and how Sasa's little brother was murdered in a singularly strange way. He even spoke of the remarkable dog that helped Sasa to figure out where the evil was coming from. Finally, he related who Jackson Halley was and why he was a most important friend to the People.

Coyote was silent for some time after Joseph finished his tale. *There must be something I can learn from this that can help my people. I don't know enough yet to take back. I am not even sure that I should,* he thought. So, he rode quietly beside Joseph. He watched as they passed much dry prairie with red soil in some places. It seemed to glow as if it were throbbing under the ground. He wondered why there was red soil in some places and not in others. This place was not like the tall grass prairie he was from to the far north. Yes, there was some tall grass here, but on the plains by the Big River, it stood higher than a man's head. He wanted to get down and walk so he could inspect the plants, taste them and see what medicinal properties they had. As he rode along, his heart was filling with a need and an excitement. This land was so unlike where he was from that he was eager to learn as much about it as he could while he was here. Then suddenly he burst out in a prayer song as he stood up, turning his body to the east. Joseph had to grab hold of his pants to keep Coyote from pitching off of the wagon, but he did not utter a sound, knowing that Coyote was having a sacred moment with the Creator.

"Oh, great Wakan Tanka, Creator help me to see the things I am needed to see. Oh, great Wakan Tanka, Creator, help me to open my eyes and open my ears. Give me wisdom that I may be of help to my people. Oh, great Wakan Tanka, I fear my people will fall into the same pit of evil that these Cherokee have fallen into. Like quick sand, they wiggle and struggle, yet they sink lower into the hole in the earth. Oh, great Wakan Tanka hear my prayer," he chanted many times raising his arms above his head, beseeching his God. Then he slowly sat down and remained quiet.

They rode on, side by side for some time, then up ahead, Joseph could see two people walking, not particularly fast, but still walking. As he got closer, he could see they were elder Indians. Recognition bloomed finally, and he hailed them.

"Medicine Man, Poison Women, we are going your direction. Will you not let me do you some good? Please let me help you up into the wagon, and you can ride the rest of the way," said Joseph.

"Ah, my son, I am not as young as I used to be and today our destination is far. We are going to see Jackson Halley," said Medicine Man.

"Yes, grandfather, we are going to the same place. So why don't we have your sister to sit up beside me while you and Coyote sit in the wagon. I am sure we can be there much faster than if you had walked," said Joseph.

It seemed wise to both the elders, so they allowed Coyote to help them up into the wagon. Coyote was all smiles, seeing the faces he had become familiar with while in this strange place. There were still quite some miles to go yet, but the group had a pleasant trip as they talked, helping Coyote to learn the English of the trees, plants and animals they passed. Poison Woman was pleased that Coyote was so quick to pick it up, and already he had given her some insight to some of the prairie plants in Indian Territory that also grew further north and their medicinal uses.

With Medicine Man, Coyote spoke of the rituals and customs of the Shaman, Forgets Things and explained about the yearly gathering of the Sioux for the Sun Dance. Medicine Man was aghast when Coyote explained how the braves allowed skewers to be pierced in either breast above the nipples. These skewers were tied to a thong that was attached to a pole in the middle of the dance ground. Medicine Man winced as Coyote spoke about the brave leaning back, blowing on a shrill whistle as the skewers eventually ripped through the flesh. Any brave who went through this ordeal was never again questioned about his bravery. He had proven it once and for all. When asked if Coyote had undergone this ritual, he shook his head slowly from side to side. Then said, "This is for warriors who wish to earn honor among the people for their bravery in battle. I have never felt that was my path, for I do not see the need for blood-shed when living in peace would benefit us all."

This, coming from what they called a Wild Plains Indian, was contrary to everything they knew about the plains tribes. Could it be that there were peaceable men within those warring tribes to the west and north? From that time on, Medicine Man looked with great respect at Coyote and knew that he had been sent on this journey to help him find a way to save his people other than war. Time would tell if what he learned here would be success-ful since it would depend on the varied Chiefs of those tribes to come to peaceful terms with their enemies. Even some of the clans of the Cherokee had not put their weap-ons down. There were still skirmishes and deaths between them and the Osage, and it would probably go on for some time since the government saw fit to place them side by side forcing them to be neighbors.

As they rode along on that clear morning, Medicine Man enjoyed listening to Coyote's animated talk, his youth-ful exuberance and his all-encompassing curiosity. At the same time, Coyote listened with proper respect any time Medicine Man had anything to add to the conversation. Poison Woman looked on with awe at the change that had come over her brother, realizing it was all due to the pres-ence of Coyote. Just when she thought her brother had given up, the Creator gave Medicine Man a job to do, that of teaching Coyote, and it was a blessing in disguise.

Chapter 22

Breakfast at Jackson Halley's had been full of smiles and conversation. Anna was completely at ease and obviously enjoying her visit. Jackson was likewise happily engaged. Arch, who was well acquainted with Anna, had been persuaded to tell a few funny stories of his family, before the forced march had ripped them apart. Sasa was content to sit and listen, enjoying the camaraderie with Wheezer at her feet, and seeing them so happy together. The only one at table that seemed ill at ease was Lucius O'Malley. The others did not seem to notice his shy behavior for they were all concentrating on the stories. Laughter went round the table like a whirlwind, and even Lucius found himself chuckling. Before breakfast was over, he had actually forgotten that he had been sitting at the table with a competitor for the charms of a wonderful lady. Partly because he would remember that he virtually had no chance to win her.

On the other hand, Jackson, although laughing and conversing easily with them all, believed he sat at across from the man who had replaced him in Anna's affections. He tried hard to keep the tragedy he felt from his countenance.

"What have you done to this dining room, Jackson? It looks completely redone. I love the wallpaper," said Anna as she rose from her chair and ran her fingers across the closest wall.

"Thank you, my dear. I had a devil of a time getting the right things all the way out here. Actually, I wrote to my Aunt Mildred back in Boston, gave her the dimensions and the things I wanted to decorate, and she did the choosing for me. The only thing is I had to wait until someone moved out here who knew how to paint and put up the paper. The furniture was easy enough. I ordered it from the same woodworkers my family has used for years, and they shipped it out here by steamboat. The deuced shipping costs were more than the cost of the furniture," replied Jackson.

Anna admired the large pink and white cabbage roses in the paper which was hung between wide white moldings. The drapes were of a soft silk in a light shade of pink and white glass curtains behind them. When the drapes were pulled open, the sun was filtered through the glass curtains which softened the room, making it inviting. Besides the dining room table and chairs, there were various and sundry other pieces of furniture placed around the room which was fairly large one for the area. In one corner was a large settee and ottoman with small stuffed chairs to either side. A large side board buffet with a matching crystal cabinet with curved glass sat opposite the large fireplace. Hidden behind the new drapes was a long window seat with many drawers and cabinets under it. All the wooden pieces were of a mellow cherry wood with its dark, rich color. The floor was hardwood stained the same as the furniture with a large oriental carpet covering the majority of its expanse. All in all, Anna thought it very nice, in fact, so nice she wondered if some female a little closer to home had helped...but no, she would take him at his word.

"I can't want to be shown around the ranch. I want to see everything," said Anna.

"Everything? Are you sure, Anna?" said Jackson.

"Quite," said Anna.

"Yes, I would like that as well, Jackson," said Lucius.

She took Jackson's proffered arm as Arch led the way with Lucius bringing up the rear.

Sasa excused herself from the tour as she had promised Wheezer they would go exploring on the acreage. She could hear Jackson explaining as he went. Maybe later she would be able to have a short talk with Anna. There were some things puzzling her. In fact, it was hard to put into words. Sasa was feeling as if the pressure were building, tension in the air made her somewhat wary.

Today she had put on her deer skin dress and some worn moccasins. Wheezer was all aglow with excitement, ready for whatever game Sasa would think up. He bounced along beside her until she stopped, thought for a moment, then turned around, going back the way they had come.

"I will be back, Wheezer. I forgot something; wait here," said Sasa.

Now that was something that Wheezer found hardest to do. Waiting and standing still was impossible for him, so he charged off to run around the tree a few times until Sasa emerged out of the front door at a trot.

They walked along a path lined with young Mimosa trees that led out into the pasturage close to the beginning of a forested area. Looking in all directions, she walked, taking care not to make much noise. Wheezer stopped and stared at her for a moment until she turned around and noticed he was not following. She crept back to him, knelt down and whispered into his ear.

"White and Black Whiskers, there is something different about today. I am not sure what it is, but it is wise to be cautious. I went back in to get my knife and sheath. So my friend, you may help me keep watch as we go. Once we are in a clear area, and I know we are alone, we can play any game you like," said Sasa.

Wheezer immediately began scanning in various directions. He placed his nose to the ground, but nothing alarmed him. He looked back up at her with one ear standing up straight and the other folded over, tilting his head as if to ask her "Is this what you want?" Sasa nodded to him, and they continued their walk.

She had been pondering on the recent murders of her people so close to where she lived. She was beginning to feel there ought to be something she should do to stop this violence. She thought, Was not this move supposed to bring us into a peaceful land that would belong to our tribes 'As long as grass grows and water runs?' At least that is what Chief John Ross said the white man's government had promised. If this were true, then why are my people being murdered and starved to death? Have we not given up everything we owned, our farms, all our belongings and then finally our blood? What more do they want from us that they must continue to kill us? Some rumor had said the Cherokee were being punished for fighting for the British, and yet the Chickasaws, who were also removed to Indian Territory had fought for the new republic. So, it did not seem to matter what our tribes do. It seems we are being extinguished; sometimes one at a time and other times in large groups. Sometimes death is violent with a gun, knife or a hanging; other times we just left to starve.

But, in her young life, she had not known the history of the land she now barely called her native land, and there was more ways to accomplish the white government's aim than the ones she saw firsthand. Now she was learning about the whiskey. *Yes*, she thought. *WHISKEY! It is a silent way of killing us, a slow way of wiping us away.* Now she was actually glad that her parents had not lived to see what happened next. True, she had fared well compared to the rest of her people, who had nothing. *But, I did not decide these things. I seem to have been placed in the middle of two opposing sides. If this is what the Creator has planned for me, then I have no right to turn down the opportunity to help my people. The only thing is, will I live through it?*

These musings kept her occupied as they glided along the path, but in an instant the sounds of the surrounding insects stopped cold and with it, Sasa stopped, as well. Something was close, deadly close.

*****

Joseph pulled the wagon up to the front yard of Jackson's ranch.

"Ho, the house!" he yelled and then waited.

Coyote thought this a strange way to announce one's arrival. However, he did not voice his question, but sat and waited to see what would transpire. After a few moments, an unusually short black human emerged from the house and upon seeing it Coyote exclaimed in what

214

was probably a Lakota epithet of some kind. Quickly he grabbed hold of the knife at his side and raising his arm high and proceeded to launch the blade at the apparition, but Joseph had caught Coyote's arm just in time so that the blade sailed and landed some feet before the house and stuck deep into the ground. Upon seeing what was almost her fate, Masey jumped back into the house and, without poking her head out, she hollered, "Jackson be out back with company Mastah Joseph. You goin' ta hafta' go an' fetch him yo'self, cause I ain't a-goin' ta be nobody's pin cushion today, no how."

Joseph, Medicine Man and Poison Woman began to laugh, first in a low chuckle and then uproariously until tears filled their eyes. Coyote could not understand what they were laughing at and on top of that, he was totally unsure about what had just happened. He had never seen a human that color before. The only thing he could think was that it had been a warrior who painted himself black all over as the Lakota did their faces sometimes and that his party had been in danger. Now it seemed that he was mistaken. Joseph said he would explain later, but told Coyote not to kill anybody that day if he could help it, then got down from the wagon still chuckling.

After retrieving Coyote's knife and returning it, he said, "I must go find Jackson. He is in another part of this place. You may look around if you like, but these are our friends. There are Cherokee who also live here and… uh… the black people as you saw. They will not harm you. That is truly the color of their skin, just as yours is brown and a white man's skin is white. Understand?"

"Yes, Joseph, I will not kill your friends," said Coyote. "I would see this black man."

"Uh, no, Coyote. That was a woman. She works for Jackson doing work in the lodge for them. I doubt she has met

215

a Lakota either. I will see if she will come out," said Joseph.

After a few moments, Joseph stepped off the porch and into the yard, beckoning Coyote to climb down from the wagon and approach.

"Coyote, this is Masey. She works very hard and is a fine woman. She is also a friend of the Cherokee. Please greet her," said Joseph.

Coyote tentatively stepped forward, then, looking down the full length of his nose said, "I am Coyote of Lakota Sioux and Blackfoot."

Masey was a bit nonplussed at this introduction. She did not know what it was he said he was, but he was a remarkably handsome looking young man and his clothes showed his muscular body off a little more than she was used to seeing.

She said, "Well, I declare. I never heard of whatever it was yo said, suh, but I is glad you didn't kilt me, and it's good to be alive to meet you. So, Mastah Coyote, does yo wants some refreshments?" said Masey, blushing under her dark skin.

Coyote looked to Joseph for an answer who nodded his head and Coyote in turn said, "Yes".

While the others sat and sipped lemonade, Joseph went in search of Jackson. It was a large ranch, and he had no idea where to look first. Masey had said that Miss Anna Edwards was with him, and he thought it would be pleasant to see that lovely young girl again. People said she had been a real help the year before, even though it was her own father who had been the criminal. He walked around the side of the house looking every which way. Hopefully he would find what he was looking for quickly.

Coyote told Medicine Man he wanted to stroll around the area. Especially after the drink he just had which puckered up his lips and at the same time was sweet as honey. Actually, it had been a long ride, and he needed to find a place to relieve himself, but upon looking around the outskirts of the house, he could not find the place where people left their excrement. So he chose an obscure place, and when that was done, he began to wonder what a ranch looked like. There were several paths out into various parts of the area, so he chose one and began down it.

*****

Wheezer laid his ears back, making a low growl. He slowly crept into a patch of overgrown wild grape vines which had mounded up over some object, completely covering it. After a good sniff, he stiffened and began barking furiously, running from one side of the mound to the other, then clawing at the ground to find a path into the mass of branches. Sasa heard a few squeaks, then suddenly three jackrabbits darted out of the mound and were gone faster than Wheezer even knew what happened. Sasa smiled, knelt down to pet him.

"Shssss, we must be quiet now. My spirit is uneasy too, but I do not think it was the rabbits that I am feeling nervous about, so we must keep on the watch. I am not worried that you won't protect me, Wheezer. You are my White and Black Whiskers, and we have a bond, you and I. We both know things others do not, and that is why I trust you. We may not be able to play today because I feel we are in danger. So, let us circle around and head back to the ranch while we stay on our guard," whispered Sasa.

She stroked Wheezer again, but before she could rise from her kneeling position, something hit her violently at the back of her head. Sasa fell to the ground. Wheezer's fur stood straight up on his back as a fierce snarling growl came from his throat. He turned quickly to locate the assailant and caught a fleeting glimpse of a person, but it had a hood and a cape. It whirled away as Wheezer started out after the retreating form when unexpectedly, the form spun around smacking Wheezer across the snout with the butt of a rifle. The blow connected with a thump, sending him flying. He landed, unconscious not too far from where Sasa was laying. Sasa, began to stir, then slowly sat up, placing her hand behind her head, feeling something wet and sticky. She saw Wheezer some small distance away, laying on the sandy soil and weeds, not moving a muscle. Sasa let out a howl that would have given anyone hearing it the cold chills.

From the direction of the Ranch, running through the bramble, blackberry vines and tall grass, came a form. Sasa found her knife in the grass and brought it up to defend herself and Wheezer. She had no time to think when a tall and lithe Indian, with his own knife drawn, ready to do battle emerged through the tall grass. There was no time to think, just react as Sasa let fly her Green River knife. As smoothly as a waltz, the Indian bent his form away from the sailing blade, then quickly held a defensive stance for what might come next. Sasa was so astonished she could not speak, and took no notice of another form which trotted through the foliage from the forest side, parting the blades of grass and brush as easily as cutting butter, but stopped short of the last layer of concealment while he stood watching, himself unseen.

Coyote stood over the scene, trying to understand what he was seeing. An Indian girl also stood in a defensive stance; at her feet lay a small form, a dog. For a moment, Coyote thought she was protecting her dinner.

When Sasa saw that this warrior had not let his knife go, she decided he had not been the original attacker. With a groan of pain, she sat on the ground holding her head; the small dog still lay motionless at her feet. He heard the sounds coming from the forest and looked up just in time to see the wild coyote emerge. He was still holding his knife, but something stayed his hand as he stared at the aberration before him. Yellow Eyes stayed calm. He did not run, nor did he growl, but continued to watch the man. Yellow Eyes brought his golden eyes up to meet the man's intense dark brown eyes. They held each other's gazes, caught up in each other while the world spun around them. After a short time, Yellow Eyes looked down at Wheezer, knowing that something must be wrong if Wheezer did not get up and greet him.

Sasa had watched the encounter and was loath to interfere for she had never seen this man in her life and Yellow Eyes was not even baring his teeth. Coyote finally looked down and said in English, "I am Coyote of Lakota and Blackfoot. Are you... uh (then he signed) in danger from this coyote? Is this animal a spirit so that it does not tear you apart?"

Yellow Eyes had slowly advanced and had stepped closer to Sasa. He would have to pass between Coyote and her to get to the, as yet, unmoving Wheezer. He stopped for a moment next to Sasa as he cautiously watched the man. It occurred to Sasa that Yellow Eyes could actually kill this man who she felt had done nothing to harm them, so she calmly raised her hand, stroked Yellow Eyes and said to him, "Thank you, Yellow Eyes, for coming to help us. We will see how Wheezer is. I do not think this man is here to hurt us. *Wado*, my friend."

Coyote watched in awe as the girl stroked the wild coyote. He wondered if maybe he was having a spirit dream, for nothing like this had ever happened in his nation. Yellow Eyes had not taken his eyes from Coyote. Sasa's loving touch told him he should not be frightened. Slowly and cautiously, Yellow Eyes stepped towards Coyote, who stood dead still, not knowing what he should do. Kill it while he could or run? No, he was no coward, so he stood his ground, standing straight and tall while Yellow Eyes sniffed at his legs, then pawed the ground.

"Yellow Eyes is asking you to kneel down so he can get a better look at you," said Sasa as she began to scoot closer to Wheezer who was beginning to move. Coyote knelt on one knee, both sets of eyes still locked on each other. It was at that very moment, when years later Coyote would tell the story that he felt something change in his life.

Finally, Sasa began to speak. She knew something remarkable had just happened, but for now she was more concerned for Wheezer. However, when she tried to get up on her feet, she swayed and sat down hard on the ground. She raised her hand to stop the man from coming forward. As she began looking for the damage done to Wheezer she said, "Who are you? What tribe?" He seemed puzzled, so she began the introductions herself.

"Oh! I am Sasa. I live with Jackson Halley, over yonder a-piece," Sasa said.

"Jackson - Halley? That is the man we are here to visit," said Coyote.

"Really? Who are you with, does he know you are here?" asked Sasa.

"I am with Joseph. Joseph went to find where this man Jackson Halley is while I walked to look," said Coyote.

Sasa was now hovering over Wheezer as she sat on the ground. He did not appear to be badly hurt, and he was beginning to wake up fully. Wheezer looked up at Coyote and showed him a terrible snarl.

"No, Wheezer. This is not the bad man that hit us. This man," she thought for a moment, "is a friend of Yellow Eyes. You must treat him well. Do not get up, Wheezer, we will carry you to the house," said Sasa.

She tried to stand up to carry Wheezer, but it was useless. Coyote made a motion like picking up, and finally she understood what he wanted.

"First, put little dog in lap," Coyote signed.

He gathered her and Wheezer up in his arms with no effort at all, not even a grunt, then he turned to Yellow Eyes who had not moved. Coyote remembered how the girl spoke to the animal, so he followed suit.

"I am taking Sasa to her home," said Coyote.

Sasa was in total amazement. She thought she was the only one who would dare talk to a wild coyote like Yellow Eyes, but her head hurt, and she could not think for the pain and worry over Wheezer was uppermost on her mind. The question remained who attacked her with deadly intent and why?

*****

The attacker could have kicked himself for missing his best chance for getting rid of Sasa and her interfering dog. He had never seen anyone so hard to kill. It was not a help to have had that third party show up. If he had not been there, he would have had more time to finish the job. Now he would have to tell his employer that he messed it up again. However, he was not worried to the point of panic. He knew that his employer valued his singular position, and there was no one like himself who could be in both camps, and no one was the wiser. The fools still had not figured out who had killed James Koni, and they never would if he had his way about it. For now, he would have to be satisfied, knowing they were all still in the dark.

Chapter 23

Anna watched as Jackson showed them how he broke the mules they would use for pulling wagons, which was different, he explained, from the way he would break them for a saddle. Sometimes a mule would do both, but only if it wanted to. Mules were exceedingly stubborn, he explained. She thrilled at seeing all the excitement, the roping, the coaxing and teaching some of the finest mules available. Jackson had said that his orders from the Army were from as far away as Virginia. She could tell how much he loved what he did for his living. She wanted so much to be a part of it, as well.

Lucius had to give Jackson grudging respect for the way he handled his animals and his business. He had spent some time behind the plow with a mule pulling him down the field when he was much younger. It taught him to have a healthy respect for the mules because if you did not, you would pay later. Mules could be devilishly cantankerous in the best of times and tenfold worse if treated badly.

He also watched Anna watching Jackson and wondered why the man did not see the love in her eyes. Well, if Jackson was not going to value this wonderful woman, then he just might fill that need, just as soon as he got his life on the straight and narrow. He would be putting her in danger if he tried to court her now.

Jackson hopped off of a young mule in training for saddle and briskly walked over the corral fence where his company was watching.

"This is what we do every day, and this little molly mare will still require quite a bit more training before she is saddle ready for the Army. She is coming along fine, though; so far, she has not damaged any of the trainers, but she is easily spooked," said Jackson to all his guests.

"Jackson, could I try?" said Anna.

Jackson was nonplussed. He had never heard of a woman training anything larger than a dog, but how was he to refuse her request?

"Uh… Anna, I don't think that is wise. She is pretty skittish yet, plus she has never even been around the fairer sex. I have no idea how she would react," pleaded Jackson.

"Oh, I think I can manage," said Anna as she slipped through the space between the fence rungs.

Jackson hastened to try to head her off, but outside of putting his hands on her, he was at a loss of how to dissuade her. Quickly he motioned to Arch to enter the enclosure. Jackson and Arch moved over to the molly and tried to keep it from shying away as Anna approached. The more they tried to steady the mule, the more skittish it became. The mule's large eyes rolled in its head so that the whites seemed enormous. It began to snort and dance around some; Jackson was aware that he might have to grab Anna to take her from harm's way.

"Jackson, please step back from her. You are making her afraid. You, too, Arch, just back off and let me approach by myself," said Anna as she began making a soft shushing sound.

Jackson looked over at Arch for an answer of what to do; Arch just shrugged and backed up slowly to wait at the fence line. Jackson saw no way but to acquiesce, but his blood ran cold, picturing in his mind all the things that a fifteen hundred pound beast could inflict on a mere female. He visibly shuddered, then, watching Anna and the mule with earnest intensity, he also backed off to the corral fence line.

Now, all eyes were on Anna and the molly. Anna had stopped ten feet from the mule and picked up the training reins lying in the dirt. She began a faint sing-song of words and music, making complete eye contact with the animal.

"Now, now, now... shush my baby girl, now, now, now... shhhhh my little lady. Lo, lo, lo... Mommy is here to love you... lo, lo, lo... she will not hurt the baby girl," sang Anna low, almost unintelligible to the onlookers.

Every breath was held, every eye on the drama of the dance Anna was creating. Even Jackson was mesmerized. She took a new step with each new repeat of the sing-song notes. That morning, Anna had donned her Kelly green split skirt riding habit which included a light gold tweed jacket with flecks of green, black leather riding boots and black kid gloves she had brought, just in case she had the opportunity to ride. From the pocket, she pulled out a few pieces of apple and held it out in the palm of her hand. Finally, she was at the mule's head. The molly mule watched Anna, eye to eye and had stopped its skittish moving and snorting. The molly tossed her head up and down as if to say, yes, yes... come, and I will take your offering.

Without Jackson and Anna seeing, Medicine Man and Poison Woman had approached the fence from the far side of the ranch and the house. As Anna finished her chant, Medicine Man began one of his own. The mule briefly looked for the sound and was not disturbed by it. Then, while Anna reached out with the apple in one hand, she began to stroke the side of her face with the other. The molly made no move to evade the encounter. Medicine Man continued his song while Anna stepped closer to the mule, bringing her chest up against the muzzle of the molly.

Anna's pale hazel eyes gazed into the steady brown eyes of the mule and softly said, "I am not here to hurt you. Would you allow me to sit on your back?"

The mule made no sign as to whether it understood her or not, but it made no sudden moves when Anna stepped near the saddle area. The mule was of medium height, sleek and trim. Anna had no trouble putting her foot in the stirrup on the left side of the animal. Momentarily, the molly turned to look at what Anna was about to do and then turned an unconcerned gaze straight ahead.

Jackson's every muscle was tight; his hand gripped the fence with white knuckle intensity. This mule had just barely started her training, and almost anything could happen, most of it not good. Lucius made his way over to Jackson, who stood on the inside of the fence.

"Jackson, me boy, I do not think this is the best thing for the lass. Can you not do something to stop her from this folly?" Lucius asked.

Without turning his head to answer, Jackson said, "If we rush in now, it will surely spook the mule and Anna will most definitely be hurt. No, there is nothing we can do now, but watch and rush in when the molly throws her to the ground, as indeed she will."

Lucius was aghast at the thought of Anna being thrown and trampled and began to climb the fence when the firm grip of Medicine Man prevented him from mounting the first rung. The Indian continued his chant all the while, and Lucius was forced to watch like everyone else.

Anna placed her tiny foot in the high stirrup, so high that Jackson was amazed that she could bend that way. With a quick leap, Anna was mounted, sitting in the saddle astraddle like any man would ride. No one had bothered to think about the fact that the saddle was not meant for a lady. However, Jackson did not possess a side saddle so that question was moot. A general intake of breath from the onlookers was heard by Anna. She bent forward, whispering in the molly's ear, stroking its neck all the while. Then, with deft hands and without kicking the side of the animal, she encouraged the molly to move forward around the enclosure with clicks of her tongue. With each round, she coaxed her ride to move faster until finally it trotted as fast as it could within the relatively small corral.

Anna eventually slowed her mount, bringing the molly close to where Jackson stood, dismounting. Stroking the mule's neck, she again brought out of her pocket a handful of cut up apple to reward the mule.

"Thank you for letting me ride you. You are a beautiful thing, aren't you?" she cooed in its ear, then turned and placed the reins gently into Jackson hand.

Jackson looked after her with admiration in his eyes, seeing how her wheat colored hair had fallen out of its pins and framed her lovely, translucent face. She was

226

strong, clever and unafraid -- nothing like his first impression. Leaving the molly to the ranch hands to rub down and lead to her stall, he crawled through the fence.

Joseph appeared from the side of the barn. He stopped to smile and nod a greeting to Medicine Man and Poison Woman.

"Where have you been, you missed all the fun," said Poison Woman.

"I was looking for Jackson. This is a big place, this ranch. It took a while to locate him. I see you found him. You must have come around the other way," said Joseph.

Jackson had run to catch up to Anna, then easily walked beside her.

"You didn't tell me you knew anything about breaking a mule or a horse for that matter," he said.

"You never asked me. I have been riding since I was three. I spent many a day helping out at the stables in Boston, learning from the ranch hands. If my mother had known, she would have been scandalized, but she never found out. She thought I was visiting the ranch owner's daughter for tea twice a week. I had always dreamed of living on a ranch. I have just not ever had the opportunity. I hope you will allow me to come from time to time and help out," said Anna, then strolled away.

Jackson stood open mouthed, almost not believing what he had heard. Could it be that the woman he adored and denied would be happy to accept a life on the frontier? The idea was so new he could not absorb it.

As the group walked toward the house, the tour of the ranch being over, they all stopped in unison when Coyote, carrying both Sasa and Wheezer, emerged from the footpath. Jackson was immediately concerned, he had no idea who this Indian was, and was immediately enraged seeing the man actually holding his ward in his arms.

Medicine Man quickly stepped forward and said, "Jackson, my son, this is Coyote who is visiting us from the far north. He is an honorable man. Let us find out what is the cause of him having to carry your daughter."

Jackson lowered his gaze, realizing he had jumped to conclusions, "Yes, Grandfather."

Coyote said, "Sasa hurt. Dog hurt. Where take her?"

Without the use of his hands to sign, his language was clipped and stunted, but he successfully made his request known. Jackson motioned him inside the house to a place where Sasa and Wheezer could be placed on the couch in the library. Anna called for Masey to bring a bowl of water and clean cloths.

Anna carefully began to ascertain the damages. As she bathed the head wound Sasa incurred, Wheezer did not seem inclined to get off Sasa's lap; both of them seemed to have come through it with no life threatening damage. Sasa related the sequence of events.

"Damnation! This is going too far. Coming onto my own property and attacking us is a serious miscalculation, indeed. I can't imagine who would be that desperate. Why would anyone want to hurt Sasa?" said Jackson.

"Are you sure it was Sasa they were trying to eliminate? After all, Wheezer has been the one to lead you to each of the bodies, so far, and he was there to protect Sasa during that blatant attack. Now that you are letting her take Wheezer with her when she goes across the river, mightn't someone think him a threat?" asked Anna in a low, conspiratorial tone.

"To me, it does not seem likely that others would know what a smart dog he is. Since this attack involved both of them, maybe they want to eliminate both," added Arch.

There was silence as Anna continued to minister to
228

Sasa's head wound. As she worked, she asked Sasa, "Do you have any idea who the person was?"

"No. He hit me from behind. From that point, I don't remember anything until Coyote came running from the road, but Wheezer saw who it was because I think he may have gotten a look at him before the man hit him. Coyote said the man hit Wheezer with something hard, like the butt of a rifle. He also said he saw a dark coat over his head, which I think means he wore a cape or cloak to conceal himself," said Sasa, still holding Wheezer in her lap. "Jackson, can you look at Wheezer, and see if he is very much hurt?"

"Oh, of course, Sasa. I was so upset seeing you hurt, I completely forgot to check him," answered Jackson, who now derided himself for not doing it sooner.

Jackson removed Wheezer to the other side of the couch while he prodded and probed. Nothing seemed to be amiss until Wheezer coughed and spit out a part of a tooth. Jackson gently opened Wheezer's mouth, and it was then that he uttered a low growl like a moan. Obviously, his mouth or jaw was in pain.

"That's fine, boy. I know it hurts, but I had to look," said Jackson as he gently stroked Wheezer's back with a loving hand. "I don't see anything major broken except for a tooth. I am sure his jaw will hurt for some time, so we will have to be careful about what we give him to eat.

The group had all found seats in the large library. Both Medicine Man and Poison Woman had never seen the inside of a white man's lodge. From his look, Medicine Man was in awe of the comfortable room and the soft furniture. Poison Woman finally elbowed him to remind him of their errand.

"Jackson, you asked me to come. I am here, and I

also have much to tell, but this place does not seem like my lodge where we can have a council," said Medicine Man.

"What? Uh, oh, I understand. You can bring out your pipe, Grandfather, and we can do the honors as we would in your own lodge. We will set our chairs in a circle, but I have to draw the line at starting a fire in the middle of the floor," said Jackson with all seriousness, but a little tremble of his supple lips gave away the humor of his little joke.

Medicine Man smiled, but Coyote was lost. He did not understand the words so he would have to wait to see what happened. Wheezer gently hopped down from his place on the couch, going over to Coyote to sniff.

Jackson noticed Wheezer's action, which gave him the answer to a question he had considered: whether or not Coyote had been the attacker all along. Wheezer showed no sign of recognition, which was a relief to Jackson. Now he could concentrate on finding who really did this. His attention was brought back to the matter at hand, having a council.

"Jackson, I do not want to disrespect your home, however, I would feel more comfortable if we did this in our own traditional way. It would not be a council of the heads of clans, but I would feel better if we asked the Creator for his blessing. The best way to do that is in the traditional circle and the smoking of the pipe. It is a nice day so let us have a council outside in a place of your choosing, then I will make it ready," said Medicine Man.

Jackson knew better than to argue, for this was a matter of their respect for God, who they called Creator or *yi-oh-wa*. He needed all the goodwill and help he could get if he were to figure out who was trying to hurt Sasa. He found a good spot to the side of the house where a small camp fire could be made, and the grass was thick and lush. He showed the spot to Medicine Man and left it to him and his sister to prepare it. In the meantime, Sasa went to her room to get something, then came back to help the elders prepare.

It was late afternoon when all was in readiness, so they all gathered around the small fire while Medicine Man began the pipe ceremony.

"First of all, my friends, I am made to say that this is not the peace pipe. If I had brought the peace pipe, I would not be able to allow any woman to smoke it. If a woman touches a Dayohi Gununaway, she will have killed it, and it would be taken into the forest and buried, never to be used again. This pipe is a Usvdoni Gunanawe, my own tobacco pipe, and all can use it to send prayers up in the smoke and for Him to be with us for our council," said Medicine Man.

Lucius had never experienced anything like this, ever in his life. Now he could see these native people as having many similar characteristics to some of the clans in Ireland. He felt privileged to be included in this ceremony and yet he also felt that he was the last person who should be here. He felt like a traitor to these people, even though he had never sworn an allegiance to them. It was getting harder to live with himself.

Medicine Man had stuffed the bowl of the pipe with a mixture of herbs and wild tobacco and once lighted, he smoked and offered the smoke to the four directions and then also to the sky and the earth. Then he passed the pipe to the next person in the circle. Each person did the same, except for Wheezer who lay quietly next to Sasa until all the tobacco had been burnt. Then the pipe was cleaned and carefully put away in a special pouch that Medicine Man always carried with him.

Without a word, Sasa drew out of the fold of her skirt a single feather, attached to a small straight stick with painted designs on it. This was what the Cherokee called the Talking Feather, used during councils so that each person would have their say without being interrupted. The feather was passed to each person, and while that person had the feather, he was allowed to speak. Another would only be able to speak when that person had the feather. Jackson had always felt it was the most civilized way of conducting a meeting. In all the councils he had been a part of, which had been quite a few, he had never heard any shouting or rudeness as he had been accustomed to hearing when groups of white men had at their meetings.

Now it was time for each person to have a turn at speaking. Out of respect for the elder, Medicine Man was first to speak.

"I come to you with a heavy heart, my friends. The children of the Cherokee are in the grip of an evil spirit. This evil is something that the white men use, but it does not affect them the same way that it does the Cherokee. I am speaking of Whiskey," began Medicine Man.

He continued on, calmly telling the terrible things that occurred only a few days before.

"And there is more. The white man spoke to me using the name my father gave to me. Very few people, even of the Cherokee, know that name," Medicine Man paused to gaze at the faces around the circle, making sure all understood the seriousness of his statement, but instead seeing puzzlement on one or two. "This knowing of my before name can only mean one thing. It means that someone of the Cherokee is helping them, and it means that this brother knows me or knows my history. Only another elder would have that name, and it could be that this person found the name out from another elder. It is not something we speak lightly about. There is someone who is betraying his people, and that, my friends, is the worst evil of all. That is all I have to say."

The faces around the circle all showed emotion at this latest knowledge. It seemed a little thing, knowing Medicine Man's before name, but in reality it showed that the fight was not just red against white. Now it was good against evil because at least one of the Cherokee Nation was part of the hurting and killing of his own people.

Sasa's face looks determined, Medicine Man thought. She is a fighter, she is strong. Coyote looks sad, for he sees the concern in the eyes of his newfound friends. Most look surprised that such a thing would happen, I do not blame them, I was surprised, as well. Joseph has an unreadable look that I cannot name. His look has anger in it, but his eyes look worried. Maybe a spy for the government has more to worry about. The newcomer, Lucius O'Malley, is watching Anna, but I can see that something is bothering him. Could it be shame I see in his face? Who knows, men can have many reasons for feeling shame and most would have nothing to do with our problem here. Anna, a woman who is steadfast and good, looks as if she might hit someone, her hands are in fists. Jackson, though surprised, is looking thoughtful. I am sure he is trying to make some sense of it. May the Creator help you, my son.

Now, Sasa took the talking feather, describing the attacks on her at the docks and the foul things the people of the town had said to her. "My brothers and sisters, grandfather and grandmother, and my new family, my father, Jackson, I feel like I am walking on a sharp mountain top. I have been learning many new things since Anna began to teach me. She also included history in my studies and it is this study that has begun to open my eyes. I see that there is good in both red and white races, but hate seems to live in this land. Even here on what the government calls the frontier, hate has already taken hold. I am made to think that if this evil and hate continue, it will spread to all people in this land and soon they will be fighting brother against brother, family against family, and there will be no safe place for the People.

"It is not just the fighting among the white man and the red, but our own people and tribes closely related to us seem to be against one another. Now it is time, if we are to survive we must stop the fighting among the Indian nations living in Indian Territory.

"When I walk to the fort for my lessons, I see many Indians from all the tribes of Indian Territory buying whiskey, begging on the streets or sitting stupefied from the drink. Their spirits have fled, and all they can do now is to drink the white man's whiskey until the body also fades away. I don't know where this will end or if any of our people will survive, but we must try to do something. If we can at least interrupt this flow of whiskey to the People, then maybe our Chiefs will have the time to speak to their warriors, reminding them of who they are and what the Creator expects of them, much like Yonaguska did for his people.

"It is the same for all the tribes of Indian Territory. There is no real peace between the Cherokee and the Creek or the Osage. It would only take a small thing to begin a terrible war where we will destroy ourselves. I am young, and I am not an elder. I am a woman in a tribe that used to value women as heads of families, but even that has been eaten away by the white man's view of their own women. It is rubbing off on some of our people, and now they beat their wives and refuse to give them the rightful place they used to have before the move here. Whiskey is a part of that, as well, for now the men do not allow the woman to hold any of the money. Then they go and drink it all up, leaving the women and children to starve, and starve they have. It is not just the stealing of the food

234

allotments that is killing our people and the people of the tribes around us, it is also the selling of whiskey that drains whatever the families have left.

"I don't know what the Chief over all the Cherokee is doing about it, because he is busy fighting a different kind of war with the white man's government. There is still hate and rivalry between the various factions within the Cherokee people. Now they call themselves the Ross Party, the Treaty Party and the Old Settlers. They are all so busy trying to overcome the other with means both non-violent and violent, they do not seem to notice our struggle.

"I am made to believe that it is because of that, we lost two elders, one Choctaw and one a highly respected elder of the Cherokee. Both tried to stop this evil, and all their deaths prove is that the enemy will stop at nothing to have their own way. What is that way? I have been think-ing about that, as well. I asked myself, why are these white people risking so much, going as far as murder in order to continue to sell and distribute their whiskey? It is true that profit has much to do with it, because the white man's world is based on the coins and paper money they use to buy all manner of things. The Cherokee saw that when gold was found on our land in Georgia. It was our land, yet we were prevented from mining the gold. White men mur-dered then, as well. So that must be one factor, but there has been something nagging at me, something more than just profit is responsible for this attack on the People, and it is an attack.

"I am made to think that some of these whites do not want us to have this new land. Now that we have it, they want it, as well. I do not claim to understand why, only that I believe this is so. I think they want us to destroy ourselves with whiskey so that they can again take what is ours which we have already so bitterly paid for.

"I am also made to believe that I have been sent two protectors so that I can continue to help my people. One is well known to you, and one is not and I will not name him for he is a secret helper. Of course, Wheezer is the first, and he is not able to speak in this circle, so when I speak I am speaking for him, as well.

"There is much evidence that we have found which may help us to catch the one who killed the esteemed Choctaw elder James Koni. One of our elders who sits here within this circle, also tried to stop our people from buying the whiskey. The evil men attacked him, and he is fortunate to be alive today. So, I am made to believe that one man cannot stop this. It will take many men, men of power to guide our people. I do not hold out hope that this will come to pass any time soon.

"In my history lessons, I learned that a war is made up of many small battles. Some are won, and some are not, but it is the side that perseveres and fights the hardest and longest that is the one that will ultimately win the war. So I am saying this: that these murders are a part of a battle, but the war will take a long time to fight. Maybe longer than I will be alive, but we must keep on fighting to preserve our nation and help other Indian nations survive as well, instead of fighting against us. We can at least keep the whiskey sellers from winning this battle."

Jackson's bewilderment was evident on his face. He glanced over at Anna. She too was completely taken off guard by this supremely adult speech Sasa was giving. Jackson had no idea that the young girl he took as ward had bloomed so quickly into what sounded like an adult woman, but it was not just the things she was asserting as she held the talking feather; rather it included her entire posture and poise. This must have been a subject she had thought long and hard about. Both Anna and Jackson were as proud as any real parents could be at that moment.

"I am also made to think that our weapons in this war are not violent ones that can kill the flesh, but does nothing to stamp out the evil behind it. In my studies, I see every day how my education is helping me to know what to do in my life. I think that education is also the key to helping others fight against that which is killing us. If we educate our young people about the dangers of even trying the white man's drink, then our nation is one step further to winning the war. I have valued every moment of my education at the hands of Anna, and I know that she is giving me a gift that I can pass on to help my people.

"But, first we must find the man or men who are murdering our people, then we can begin to educate our nations, because the truth is the white man's drink will not go away. It will always be here to tempt us.

"Those of us who can, will continue to follow the leads we have. All that I ask is that you all will keep Jackson informed of anything that you observe out of the ordinary. Open your eyes to what the people around you are doing and try to remember the things that you see. That is all I have to say. *Wado*," said Sasa.

The feather was thrust into Joseph's hand. Looking at all the expectant faces, he knew he was supposed to speak. Speaking in council was not one of his strong points.

"For those who have joined us that do not know me, I am Joseph Deerslayer, elder of the Cherokee. I do not have much to add to this council. Other than to caution you all to be careful in what you do. This is a dangerous business, and I would hate to see any of you get hurt. I know that the United States government is trying to stop the flow of whiskey and maybe it would be best if you let them handle it.

"I am very sorry for James' death, but he took the risk, knowing what might happen to him, and he paid the price. I don't know that this whiskey is killing the People. We seem to do that among ourselves very well. Most of the Cherokee are a peaceful lot, but we still have men who think of themselves as warriors first. It is true that there seems to be some type of conspiracy behind this, but whether or not it had anything to do with taking away the land that the government gave to us, I do not know. It says in the treaty, 'As long as grass grows' it would belong to the Cherokee. I see no way that they could legally take the land from us. It may also be that this will calm down and fade away if we just do nothing.

"So, I suppose I am urging you to take more time to think about what you are doing and let the people assigned to run criminals down do that. I have already lost one friend; I cannot bear to lose more. Uh... that is all I have to say," said Joseph.

Almost everyone in the circle, including Sasa, was distressed by Joseph's words. It seemed particularly odd that he would urge doing nothing, not even using the clues they already had gathered to lead them to the murderer or murderers.

Next the feather was passed to Anna. She stood up with the feather gripped in her fingers. Trying to control her temper, she searched for the words to convey what the council needed to know.

"I am sorry, but I disagree with Joseph. I may be a woman, but I have grown up around the Army and their way of doing things. The true fact is that there is no real law here. The Army cannot intervene into civil peacekeeping or justice matters unless marshal law is declared. It would have to be a dire emergency before the Army would consent to do that. The closest law is Marshall Elias Rector, and he is the Arkansas Territory Lawman assigned for a vast area of frontier. He is spread very thin, and I can tell you what he would say once he got here. He would say that he has no jurisdiction over Indian Territory, and he would not have time to run down the killer of a couple of old Indians. Especially since the Indians are so fond of killing each other, but I think that we should continue to look for clues. To quote my grandfather, 'this business of putting your head in the sand and hoping it all goes away will only get your rear end shot off' and he was right. If we do nothing, how can we expect anything good to come of it?

"I am a new friend of the Cherokee, and I feel a strong kinship to them because of all the ghastly things my father was responsible for doing to them, but yet they accepted me as a daughter. I may be selfish, but I don't want to lose that," said Anna.

Medicine Man's eyes glittered with emotion. He was immensely proud of Anna because she was full of strength and stood for truth no matter the consequences. She saw people as people first, and the color of their skin last or not at all. She was a rare find.

Anna fidgeted with holding the feather, but she felt determined to finish what she had started. She wanted to mention an idea she had, but something in the back of her mind stopped her. So she decided to keep the important stuff for Sasa, Jackson and Medicine Man after the council.

"I also have had some threatening encounters with the people of the town as well as the soldiers, but I am not afraid of marching right in to the commander's office and laying it all out on the table if I have to. It is getting to where these men think they can do anything they please, but in all fairness, I must say that Captain Stuart has been butting heads with the town merchants for some time now. His efforts and orders go ignored by his own men. It is a disgrace to the Army, and if this had been happening back East, there would be no end to the measures the Army would take to punish the guilty.

"However, we may as well be on the surface of the moon. For now, we are isolated by distance. I understand that one of the town merchants has continually sent complaints to Washington City and to the capitol of the state of Arkansas. I am sure he paints things is a decidedly different light than what the reality actually is, and the result brings orders from the Army to the commander at the fort to quit agitating the situation. So you see, even the Army is walking a fine line. They can't even solve the whiskey problem within their own ranks, so how could anyone expect them to stop its sale to the Indians?

"My feelings are that we continue to investigate these murders, do what we can to help the commander stop the sale of whiskey to the Indians and give me a chance to think of a way to encourage education among each tribe in Indian Territory. I know that there are missionary schools to teach the children, but I am talking about specifically teaching about the effects and the dangers of drinking whiskey, especially for the Indians.

"On another matter, we have assumed that the attack on Sasa and Wheezer today was done by the same murderers. I am uncertain of that. I have been thinking that we might have noticed a stranger on our land, but maybe not. So, in view of that, let us consider that we may have a second enemy whose reasoning we cannot know. Uh, I am done. Thank you," finished Anna.

The feather was passed to Arch, but he said he had nothing more to add and so then it was given to Poison

Woman. Her calico dress was worn and rent in several places, but clean. Her sparse hair shone translucent in the afternoon sun, but her face reflected the dignity and poise which
emanated from her innermost being. She took the feather
and with some effort, she cleared her throat to speak.

"I do not have any evidence to help you, but I wanted to say something that is a worry for me. It is that if these
people would do this to a Medicine Man and spiritual leader, they would do this to anyone. I am made to think that
it is possible that the white men will end up killing each
other; all of it because of this whiskey. I do not want to
spend my days worrying about what the white men are doing in Fort Smith. What do we have to do with them? This
is supposed to be a time when our tribe pulls together so
that we can survive and grow strong. Instead, I see that it is
destroying us. I am old, very old, and I want to be of help to
my people before I go. So my suggestion is...," said Poison
Woman who had to break off in mid-sentence because of
a visitor striding boldly into the yard and up to the circle.

Sergeant Willis walked like he owned the land he
stepped on. Arrogant and egotistical in the extreme. Still in
his blue uniform and dusty boots, with his shirt tight across
his chest showing off his musculature to his advantage, he
came to a stop with one foot in the circle and one out. It
was obvious he knew the implications of his action; it was
a blatant challenge and sign of disrespect.

"Well now, ain't this here a fine game you're a-play-
in', Jackson, I had no idea ya liked playin' at bein' an injun,"
said Sergeant Willis as he stood fast, partially within the
circle and with a cruel smirk on his thin lips.

Immediately, Jackson saw the intended insult, he
stood and sprang into action.

"Sergeant Willis, what do you mean by coming up
here and insulting my guests? Take yourself on over to the
porch and wait for me there," said Jackson.

241

"Oh, now wait just a goll-durned minute. What do you expect, with you sittin' down out here with this bunch of reds? I suppose, you can do as you like. Heck, I think sooner or later you is goin' to have to choose. Either you want to be white, or you want to be red. No in between about it," said the sergeant.

Jackson was fuming with anger he could hardly control until he caught sight of Anna's bright eyes watching how he would handle this blatant attack.

"Willis, I am sure the commander sent you up here to give me a message. Suppose you just do your duty, then get off my land. In the future, I will make sure that the commander will not choose you for any further deliveries to my ranch. Who my friends are and what we care to do with them is strictly none of your business. Hand me the message Sergeant, then get on back to your post where you belong. You are not welcome here again, and if you do come, expect a seat full of buckshot," said Jackson vehemently.

Willis stood in place, his fists balled; it was plain there was nothing he would like better than to provoke a fight. Possibly he could explain that it was self-defense when the matter was reported to the commander. Apparently, he was weighing over the consequences of that action and upon reflection decided there was too much risk. For a moment, he looked darts at the guests in the circle. The sergeant reached into his pocket, and threw the missive at Jackson as he turned, then retreated the way he had come.

Jackson took a shuddering breath, picked up the message and put it into his shirt pocket. Returning to the circle, he said, "I apologize for the interruption, my friends, please continue, Grandmother."

Poison Woman looked with slitted eyes at the retreating form of the sergeant, then looked around at the others seated.

"I see that there is an obstacle to your investigations, Jackson, and I am made to think that Sergeant Willis is very much involved in this bad business. He does not act like a sergeant in the Army, but like a man who believes his station in life will change for the better real soon. Make no mistake, he is a killer. I don't know if he is the murderer you seek, but I saw murder in his eyes and evil deep within them.

"Before he came, I was going to make a suggestion. I am not sure it is wise to make it known that you are looking for clues to these murders. The men who do this, I am sure, think that no one will care if they murder a few Indians. In reality, that is true of most people, but I believe that the commander at the fort has a hood over his eyes. He cannot see what is right in front of him. He would stop this if he could, but sometimes a good heart cannot see the evil in others, at least, I think he does not see the depth of the evil that he is up against. So my suggestion is to go to the commander and make him aware of what you know. You should not do this alone. That is all I have to say," said Poison Women.

Lucius was offered the feather, but declined. He had watched the sergeant with growing concern. It was obvious the sergeant had seen Lucius sitting in the circle and this did not bode well for him. Just one more thing that could be used against him and another way to blackmail him into doing things he wished he had not. His eyes crossed the circle and rested on Anna. The sweet countenance thrilled his every being, except he knew that she would never accept a lawless man and if he tried to pay court to her, others would use that also and put her in danger. *When will I be free to be my own man,* he thought? Surely there must be a way that he could gain his lost integrity, and win the woman he loved, but he had no answer to his own question, so he kept silent.

Even though Coyote was not Cherokee and had somewhat of a language barrier, the feather was offered to him, as well. He accepted it tentatively, stood and imparted his thoughts on the subject being discussed, signing as he spoke.

"I am Coyote and not from this land. I am made to think that I am supposed to learn something here that will help my people. Soon, the white man will come to the plains. His desire for owning what belongs to no one other than Wakan Tanka, the same as your Creator, is what will come upon my own people. The thing that is coming with the white man is his whiskey. I am beginning to see how the white man uses it against the tribes to gain the land, and displace the peoples who have lived there for all time. When I learn all that I can, I will go back to my people and give them the warning. They may not believe me, just as they did not believe the large cities and numbers of the white man. I watch you so that I may learn. May you succeed so that my people may also succeed," said Coyote.

He gave a quick nod of his head and gave the feather back to Medicine Man.

Medicine Man rose and said the council was over for now and that they may have another if more information made the problem clearer.

Anna felt if they did, the members of that council should be chosen carefully first.

The excitement of the day had made the thought of the noon day meal, slip everyone's mind, so by the time the council had ended; they all found themselves fairly hungry. As they all rose from their positions and began walking about and stretching their legs, Wheezer became momentarily agitated. He stood stiff with the hair on his back up and his menacing growl warned all that something was not right.

Wheezer for his part had no way of telling them that the person who had attacked Sasa and him was still in the vicinity, for he had smelled a faint whiff of his scent. It was here then gone almost immediately. Dogs are not like humans in that they do not waste time speculating if something is real or not. He had smelled it and was sure and therefore, was now on the alert. As the adults filtered back into the house upon Masey's request that they come in and have a bite to hold them until dinner, Wheezer took up his position as guard. Sasa and Coyote sat down on the steps of the porch and began to chat.

Coyote now had more time to look at Sasa at close range. He had already noticed that the Cherokee were a good looking people. His own people were good looking too, but in a different way. Sasa was not short or very tall. She had shining black tresses that came just past her shoulders. Her skin was not dark, but more golden than his, and her eyes were round and large. Her features were finely made, and he noticed that she was exceptionally intelligent.

"Does you head hurt you very much?" asked Coyote in words and sign.

"Yes, I do still have a headache, and it is especially pain-ful if I touch the place where he struck me. I think Wheezer hurts as well, his eyes show the pain and yet he still will guard us all. I cannot do without him, and I am glad that he is not se-riously hurt," said Sasa. "I was wondering about your people, Coyote. Are they very much different from us?"

"In many ways it is the same, but there are some things that are very different. If someone had hurt our sha-man, which is our medicine man, the entire village would be up in arms. There would have been a very swift attack, regardless of who it was. There is nothing the equal of the Lakota's punishments when it comes to harming our sha-man. That is why it has so seldom happened," said Coyote

245

Sasa looked closer at the young man who disdained to be called a warrior. His hair was extremely long which he allowed to flow freely with only the sides pulled back and tied with sinew. He was taller than most of the Cherokee men, and he was hard muscled. His skin was darker than hers, but had an unusually pleasant tone to it like warm red oak. His people must be a handsome tribe. His eyes seemed more almond shaped, but they were clear and alert, the iris a deep, almost black, brown, with long lashes.

"Do your people have a story teller?" asked Sasa.

"Oh, yes. We have those that tell stories well in our village, and then we sometimes have the trader who comes, and we call Storyteller. He is the best of them, and when he comes, he will stay with us for many days. Each night, we all gather around the fire while he tells us stories we have never heard before and then he always will ask him to tell our favorite stories which we already know and love. Do you have a favorite story that your storyteller always tells?" said Coyote with wonderment in his eyes. Clearly, this was a subject he enjoyed.

"Yes, I have many favorites. My father used to tell wonderful stories. My favorite is Why Rabbit Has A Short Tail. That is a story that is told over and over. We never tire of it, especially the children," said Sasa.

Coyote's eyes opened wide, and he said, "We also have a story about the rabbit. Please, tell me your story and I will see if it is the same as ours?" said Coyote.

"I am not a very good story teller, but Medicine Man is a wonderful one. Let me see if he will come out and tell the story," said Sasa as she scuttled to her feet to run into the house. Presently, she returned with Medicine Man in tow.

"Ah, I hear you want to hear one of our stories. Sasa tells me you have chosen, 'Why the Rabbit Has a Short

Tail'," said Medicine Man as he settled down on the next step up on the porch steps.

"Now, you know that one rabbit is much like another today. But it was not like that a long time ago. But, first Coyote you must know the word for Rabbit which is tsi-s-du, and Fox which is tsu-la and also Fish a-tsa-di.

"A long time ago when the world was new, tsi-s-du (Rabbit) had a very long bushy tail and he was very proud of that tail for it was longer and bushier than the tail of tsu-la (Fox). Now tsi-s-du (Rabbit) was all the time telling all the other animals about his beautiful bushy tail. One day tsu-la (Fox) got very bored of hearing tsi-s-du (Rabbit) talk and brag about his tail, and it was on that day that he decided to stop his boasting once and for all.

"It was at the time of year of the falling leaves, and it got colder, and colder still. It finally got so cold that the waters in the lake froze. Tsu-la (Fox) was very crafty, and so one day he went down to the lake carrying four a-tsa-di (Fish). Now, no use asking me where he got those fish, for I do not know. Before long he came to the lake, he stopped after walking onto the ice and then he cut a hole in the ice. Tsu-la (Fox) took those four a-tsa-di (Fish) and tied them to his own long and bushy tail, and then sat down to wait for tsi-s-du (Rabbit) to walk by.

It was not very long before tsi-s-du (Rabbit) came hopping along, and when tsu-la (Fox) saw tsi-s-du (Rabbit), he quickly lowered his tail with all the a-tsa-di (Fish) into the cold, cold water. Tsi-s-du (Rabbit) hopped right up to tsu-la (Fox) and said, "What are you doing, Fox?" tsu-la answered, "Why, I'm fishing". And tsi-s-du (Rabbit) asked, "With your tail?" tsu-la (Fox) replied, "Didn't you know, that's the very best way to catch the most a-tsa-di (Fish)?"

"Tsi-s-tu (Rabbit) said, "How long you been a-fishing?" tsu-la (Fox) lied and said, "Oh, only a short time, maybe about fifteen minutes." tsi-s-du (Rabbit) asked, "Have you caught any a-tsa-di (Fish) yet?" Then crafty old tsu-la (Fox) pulled up his long bushy tail, and there were those four a-tsa-di (Fish) dangling from it.

"Tsi-s-du (Rabbit), being very curious asked, "What do you plan to do with the a-tsa-di (Fish) you catch?" and Tsu-la (Fox) said, "Well, I figure I'll fish until I catch enough a-tsa-di (Fish) to take to the Cherokee Village and then trade them in for a pair of beautiful tail combs. There is only one set of tail combs left, and I really have to have them for my tail." Now, Tsu-la (Fox) could see that tsi-s-du (Rabbit) was thinking. Tsi-s-du (Rabbit) thought to himself, "If I fished all night long, I bet I would have enough a-tsa-di (Fish) by morning to trade at the Cherokee Village and then I could get those tail combs for myself since my tail is the longest and most beautiful tail of all."

"Tsu-la (Fox) said, "It's getting late and I'm too cold to fish anymore. I think I'll come back and fish some more, maybe in the morning. See you later, Rabbit..." Then tsu-la (Fox) loped off over the top of the ridge and was gone. As soon as tsu-la (Fox) was out of sight, tsi-s-du (Rabbit) dropped his tail down into the icy cold water of the lake and said, "Brrrrr", it really was very cold! But tsi-s-du (Rabbit) was determined and thought, "I can't give up now. I want those tail combs more than anything I have ever wanted." So, even though it was bitterly cold, he sat down on the hole in the ice and then, he fished all night long.

"The next day after the sun came up, tsu-la (Fox) loped back over the top of the ridge. He came right up to tsi-s-du (Rabbit). He said, "What are you doing, Rabbit?" The teeth of tsi-s-du (Rabbit) began to chatter. "I'm ffff-issshing, Fffox." said tsi-s-du (Rabbit) Then, Tsu-la (Fox) asked, "Well have you caught any a-tsa-di (Fish) yet?" And it was then that Tsi-s-du (Rabbit) started to get up, but he found he couldn't budge. He said, "Fffox you've ggott to helppp me. I'mmm ssstttuck."

"So tsu-la (Fox), with a big almost evil smile on his face walked behind tsi-s-du (Rabbit). He gave tsi-s-du (Rabbit) one mighty big shove. Tsi-s-du (Rabbit) popped up and out of the hole, sailed through the sky almost like a bird and landed clear across on the other side of the lake... But his tail...was still stuck in the frozen water. And that's why from that day to this, tsi-s-du (Rabbit) has such a very short, short tail."

Coyote laughed until his sides hurt right along with Sasa who loved hearing this story. As soon as he was able, he said, "I have not heard that one, but my people also have many rabbit stories. I have one I like, it is called, The Story of the Rabbits. Would you like me to tell it? I will have to sign most of it."

"Yes, I would be very interested in learning a new story to tell the children by the fire this winter," said Medicine Man as Sasa nodded her head in agreement.

"Let me see how this begins, oh yes... The Rabbit nation were very much depressed in spirits on account of being very obedient to their chief, obeyed all his orders to the letter. One of his orders was that, upon the approach of any other nation, they should follow the example of their chief and run up among the rocks and down into their burrows, and not show themselves until the strangers had passed.

This they always did. Even the chirp of a little cricket would send them all scampering to their dens. One day they held a great council, and after talking over everything for some time, finally left it to their medicine man to decide.

The medicine man arose and said: "My friends, we

are of no use on this earth. There isn't a nation on earth that fears us, and we are so timid that we cannot defend ourselves, so the best thing for us to do is to rid the earth of our nation, by all going over to the big lake and drowning ourselves."

This they decided to do; so going to the lake they were about to jump in, when they heard a splash in the water. Looking, they saw a lot of frogs jumping into the lake.

"We will not drown ourselves," said the medicine man, "we have found a nation who are afraid of us. It is the frog nation."

"Had it not been for the frogs we would have had no rabbits, as the whole nation would have drowned themselves and the rabbit race would have been extinct," finished Coyote.

"I have another you also might like. It is called, The Rabbit and The Cricket.

"On a cold fall night, as coyotes howled nearby, a very tired rabbit sat alone in the brush doing his best not to fall asleep.

"Then out of the darkness came the chirping of a cricket. The cricket sang as loud and as hard as she could, giving one hundred percent of herself. Well, needless to say, the rabbit did not fall asleep.

"As dawn approached, an owl appeared and spoke to the rabbit. Telling the rabbit, 'You are very lucky the cricket sang for you all night.'

"The rabbit responded to the wise old owl, "Yes, but why did she sing for me? I did not ask for her help and had nothing to offer her."

"The owl twisted his head, pondered for a minute and then hooted, "Help can come in many shapes, sizes and sometimes where you least expect it. She gave you the only thing she had, her voice. What could you do, rabbit, if you gave one hundred percent of yourself to help another and asked for nothing in return?"

"The wise old owl then flew off, leaving the rabbit to himself."

"That is a story that makes you think about helping others," said Coyote.

Medicine Man smiled to himself and was happy to learn these new stories. Then something occurred to him he had not considered before. He excused himself and went in to speak with Jackson while Sasa and Coyote enjoyed the late afternoon breeze with Wheezer guarding them.

Wheezer had not turned to look at Sasa for some time and was staring out at the tall grass. Sasa followed his gaze and was not surprised to see Yellow Eyes, resting in the grass. She nudged Coyote and directed his gaze. The sight of Yellow Eyes made the hair at the back of Coyote's neck stand on end. There was something about him, but he could not put his finger on it. One thing Coyote knew. He had a connection with Yellow Eyes, but was it good or bad?

Chapter 24

After the council Jackson realized that Joseph and Medicine Man had actually come for the bodies now lying in their ice house. First, the body of James Koni, a Choctaw which had yet to be removed and be taken to the Choctaw part of Indian Territory and Sam Bushyhead, the Cherokee elder, to be taken to Tahlequah. Both had tried to stop the sale of whiskey to their people and died for their efforts. The Choctaw needed to be taken to Tuli Hina near the Kiamichi River. Joseph had said he was here to pick up Sam Bushyhead's body to take to Tahlequah. He would see if Joseph would also deliver the other body as well instead of waiting for his family to come and collect it. The Choctaw Nation was not very far away. Their border followed the Arkansas River until the Canadian River diverged from it. If Joseph took it to the first village into the Choctaw territory, the elders at that village would be able to deliver it where it needed to go from there.

Jackson made the arrangements with Joseph, but Medicine Man, his sister and Coyote wanted permission to camp on the grounds for a while. Of course, they were welcome to stay in his house as guests, but they felt uncomfortable doing that. So he gave them permission to cut the branches and vines they needed to make a brush lodge. Sasa offered her help, which was accepted with thanks. Joseph left with the bodies and now Jackson had time to take a breath.

The message Jackson had received from Sergeant Willis was indeed from Captain Stuart, who was informing him that Jackson's father had arrived with a friend. They were waiting at the fort for Jackson to come, because Andrew had wanted to be taken on a tour of the rebuilding efforts of the new fort first, Stuart had sent Willis to deliver the message. Andrew was a great deal surprised because he had expected more to have been done at this point. The projected date for the finish for the new fort buildings was long past and the new brick buildings, palisade and parade grounds were not done by half. Instead of a palisade of the sharp ended posts that normally surround a fort on the frontier, there was a rock wall of native stone still unfinished and at the moment he saw no tradesmen at work.

"What has happened to all of your men, Captain?" said Andrew.

"The confounded Congress keeps dragging their feet about paying my tradesmen. So much so that I am forced to pay them off and send them home. This is not the first time this has happened. It slows the work down so much that I don't know if I ever will be finished. Mind you, the Congress will one day want to know why I did not finish and they won't take any of the blame. It will fall all on my head.

The tour of the facility was almost complete and Andrew wanted to get back to the Captains office since Nathan Boone was there taking charge of the ever excitable Penny. Already some of the men had taken a shine to her. Penny was the friend of anyone who would play with her. Nathan had said they ought to make that her middle name, Penny Play Halley. They all got a good chuckle out of that during the steam boat trip from St. Louis.

Andrew and Henry Neugent made their way back, just in time to see Jackson disembark from the ferry at the Fort Smith dock. He came up to his father with a very big smile on his face, and they embraced most heartily. This was Andrew's first visit to his son's new ranch, and he was anxious he should like it. Introductions were made all around and Jackson was extremely in awe of meeting Nathan Boone, but as they were shaking hands, Jackson noticed something was tugging at his pant legs and growling for all it was worth.

"Well, well, what do we have here?" said Jackson as Andrew bent to pick up the Jack Russell pup. "I believe, father you have had a stowaway on the boat. Would you mind introducing me?"

"Certainly, my boy, happy to do it. This little girl is Penny. She is a gift from the Reverend John Russell who, as you well know, is credited for the making of this new breed, the Jack Russell Terrier. He has sent her so that Wheezer might have a mate and thereby not dilute his efforts for expanding the breed. He assures me that she is of a different line of stock so they will be completely compatible," said Andrew holding Penny up so that Jackson could shake her paw and pat her on the head.

"Well, that will be up to Wheezer. We can certainly give this a try, but Wheezer is inclined to decide who his friends are. Besides, she is still very young yet, is she not?" said Jackson.

"Yes, yes, she is still young, but you will see. He will come round," said Andrew. "She has a way of getting under your skin."

Nathan Boone took his leave. He had received orders, which were waiting for him at Fort Smith, to proceed directly to Fort Gibson.

"I was mighty happy to meet you folks. Remember, Jackson, when you do have a litter, let me know. I think that a pup like Penny could give a man a new lease on life. I am much obliged for the company on the river boat, Andrew, and you too, Henry," said Nathan. He picked up his gear and headed to the stables where he would choose a sturdy mule to take him the rest of the way.

Andrew introduced Henry to Jackson who was so pleased that his father had chosen a traveling companion. Jackson excused himself to speak to Captain Stuart, who wore a fierce scowl by the time Jackson took his leave. Having all the formalities settled, they departed for the Van Buren docks on the other side of the town. As they walked, Jackson informed his new guests that he also had a houseful of other dinner guests waiting for them.

Jackson was loath to discuss what had been happening while they were still yet on the ferry, so he waited until they were on the Van Buren side and were walking the path that lead to his ranch.

"Well Jackson, the Army informs me that there has been trouble, but I had no idea you were in the middle of it, my boy. Even so, I have complete faith in your abilities. Heaven knows the terrible blows all the Indian nations of

Indian Territory have suffered. This problem has the potential to finish them off, and I would very much hate that.

"Actually, Son, I am here not just to see you and deliver a puppy; I came because I am now more financially stable than I was and I have decided to come and invest some of my capitol in helping our friends start their businesses up again. I plan to seek out the ones who were giving the most employment to the tribal members before the removal and get them back up and running again. Even if it means that they have to plant a different type of crop or raise a different type of stock. I regard what the Army is doing to help as totally ineffectual. I figure that since our Indian partners and I both lost our investments back east together, we may as well rely on each other to begin again," said Andrew.

Henry had been a little quiet on the walk, but finally the subject raised was something he also was interested in.

"My interests are purely philanthropic. I would like to help some of the families recover their necessities. Giving them what they need to plant their gardens and build their lodges. I won't be able to help everyone, but I plan to make a dent. Plus, I am interested in investing in education. Schools are what is wanted and I don't mean missionaries. Of course, they will be operating in Indian Territory, but what I want to do is help them set their own schools up that are taught by their own people. I plan to approach the Cherokee first and see how it is received, then maybe I can help other nations. After all, my father was fond of saying, 'You can't take it with you, so you better do something with it that means something instead of throwing it all away just to have your name put up on buildings,' you see he had no patience with those who give to charity so that things could be named after them. Ha, ha, ha, he was

256

a cantankerous old bird, to say the least," said Henry.

Jackson felt a ray of sunshine enter his thoughts now that these jolly men were here. He never had to wonder about his father, who loved everyone equally; if they were good human beings, then he was good to them. Race and color of skin took no part in this whatsoever. Jackson had been raised to have the same ideals. It hurt both son and father to see members of their own race treat others as lower forms of life and that is why Jackson had left the east; he found he could not stay and watch the greed build to the point of avarice. Now, it seemed, all that he had run from had followed him all the way to the frontier.

Andrew was certainly looking forward to meeting Anna, whom he had heard so much about, and also Sasa, who was now a part of the family. Andrew had been delighted when Jackson wrote of his intentions of making Sasa his ward. He also knew that Jackson would not bother to write about Anna, if she had not been much on his mind. He was keen to meet the woman.

Henry trotted along somewhat behind, since his legs were a bit shorter, until Jackson noticed and slowed his steps.

"Forgive me Mr. Neugent, I find that the speed I walk goes with the agitation of my mind," said Jackson.

"No problem, Jackson, but do call me Henry. I am sure that your father, as am I, are anxious to help you in any way that we can. Maybe two new sets of eyes and ears will shed some light on this ghastly business. And I for one, am extremely keen on helping you unravel this mystery," said Henry.

They topped the ridge that was not too far from the ranch. Jackson explained all the different part of his operation as they went, then headed to the house for dinner and fine company with new friends. Since they were nearly late for dinner, he asked Arch to take Penny and kennel her in the barn until later when they had the time to introduce her properly to Wheezer and Sasa. Sasa did not see them until after they were in the house, and the greetings and introductions took Jackson's mind off of the news, so Sasa and Wheezer were unaware of the new arrival. Even after dinner, Arch had excused himself to tend to duties and check on his family. The news about Penny would have to wait until tomorrow.

Chapter 25

"I tell ya I don't like it, no, not one bit. Them Injuns was up there with that Halley crowd, an' they was a-havin' themselves a Pow Wow. I didn't hear what they was a-talkin' about, but I sure as heck felt the cold chill when I walked up," said Sergeant Willis as he sat at the kitchen table with Robert at the Reardon's residence behind the stables. "And that Joseph was up there with them too."

"Well, he was supposed to be up there. Did you see that Sasa girl and her dog?" asked Robert Reardon.

"Yeah, they was sittin' up there as pretty as you please. I don't know what happened, but somethin's got them all riled up like wet hornets. I thought you said you were gonna' have her and the dog taken care of?" said Willis.

"I did, but something must have gone wrong if'n you saw her up there alive and well," said Robert, slamming his fist down on the table. Some of the dinner dishes that Patricia had just put on the table came crashing down to the floor.

"Now look what you did. How am I supposed to entertain the society ladies if all my good china is all broke up?" said Patricia.

Robert jumped to his feet and grabbed Patricia by the neck of her dress and drew her close to his face. "Now hear this, Patricia, whoever your name is, I told you for the very last time that we ain't play actin' no cozy house keepin' here. I am tired and fed up with your hair brained notions. I want you to pack up your bags and head on out on the next boat up the Arkansas," he said through clenched teeth.

"Robert, you don't mean that. After all the time, I spent trying to make a good home and all and..." said Patricia.

"Shut up, you silly stupid woman. You were only a means to an end. Things seem to be coming unraveled here and I want you gone by tonight. So pack a bag and get," yelled Robert.

Willis' eyebrows rose. He had never heard him talk that way to anyone. He was beginning to believe he was in over his head, but it was too late now. "So what do ya think I needs to do now?" he asked.

They all started when a faint knock sounded at the door. Robert motioned Patricia to open the door with a warning look that she better not slip up. She opened the door to Joseph, who walked in while looking behind his back and down the street.

"Whew, I don't think anyone saw me. They think I am on the road with that wagon with the two dead men. I am supposed to be taking them back to their families. I hid the wagon in the woods about a mile away and then I ran back here to tell you what happened," said Joseph Deerslayer.

Joseph went through the explanation while Robert listened with mounting agitation.

"I had only a little time before I would be missed. It was the perfect time because she was alone and even her dog did not see or smell me coming. I don't understand what happened because I hit them both very hard. Hard enough to have split their skulls and I would have stayed to make sure it was done good and proper, but that Lakota showed up. I am just thankful he did not follow me. The two old ones had spent so much time telling him about the girl on the way over there, I think he felt taking her to get help was more important. I circled around and got to the training corral where Mr. Halley was entertaining his other guests, but not before the old ones showed up there too. I don't think they thought anything of it," said Joseph as he nervously fiddled with his hat. "Then at the council, the way some of them talked, I think that maybe they have some clues, but they did not talk about them specifically, just whether or not they should look for the murderer of those men.

Robert, with an effort, had contained his terrible temper. Killing Joseph for his failure was not going to help him one iota. Anyway, he still needed his confederates if he were going to finish the job. The idea to kill the girl and her dog came to him when he knew the dog had seen him at the dock that night. Something in that rascal's eyes told him the dog was a liability. The girl, as well, was too curious for her own good. He knew that if he killed the dog, it would just spur the girl on to looking even harder for clues.

Now, however, the situation had changed. He was going to have to make some sort of contingency plans to get away clean, not leaving anyone behind that could bring the law down on him if it became necessary to leave every-thing behind. He already had a place on the south bank of the Arkansas where a cut bank had been eaten out by the spring floods. He could stash his inventory there and re-turn any time before next spring to get it if he were forced to stow it. The place was not far from the Fort Smith mili-tary dock, but it was a place that was never used for land-ing since the bank was too unstable and high to unload anything or even set a gangway on. He was sure, as long as he hid it well and covered it, no one would be the wiser.

He had no qualms about killing a woman. That was how he had got into this mess in the first place, and if Pa-tricia did not take his unusually pointed hint to get herself away, he would be forced to kill her, as well, and leave her to float down the river.

Now, tonight would be the time to lure away the girl and get the dog. If she went missing, no one at the Halley ranch would know where to look so he could take his time about doing the deed. He barked out orders to Joseph and Willis. This was top priority. After they secreted the girl away, they could stash the whiskey under the cut bank. Then he could arrange for the girl's demise and the dog's, too, and Joseph could put them under the blanket and keep going on down the road to deliver the other bod-ies. He would dump the girl first as soon as they got to the confluence of the Canadian and the Arkansas River. Even if she were found, no one in that direction would know who she was once she had bumped along the bottom of the river for a while. When Joseph returned to find Robert gone, he would not be able to say anything unless he con-fessed to his own part in murder, and since neither Willis nor Joseph knew who he actually was, they would be hard pressed to find him, as well. It was the perfect plan.

*****

Anna handed Lucius a fresh cup of tea as they settled down in the comfortable chairs of the library. Lucius was so in awe of Anna that he felt like his mouth were full of chicken feathers. Jackson's Indian friends were outside building a temporary lodge and the others were taking a tour of the house. If he were going to approach Anna, he may as well get his feet wet now.

"May I ask Miss Edwards, if the Edwards family have their roots in Ireland?" he asked.

"Why, yes, Mr. O'Malley, I believe they do, but how far back I really could not say. I don't have much contact with that side of my family. You may not be aware that my father was not truthful when he told my mother of his family connections. Now that he is gone, I really have no way of knowing who or where his kin are," said Anna.

"May I be very bold, Miss Edwards, but why have ye not got a husband, a fine looking lass as yourself should have been snatched up a long time ago." said Lucius.

"I have been busy. I was too interested in education when I was younger, then I just did not find the kind of man that interested me. You see, I don't want to be the simpering wife, having society parties every week and hosting the ladies aid for who knows what. That kind of life does not appeal to me at all. Now that I have lived a year on the frontier, I believe I am captivated. I could not dream of living anywhere else. There is so much to do and build. It is like having a clean slate and beginning afresh," replied Anna with a side long look at Lucius.

"Speaking of clean slates, Miss Edwards, may I speak freely about some personal, confidential information?" said Lucius.

"Mr. O'Malley, I am flattered you feel you can confide in me, but I am not sure I am the best judge of other peoples' circumstances," said Anna.

"I am not a lad to be used to talking to a young lady, and I am not sure how to say this, so I'm begging your pardon afore hand. I would like to ask, would you be opposed to allowing me to escort you to dinner sometime?" O'Malley asked.

Anna began to open her mouth to speak, when Lucius quickly preempted her answer.

"I would not be living with meself if I did not tell you first something that no one else in America knows. I am hoping you will not be finding me too repellent after you hear my secret. Lord knows that I have lived with myself for some time now, knowing that I can never go home to my own Ireland." Seeing her questioning look, he continued, "I am a wanted man, Miss Edwards. I have not done any human any harm. I freely admit that I fought for independence for Ireland against Imperial Britain. I was apprehended and sentenced to live the rest of me days in Australia, but I eluded my captors and came to America, and it is this secret that I have been living with and fearing to be found out. I had to tell you before you answer my dinner invitation, and I will respect your answer."

Anna was somewhat amused at his honest concern for telling her the truth. She did not want to lead this good man on because she knew the man she wanted. She was not the type of woman that would coyly play one man against the other, so she sought a way to soften the blow.

"My dear Mr. O'Malley, I cannot say that I have had a more pleasant request. I do not think that the government of the United States is concerned about who Britain is seeking since it is well known that they have been at odds with that country for some time now. We Americans understand a patriot, sir, and I doubt very seriously if anyone would bother about your efforts for your homeland, just as long as you did not break the law in this country or committed murder anywhere. America is being filled up with many nationalities of people coming from all corners of the earth. Many have found that their own countries are a danger to their freedom, so they have come to America," said Anna. Noticing the delight in the man's eyes she quickly went on, "However sir, I do not turn down your request for a public meal, but I must turn it down if it is to take the form of paying court to me. It has nothing to do with you or who you are; in fact, I admire your candor, and the trust you placed in my hands. It is just that I have my own goals in life and a path that I want to follow. I know this is unusual for a woman to make this type of declaration, but there are things I want out of life that I am working toward. However, I would be happy to call you my friend, sir. You are welcome to call me Anna if I may call you Lucius. I am not saying that I would never allow someone to pay court to me. I hope you will understand," said Anna sincerely.

Lucius was momentarily stunned into silence. She did not exactly turn him down altogether. She seemed to leave a small window open and maybe if he could show his integrity she might someday find he occupied a place in her heart. Then he realized that he had no integrity as long as he participated in the illegal whiskey trade. And then it dawned on him what she had said about the U.S. Government not caring about his particular differences with Britain. If that were true, then he had handed an enormous many months of his life over to Robert for no good reason, and realizing this built a fury within him for being cheated and manipulated. He determined then and there to get himself out from under the influence of the group of men selling the whiskey and show Anna he was truly a man of integrity.

"Of course, uh... Anna, I understand. I will respect your wishes, and I am pleased and proud to be calling you, me friend. Please, rely on me anytime you need anything as friends are like to do," said Lucius smiling brightly.

Anna was relieved after seeing Lucius smile, and looked up just as Jackson, Andrew and Henry walked, into the library, to join them for tea.

Jackson paused momentarily, seeing Anna and Lucius with their heads together so amiably. "Are the others still outside working on the wigwam?" he asked.

"I believe so. I saw Sasa out near the forest line cutting saplings and wild grape vines to lash the sticks together. I assume it will take them a little while more, but the sun is just now beginning to set, so they should have the lodge for Medicine Man, Poison Woman and Coyote ready by bedtime. I see he is working furiously. I guess that kind of lodge is known universally among all the tribes because Coyote didn't need much instruction. He seemed to know just what to do," said Anna.

"Would it not be interesting to compare the various tribes to see how many things are common among them and what differences there were?" said Henry.

"I think we might find the differences would have a lot to do with where they live and what natural resources they have at their disposal," said Andrew.

Anna arose to refill the sugar bowl from the box on the buffet table. Jackson took the opportunity to talk privately with her. "Have you been enjoying your visit, Anna?"

"Why, yes. I think I have enjoyed this visit more than any of the others," said Anna.

"Uh, why so?" said Jackson, hoping her answer had nothing to do with Lucius, and if it did, he wondered if she would say so.

"Oh, I had a marvelous time working with the mules. This is my idea of the perfect life," said Anna sweeping her arm to indicate the entire ranch. "I envy you, Jackson. Ranching is not something women get to choose for a vocation. I was not raised to it; however, I have always wanted to experience it. If I could duplicate any part of this visit over and over, it would be when I was in the corral with those magnificent animals."

Jackson was dumbfounded. Her answer was so un-expected; it took him by complete surprise. He looked at Anna as if he were seeing her for the first time, or as if he had never actually known her. Could he have been guilty of assuming, because of her gender, she could not fit into his frontier dreams?

Anna gazed into his open eyes as if to say 'Do you see me now?' Happily, she could see from his expression that recognition was dawning. Maybe there was yet a chance for a happy life.

Chapter 26

Sasa laid a long piece of canvas on the ground, loading it with the vines and supple saplings she had gleaned from the woods. Picking up two of its corners, she dragged it about fifty yards to where the elders were erecting their temporary lodge. Coyote was there, placing the straight sticks and bundles of last year's dry tall grass against the bent wood frame that made the foundation for the wigwam. Each bundle was lashed onto the frame using the wild grape vines Sasa found growing freely in the woods. Where he was from, there were extremely few vines for building a stick lodge, so they used animal skins for the

268

covering. Buffalo hide stood the test of time the best, but any animal hide would do in a pinch.

Further north into the colder Canadian region, Coyote knew they used the bark from certain trees that grew large and which would also regrow their bark year after year, but the wigwam concept was essentially the same. Sasa arrived with the last load, dropped the canvas and knelt on her knees by the lodge next to Coyote. From her side pocket, she pulled out her Green River knife and helped Coyote trim the saplings and remove thorns from some of the twigs. They worked in harmony, side by side, and Poison Woman looked on with a deepening sorrow.

Medicine Man let down his old bones next to Poison Woman as she watched the lodge being built. Seeing the sad look on her face he said, "What troubles you sister? You are not letting that soldier's words from today at the council penetrate your tough skin, are you?"

"Bah, of course not, my brother. No, I am just sorry that this young Lakota must go away to his people. Look there, see how well they work together, they do not even have to speak. That is something special that does not always come along, but his people are going to need him, even if they do not realize it now, and even if he completes his journey, he will find many closed minds to what he must tell them. This I know. It took the Cherokee many generations to see we would lose it all to the invaders; once we were caught, the harder we struggled, the faster we were overcome, like quicksand," said Poison Woman.

"Yes, I have seen it also. Coyote has a chance to warn his people, but if they are as stubborn as we were, they will not listen until it is very much too late. They might have a chance if they do not begin drinking the white man's drink, and if they stop fighting among each other on the plains, but I am afraid that Coyote will have no effect on what is to come to his people, and it will break his spirit I think," said Medicine Man.

"No, not that young man. They will not break Coyote's spirit. This I know," said Poison Woman.

The lodge was almost finished. It was a good summer lodge, just large enough for three or four people to sleep in. During the day, they could sit under the brush arbor Sasa would build in the morning. It was also made of sticks and leaves, but it was remarkably pleasant. Before the long walk, Sasa liked to sleep under the brush arbor on nights when it was not going to rain. There was nothing like going to sleep smelling the sweet night air and hearing all the forest night animals call to each other, but it was getting late and she wanted to have time to get to know her foster grandfather, Mr. Halley Senior and his friend Henry.

She tidied the mess of leftover twigs and leaves into a mound, then swept them up in her arms and headed for the edge of the woods to leave them there. Before she went terribly far, she noticed Wheezer was not there. She called for him, but still there was no sign of him. However, she was not worried because Wheezer sometimes went out investigating scents and noises at night. She was sure he would be back soon. She carried her armload of leaves out to the woods and just as she was emptying her arms of the load, she thought she could hear Wheezer's bark. She did not want him to go off, chasing who knew what, at night.

"Here is the last load, Grandmother. Please excuse me. I must call Wheezer in so we can go in for the night," said Sasa.

"This is fine, Daughter. Coyote is almost finished, and after that, we plan to lay our blankets down on the inside and go to sleep. We will say good night now and see you in the morning. Thank you for helping," said Poison Woman.

"He has stopped barking, I think he may have caught something; I had better see what it is. *Wado*, Grandmother," said Sasa as she headed into the woods where Wheezer had gone.

Sasa called for Wheezer, but he did not come and she could no longer hear his barking. She hoped he had not gone down into a burrow. It would take forever to find him since it is hard to hear the barking of a dog when they are underground.

*****

Wheezer had heard something rattle the bushes, so he went to investigate. He sniffed around the bush but could not latch onto any recognizable scent. When, he saw a figure running through the woods further ahead, Wheezer could not resist joining in the chase. He went off barking into the woods. Doing what Jack Russells do best, getting into trouble.

*****

She became aware first of a smell. Something musty, cloying and sweet. Then the next sense to register was hearing: loud thumps on a wooden floor sounded close, but not in the same room. Hot. She was terribly hot and uncomfortable, and she vaguely sensed she could not move; not her arms, her legs, she was not even able to move her head from side to side. Something foul was in her mouth, and it was shoved down so far she occasionally gagged. Finally, she opened her eyes, but all she saw was black, all-consuming darkness. Even though the sounds from some other room frightened her, the sounds also gave her the only hold on reality she had at the moment.

As she lay there, taking stock of each part of her

tethered body, her eyes became accustomed to the dark, and she was able to see that the room was not completely dark. A pale fluttering band of light could be seen through a small gap at the top of a door. She had to concentrate on breathing because she found when she panicked, breathing became difficult. The gag in her mouth also partially covered her nose. Her hands were bound in front of her, but her arms were tied down at the elbow so tight, she could not wiggle her hands to loosen her bonds. The same seemed to be true of her legs, and she gradually became aware of her need to urinate.

After what seemed like hours, the door with the dim light behind it creaked open, but not being able to turn her head, she could not see the person who entered. Soon, a dark form loomed over her, chuckling softly. The man, for that is who it seemed to be, took the gag out of Sasa's mouth. Her mouth was so dry she could barely work up enough saliva to swallow. The man removed what appeared to be two heavy wooden boxes from either side of her head, then lifted her shoulders up to give her a drink of water. Trying desperately to see the person's face, but failing, she said, "Who are you? What do you want of me? Where is my dog?"

The man chuckled again. "Now I reckon it don't do no harm in tellin' ya who I am cause you ain't gonna' be leavin' here - alive anyways," the man said.

He stomped heavily into the next room and retrieved the flickering lantern. He set the lantern on the same slab of wood she lay on, up above her head. With a gasp, she realized she knew the man and shuddered.

"Sergeant Willis. Why have you taken me? I don't understand what is happening," she said, beginning to sound hysterical.

"Now, now, little squaw, you best be savin' yourself for

272

what's to come," he said with what sounded like pure enjoyment. He leaned over her so that his face was above hers. "Normally, I prob'ly wouldn't resort to violence, but you have become a mite troublesome, you and your scrappy dog."

The man opened a nearby crate and pulled out a brown crockery jug with a cork in the spout. After taking a long swig, he offered her a drink, which she refused.

"No? You see, missy, this here is the stuff that is gonna' make big men of us round these parts. Soon's I retire from the Army, I'll have plenty to live comfortable like. All from the sale of the liquid in this here jug," he said.

Her fear was getting the best of her, so she began to scream. The man did not even start. He just sat there smirking at her until she subsided.

"No use doin all that a-hollerin', no how. We are way back in the woods, and there ain't nobody knows where you are, 'ceptin' two others which you will be seeing directly. Then we is gonna' have us a party. So save your strength, cause you gonna' need it," he said.

Outside the little shack in the woods, Wheezer was struggling to get out of cage made of thick hard wood. The rungs were too large for his mouth to get a good bite and he was beginning to lose strength. Finally, he lay down to wait. He had already barked until he was hoarse with no results.

Wheezer was not sure how the trap was set. All he remembered was running through the woods, chasing a running form when something had been flung over him, a blanket or a canvas bag. No matter how he struggled, he could not break through as his captors carried him for some while to his present cage. It had been very much too late when he recognized two of the miscreants. One he knew as an enemy, but the other confused him since he had just been at Jackson's house enjoying the day with his family. What worried him more was not knowing where

Sasa was. He could smell her scent faintly, but he could not follow the clue. So he circled the cage whimpering and whining for a time, then lay down for a while, then back up pacing again.

As he now lay quiet, he was able to hear a rustle in the grass by the nearby bushes. Being a Jack Russell, he was at once eager to go on the chase again, but was prevented. The grass parted slowly. Creeping low to the ground was a shadowed form, stopping at intervals, then continuing on up to the cage. Wheezer looked into the eyes of Yellow Eyes.

Yellow Eyes saw at once the predicament Wheezer was in and tried with all his own strength to gnaw off a rung of the cage. If Yellow Eyes had had enough time, he would have succeeded. Yellow Eyes became alert, stopping to listen, then scurried away back into the grass.

Chapter 27

"But, I just don't see why we cannot figure out who is doing this. I mean, there aren't that many people living in the town. If the whiskey is flowing, we ought to be able to deduce who is supplying them with the corn to make it," said Jackson.

"That would seem like a logical way to proceed, Jackson, however, when we were at the fort today, I noticed the exceedingly large amount of activity between and on the border. When Captain Stuart showed me the Commissary building, I noticed several Indians there trading. And when we were let off at the fort docks, there seemed to be quite a lot of traffic on the river with boats coming and going. How in the world can one man keep track of all that?" said Andrew.

"Exactly my own question," said Anna.

"That is just the problem; even though the Army wants the Captain to stop the sale of whiskey to the Indians, they have made it impossible for him to do so. Because of the strict Army regulations, he cannot interfere with any civilian transactions on the Arkansas side. The only thing he could stop would be preventing a wagon load of whiskey from going over the border into Indian Territory. So unless these men are stupid and go over in broad daylight at the most convenient crossing place, the Captain would never catch them unless he knew where and when the law would be broken, and that is just silly," said Jackson.

"So what you are actually saying is that the orders that were given to Captain Stuart were doomed to failure before he even got them. That poor man, he must be feeling very frustrated by now," added Anna.

"Have there been no clues to the murders you spoke of earlier, Jackson?" said Henry Neugent.

"Well, yes, there have been, but I have not had any time to stop and give any of them much thought. The first body was that of James Koni, the Choctaw man who was hired by the government, to try to join the group selling the whiskey. We found him holding a piece of blue cloth, and Sasa found a poem written by him in the pouch hanging from his neck. We could not make heads or tails of the poem; it may have nothing to do with his murder. The other man was still alive when we got to him. He was Sam Bushyhead. He whispered to Sasa that there was an evil man who was an Irishman behind a mask, who was a murderer. Then he also said there was a man who gives orders to soldiers and one last man who had the skin of a Cherokee. Very enigmatic.

"Then Sasa was accosted at the docks. Wheezer came to her aid and ripped a patch of one man's shirt. She claims that a wild coyote also helped but I have never seen such a thing. The coyotes here are not friendly. But, that is beside the facts; she kept that piece of cloth, but forgot it until recently. When she thought again of it, she compared the two scraps of cloth, and they were identical. We know that the pieces of cloth are from two different but identical, blue shirts from the Army uniforms of enlisted men. I have nothing more to go on," said Jackson.

Lucius felt like he was invisible. He had no idea all of these things had gone on in the last few days. The idea dawned on him that something was going terribly wrong and that he must be involved with a pack of murders.

"Jackson, you said the first man had a poem written on a piece of paper? Could we see it?" asked Henry.

"Sure, but there seems to be a couple of words missing at the end, plus I can't figure it out and I think I am fairly well read. Let me go get it," said Jackson.

Jackson returned with the poem and the pieces of cloth and handed them over to the two older men.

"I am a bit of a poetry enthusiast," said Henry.

The poem was handed over to Henry's examination while the pieces of cloth went to Jackson's father. Henry seemed to be fully engrossed in his reading. Then Henry abruptly jumped out of his chair.

"Great Jehoshaphat! Jackson, this is not just some idle poem. This is a clever way the man concealed the clues he had found out," said Henry, who then settled back down in his chair breathing heavily.

"You see, I have done quite a bit of traveling, but especially to Ireland. I go there from time to time and look for enterprising young persons that I can set up in American

277

businesses. There is so much poverty over there, and a great deal of industrious talent. It was one way I could help.

"To continue, a few years ago when I was there, there was a scandalous murder that happened which was talked about for quite a while. Murder happens every day with all the unrest going on, but this murder happened within the highest of the lord classes, in one of the land owner's family. In point of fact, a family that ran in the same circles that I enjoyed.

"It seems that there was a very sought after young lady, with a very nice sized dowry, who was to be wed to a man of her father's choosing. Unfortunately, the man of his choosing was not the man she would have wanted, but the plans went on anyway. It happened on the eve of their marriage that, evidently, the young lord came upon his intended in the arms of her lover. You would expect a man to lash out at the other man, but that is not what happened. He knocked the other man aside, thrust his sword into the heart of the lady and he ran. Since he had left the other young man, staring and brokenhearted, he had actually left an eye witness to his crime. He eluded the authorities and no one has seen hide-nor-hair of him since. Not even his own family has heard from him, not that they want to, mind you," said Henry.

"But, what does that have to do with the poem? I don't get the connection," said Anna.

"You will when I show you. You see, this poem is highly cleverly written. Only someone who was familiar with the crime would understand the clues. I am assuming that James was going to send this to his contact in the government who would have been able to figure it out, sooner or later.

"See here, the first stanza of the poem explains the crime, but the clues are in the very specific words he uses.

The rapier swirled down, he was deaf to her plea,
her heart blood he did smite.
Down the coast he dashed by the dark angry sea
the Royal Bard did run from his plight.

Like 'rapier' in the first line of this stanza, the family crest uses that image on its shield, and it also is the murder weapon. Then there is the mention of the 'Royal Bard', which is even more telling. You see the murderer's name was Richard O'Riordan. The name may have changed some if he came to America and it could be some convoluted form of his name, like Rordon. James' clue, though, must mean that this person's name is still recognizable. In Ireland that name translates from the Gaelic as 'descendant of Ríoghbhardán' which is the Irish word for 'Royal Bard', said Henry, excitement building within him.

Lucius was now paying strict attention to the conversation. Light was beginning to dawn in his brain that he had been duped by this very same 'Royal Bard'. However, he did not deign to interrupt the flow, for he also wanted to know what the rest of the poem meant.

"The second stanza tells where the fool went. See, it says:

Off to the far West the Royal Bard did go
his unreasoning hatred consumed him.
He may run fast and deep, but how far can he go
when he is running away from his sin?

"So you see, James found out that this man had come to the frontier, or 'the far West'. That must mean that he is here in this area or James would not have known of the connection. Then the next stanza seals his identity and where the murder happened, thus giving the authorities something to base their search on. See, it says:

Tis fitting the emblem his family does carry
two lions, two rapiers, mighty and true.
Alas, he murdered the one he would marry
from his family in Kerry he withdrew.

"What a telling sign this is. If you saw the royal shield, it has two swords or rapiers catty-cornered top to bottom with two lions, and it says his family is in Kerry. An easy thing to trace and, might I say, matches with the family and incident I know about. The last stanza says:

Flee, yes flee, but your rapier follows thee
Royal Bard run to the setting sun,
You may have some repast, then still you must flee
For the foul deed was yours - -

"I see that James was careful to not put the man's name in the poem so that if it fell into the wrong hands, he might not be found out as a spy for the government. So the question is, do you have anyone in these parts by the name of Richard O'Riordan or anything close to that? Assuming, of course that he has not changed one or both of his names," said Henry, not realizing the electricity he had caused to go through the entire group.

Anna was the first to recover. She stood up, not able to contain her own excitement and dread.

"We have a man here by the name of Robert Reardon. I have never felt comfortable in his presence, but I have to say that he does not sound like an Irishman. I mean, not like our friend Lucius here," said Anna.

Finally, Lucius felt he had something to add.

"My friend Anna, please do sit down. I have something I wish to say, for sure it will require all of my courage to say it," said Lucius.

Lucius then explained to the men what Anna already now knew, that he was running for his political views. But now, he was forced to reveal the rest of his own dirty truth. He stood with an apologetic look to Ann and a corresponding look from her, and began with shaking voice and head bowed.

"I have more to tell and it is not pretty. This man Robert Reardon became friendly with me early on, and I confided in him about my past. Well, I am ashamed to say that I fell victim to blackmail, and now I see my deliverance ahead. Robert has been forcing me to take part in this whiskey running," said Lucius as whispered gasps erupted round the room. "However, he keeps saying that there was someone else in charge. I have tried to get loose from his grip, but to no avail. I have detested myself ever since, because I was known in me homeland as a man that stood for what was right. And now, I have fallen down to wallow in the muck. I don't know much about their plans, but if there is anything I can do to help, I pledge myself to it. After listening to all of this, I believe that Robert is this Richard you are speaking of and when he was blackmailing me for being a wanted political person, he was at the same time a wanted murderer, and the murderer of a lovely lass as well," said Lucius.

Jackson was astonished, but recovered enough to reach his hand out to Lucius and they shook hands.

This was a happy scene, until Coyote burst in the door and in his halting English he said, "Sasa and Wheezer not here. We call, no answer. She gone, long time now," said Coyote.

Pandemonium broke out within the house.

Chapter 28

Wheezer whined from time to time, then lay quite for a while. He had not seen Yellow Eyes since he had been scared away. From his cage deep in the woods he could see nothing but trees and brush. He had heard voices at one point, but they were muffled and seemed far away. He had been thinking of Sasa and those thoughts were beginning to make him frantic with worry. Sometime after he was left in his prison, he heard Sasa cry out, but since that time there had been no human sounds at all. All it meant to Wheezer was that Sasa was in danger and he could not get out to help her. He had no way of knowing why she had cried out or that she was being held by the same people that put him in his terrible cage.

His worrisome thoughts of Sasa caused him to begin barking again. Maybe someone would hear him. Then, from the bushes slunk Yellow Eyes again. Wheezer was relieved to see his friend. Yellow Eyes began again to gnaw on the rung he had started, before he was scared away. Yellow Eyes worked hard to get the job done, for he knew he may not have much time to accomplish the task. His gums began to bleed from splinters pinching into his flesh with each bite. As he bit down and tore out slivers of wood from the hardwood rung, he continued to keep his ears and eyes alert for movement or sound. Finally, he broke through, but the rung still did not fall out. Then Wheezer bit down on the upper broken rung while Yellow Eyes did the same with the lower. Each pulled and tugged pulling opposite directions and finally it was parted enough for Wheezer to squeeze through; it had been a tight fit since Wheezer left several tufts of fur stuck to the ends of the broken rung. Yellow Eye licked the blood from his damaged mouth.

Once out, Wheezer wanted to find Sasa, but Yellow Eyes had a different idea. They passed by an old shack. and it was there that Wheezer caught Sasa's scent, but Yellow Eyes came quickly and bit down on Wheezer's collar, tugging him away from the shack. With somewhat of a struggle, Yellow Eyes succeeded in getting Wheezer to follow him. Wheezer did not recognize the area until they had traveled for some time. Then things began to seem familiar although it was a little hard to tell in the dark.

When they finally arrived at the Halley ranch, Wheezer went bounding up to the house, while Yellow Eyes hung back, still fearing all the humans he saw at the house. However, there was one person he saw standing outside of a structure of some sort that had not been there the day before. The person was alone at the moment, watching Wheezer rush into the frantic scene, so Yellow Eyes crept up on silent feet.

Coyote was standing next to the summer lodge he had just helped to build, watching Jackson Halley and his friends scurry around trying to figure out what to do. He stood with his arms down by his side, waiting to be called if needed, when suddenly he felt something cold and wet slip into the palm of his limp hand. Coyote looked down to see a sight he would never have thought possible. Yellow Eyes had just put his muzzle in Coyote's hand. It was a gesture of trust from a wild animal and Coyote was very aware of the honor implied. He knelt down so that he was eye to eye with the creature, and spoke to Yellow Eyes in the language he knew best, Sioux.

"Ah, I see you have come to help us my brother. Was it you who helped Wheezer to find his way home? Aaaee! What is this, you are bleeding? We must take care of this first, then we can decide what to do about finding Wheezer's friend Sasa," said Coyote.

Coyote motioned for Yellow Eyes to follow him into the lodge. Yellow Eyes had never been inside of a humans den in his life and he was very unsure if it was a way to trap him. But Coyote continued to speak softly to him, reassuring him that it would be fine. There were two other humans inside the lodge when Yellow Eyes crept on his belly through the doorway. Poison Woman was in shock, but she recovered quickly, seeing that the animal was with Coyote. Medicine Man looked as if he had seen such a thing every day of his life. When Yellow Eyes came before the two elders, Medicine Man greeted Yellow Eyes with a nod.

"Grandmother, my friend Yellow Eyes has come to help us find Sasa. He has already brought Wheezer back to his home, but in helping him, he has injured his mouth. It is bleeding. Do you have something that would help stop the bleeding and help him with the pain?" asked Coyote.

"I can make him some tea that will clean the wounds. That alone will probably stop the bleeding and help with pain, but how can you get a coyote to drink tea?" said Poison Woman.

"All we can do is try it and see if he will trust me enough to drink it," said Coyote in English and sign.

Coyote needed to tell Jackson about Yellow Eyes and that the animal might be the only one who knew where Sasa was. He began to leave the lodge, and Yellow Eyes began to follow.

"I am sorry my brother. You must wait for me here while Poison Woman helps you with your bleeding mouth. I will go and get others to help us. We will follow you, but you must stay here and wait for me," said Coyote.

The animal seemed to understand, if not the words, the hand gestures. He sat down and turned his head to Poison Woman.

"Yes, Little Brother, I will not harm you. Stay here for a while and I will help you. Coyote will be back very soon," said Poison Woman.

The elder set about preparing the medicinal tea for her new visitor, making sure it was cool enough for him so that it would not hurt his wounds. She put it into a low wooden bowl, then gestured to him that it was something for him. He sniffed at it, then seemed to make a decision and steadily drank the tea.

*****

Sasa had been moved to a chair, after she had been given a bucket to urinate in, still with her hands tied tightly

285

in front of her. Willis had tied her to the chair, for what purpose, Sasa could not fathom. Soon, she heard a door open, with muffled voices from beyond the room she was stashed in. She had taken what time she could to look at her surroundings. She still did not know where exactly she was, but she recognized the type of barrels and jugs sitting on the floor and stacked onto rickety shelves surrounding her. All of it was whiskey. Knowing that, she began to realize what this was all about and it did not bode well for her at all.

She was not sure just who she expected to walk through the door, but could never have imagined that her captor would turn out to be the next person to come in the door.

"You? Why? Why would you do this to your own people?" said Sasa.

"You ought to know the answer to that. All my life I have been pushed around by white men, unable to do anything about it. It finally dawned on me that I may as well figure out a way to join them and it would not go so hard on me. And you know what, daughter? I think it has worked out very well," said Joseph Deerslayer.

"Do not...do not call me daughter. You do not even deserve to be called a Cherokee. You must be filled with dark evil if you think it is better to turn against your own blood to join with criminals," said Sasa almost allowing her emotions to bring tears to her eyes. "Especially men who poison our nation with their vile drink."

Sasa steeled herself, so that she could guard against whatever this renegade might say to her. She refused to allow herself to cry.

"Do you think that I care what you or any of our tribe think about me? I lost my respect for them a long time ago. Especially those men who signed that false treaty that gave our land to the white man. Well, most of them

286

paid the price. I helped to see to that anc it was very satis-
fying," said Joseph, gloating.

"You murdered your own people?" asked Sasa,
aghast at what Joseph had said.

"And why not? They had no right to give my land
away. Nobody asked me, did they? After the march, my
eyes were opened. I saw then that the only thing that
speaks loudly is money, and a good gun. The white man's
money and the white man's guns. Now I have plenty of it,
and am planning on having more. And, if you think that I
will let you interfere, you are mistaken.

"Ha, ha, the government thought they were so clever. They thought they could use me to help them stop the
whiskey trade. They supplied me with money so that I had
time to devote to finding the whiskey runners. I fooled
them all. Even James was fooled. He had no idea that I was
one of the gang until the day I killed him. But, he did not
have to die. I offered him the same deal I got. He only had
to keep quiet, and not report what he found. But he would
rather do the bidding of the white man's government than
get back the money and land that was stolen from him. He
refused, and I had no choice but to prevent him from pass-
ing on his information," said Joseph.

"What information? What are you talking about?"
said Sasa.

"That is another great joke on the white man. They
have James' report; right now it is in the hands of Jackson.
But they have no clue how to read that stupid poem. Yes,
James told me about it, but I had no idea he had it in his
pouch, or I would have removed that little piece of evidence.
What do I care anyway? That poem does not incriminate
me, it only is the possible lead to the leader of our gang, and
believe me, they will never figure it out," said Joseph.

Sasa had listened as calmly as she could. She knew that
she was at the mercy of this man who had given up his peo-

ple for his own greed. He probably did not feel so bad about murdering James Koni because James was Choctaw, but his admission that he helped to murder some of the signers of the New Echota Treaty showed her that he would rationalize anything, anything at all, if it furthered his own plans.

"Now I am here to find out some things from you. I hope you will cooperate, Sasa, because I would hate to mess up your pretty face," said Joseph.

"I don't know what you are talking about. But, even if I did, you probably plan on killing me anyway," said Sasa.

"True, but you have a chance to go easy or painfully. That is your choice, because you are not leaving this place, ever. There is a room under the floor and that is where you will be buried. So you see Sasa, even though you are friends with those whites, it did not benefit you," said Joseph.

Willis was in the next room still, and was listening carefully. He was getting some pleasure out of listening, because that stupid Indian, Joseph, thought he was going to escape this alive. As if good white men would accept a redskin as a partner. He had served his purpose, and was one more loose end to take care of.

His orders were to allow Joseph to extract what information he could from the girl before killing her, then, after moving all the whiskey to the cut bank stash on the Arkansas River, he would take care of Joseph as well, before placing the cage with that annoying dog in the shack and burn it to the ground with a little encouragement from a jug of whiskey poured all around.

Sasa thought furiously about what she could tell them, but she honestly did not know what information they thought she had.

"Does anyone, Jackson, Arch, or anybody at the ranch know who the leader of our gang is?" asked Joseph.

"How would I know that?" said Sasa.

The slap across her cheek was like bright lightning which brought stars to her eyes and blood to her lips.

"Now, answer the question," he said.

"As far as I know, no," said Sasa in all truthfulness.

Joseph believed that statement because he had just come from there earlier that day, and there was nothing of import revealed at the council they held outside.

"Do they suspect that someone in the Army is in on it?" asked Joseph.

Now that was a question she did know, but she had to think quickly to figure out an acceptable answer.

"I think they suspect someone in the Army was harassing me. We were supposed to talk about that tonight and decide if I was going to keep going to Fort Smith for my lessons," said Sasa.

Joseph turned his head to shout at the empty doorway.

"I told those fools they were bringing undue attention to us, didn't I Willis?" he shouted to the man in the next room.

"Don't worry about that. Get on with what we need to know and hurry it up," said Willis.

"Does anybody know where we are storing the whiskey, or anything about our deliveries?" asked Joseph.

"I don't think so, at least I have not heard of anything like that," said Sasa.

"Who do they say killed James and Sam Bushyhead," said Joseph.

"They don't know," said Sasa quietly.

"Ah, but they are working on it, are they not?" asked Joseph.

"You were at the council. You know they are trying to figure it out, so why do I need to tell you what you already know," said Sasa, stating the obvious.

From the other room, Willis came through the door.

Sasa saw the look on his face. Joseph had been looking at Sasa and saw the horror sweep across her countenance. But, Joseph cared little about Sasa's fears. He still had to move more of the whiskey to its new hiding place, so he loaded up his mule and set off through the woods. Now Sasa was left alone with a cold blooded killer and she knew she also had outlived her usefulness.

Chapter 29

Coyote came running into the house again, but this time he sought out Jackson, needing a private word with him. He found him in the dining room, taking out the rifles from the gun cabinet.

"Jackson, I need... uh... talk to you now. Important, please come lodge. Come, come," Coyote urged.

Jackson saw the intensity in Coyote's face and agreed quickly. Telling the others to wait for him in the house, he followed Coyote outside. When Jackson stepped out of the house, Wheezer jumped high into his arms, licking his face furiously.

"Wheezer? Where did you come from boy?" said Jackson.

Coyote took Jackson by the arm to hurry him along. When they approached the lodge, Coyote stopped and faced Jackson. A piercing look of concern filled his face.

"This important, Jackson. Wheezer has helper. Make Wheezer free, but may know where Sasa is. Helper protect Sasa before, but you must be . . uh . . calm. Helper is wild coyote, Sasa name Yellow Eyes. He can take Jackson to Sasa, but do not frighten him, yes?" said Coyote.

"What? Are you serious?" hollered Jackson, putting Wheezer on the ground, then remembered a forgotten conversation.

"Sasa had said Wheezer had a helper and she mentioned something about a coyote, but I did not take it seriously." mumbled Jackson.

Coyote pointed to the door of the lodge.

"You mean, you left him inside with the elders? You left a wild coyote alone with two very old elders who can't protect themselves?" said Jackson, incredulous.

"Look, you see. He here to help," said Coyote.

Cautiously, Jackson moved the skin flap away from the doorway and stepped inside. Yellow Eyes met Jackson with wary golden orbs, staring intently at him, shining with the reflection of the low fire in the lodge. Coyote entered and Yellow Eyes visibly began to relax.

"Brother, this is Jackson. He is Wheezer's friend," said Coyote to Yellow Eyes.

At that moment, Wheezer trotted into the lodge and sat close to Jackson, looking seriously from one to the other.

"Coyote, I don't know the first thing about how to talk to a coyote for heaven's sakes. What do you want me to say to him?" said Jackson, not sure if he believed the animal was here to help at all, but actually came for a free meal.

292

Coyote motioned to Jackson to sit and it was then that Jackson noticed Poison Woman. She picked up the bowl she had given the tea in and seemed unnaturally calm.

"Jackson, although I have only just now been introduced, this is Yellow Eyes. I believe you may have heard about the incident at the docks. This is the coyote helper. He is a friend of Wheezer and Sasa and so, he is friend to me. Medicine Man has not said what he feels, but he usually does not allow any animals to come into our lodge except Wheezer, and he has said nothing since coyote entered," said Poison Woman.

Jackson mumbling his words said, "He may just be scared stiff." Medicine Man smiled at him from across the fire which told Jackson he appreciated his small attempt at levity.

Addressing Yellow Eyes, Jackson said, "Yellow Eyes, I am glad to meet you," and Coyote nudged him to continue, "uh... I, that is, we are Sasa's friends and we need help to find Sasa. Somebody may be trying to hurt her. Can you take us to Sasa?"

Yellow Eyes stood up immediately, but Coyote motioned the animal to wait for his signal.

"Jackson, must go quickly, Coyote do not know how many bad men. Need friends help," said Coyote pointing back at the house.

"Right, I understand. You stay here with Wheezer and... uh... Yellow Eyes, and I will gather our forces. We will be off soon," ordered Jackson.

Upon reentering the house, all eyes wore questions in their stares, so Jackson hastened to relieve their concern.

"Uh... please gather round. It seems that Sasa's story about a wild coyote who is a friend of Wheezer's... oh this sounds so impossible, even to me,... he is here and he has brought Wheezer back to us," said Jackson.

Arch and Lucius began to head for the door, when Jackson's peremptory shout stopped them in their tracks.

"You cannot just go out there and scare the beast. He is in the lodge of the elders. Wheezer and Coyote are with him and he is waiting for us to gather ourselves. He will take us to where Sasa is, but this may be a very dangerous venture. We have no idea how many there are and we may have very little time. It is obvious someone took them both. Why, we still don't know, but we must locate her tonight and...er...Yellow Eyes... will help us," said Jackson.

"Do you want me to gather any of the ranch hands, Jackson?" asked Arch.

"No, Arch, I don't want to endanger them. It is probably best if we keep this a little quiet. We don't want a huge mob traipsing through the woods. I believe you should stay here, Anna..." but before Jackson could continue, the said Anna interrupted.

"No you don't, Jackson Halley. I have had just about enough of you treating me like a wilting flower. If you had taken the time to ask me, you might know that I am a crack shot. Since last year I have made a point of becoming more useful on the frontier and the first order of business was being able to take care of one's self. I am going," said Anna, stomping her foot.

"But, my dear, you cannot go in that dress. It will trip you up," said Jackson, trying everything he could to dissuade her from going with them.

"That can be remedied. Get yourselves ready. I have my own gun with me and I will just pop into Sasa's room. I know she has a deerskin dress, moccasins and leggings, and we are the same size. I will meet you out front," she said emphatically and marched off with a determined air.

Jackson was unable to think of anything he could do to keep her from going, other than tying her up, and if he ever wanted to have her as a wife, he had better not do that.

Within twenty minutes all were assembled and waiting at the elder's lodge. Andrew had changed into the clothes he had brought for the overland trip. Henry, rotund as he was, walked with a grace normally not seen in one so large. Both men, ready and serious. Arch, of course was with his partner and friend, Jackson. He carried his knife and his bow. He was the best shot with the bow and arrow. Lucius only had the change of clothes he brought to look around the ranch in, but it would serve their purposes well enough. Anna emerged from the house, her hair pulled back and out of the way. She wore Sasa's skins and moccasins with the leggings to protect her legs from the brambles. She carried with her the little Pepper Box hand gun. It would only be useful at close range, but it would send a spray of shot which had to hit her target in some fashion. Jackson hoped she would not do anything foolish that night.

Coyote stepped out of the elder's lodge, followed by Wheezer and Yellow Eyes, who looked suspiciously at the group. Coyote spoke quickly to him and the animal took on an air of unconcern. Before they could get started, Poison Woman and Medicine Man came out of the lodge.

"My son and friends, you must be very cautious, there is much danger. These men will stop at nothing to save their own flesh," said Medicine Man.

"Yes, Grandfather, I understand. We believe we have figured out who, at least, is the leader. This will be settled tonight, one way or the other. I have written down who we are looking for and why. If we do not return, please take this to the Captain at the Fort. He will know what to do with the information," said Jackson as he handed Medicine Man a sealed envelope.

"Now listen everyone, Yellow Eyes is in the lead. You must be very careful not to overtake him. If he slows, then so do we, if he stops to listen, then so do we. Tread as qui-

295

etly as you can. Of our group, only Coyote and Arch know how to be invisible and silent, but do your very best to not give yourselves away. No shooting, unless I shoot. Is that understood?" said Jackson.

All heads nodded and before long, they disappeared into the woods following the wild coyote named Yellow Eyes.

Medicine Man stood with the envelope in his hand, puzzling over what Jackson had said. He thought, *What could he mean by, "If they don't come back"? How long do I wait? This is not good. Even if I start out now for the fort, it will take a good hour to get there.* He made his decision, put on his skin jacket, strapped on his knife and left for the fort immediately.

*****

Sasa's thoughts swam in her mind. She saw Sergeant Willis walk slowly towards her.

"Now squaw, I reckon it's just you and me for a tad bit. What do you think we should do with the time? Oh, I have lots of ideas. Do you want to hear them?" said Willis, leering at her.

"Please do not do this. I have never hurt you. Why would you want to hurt me?" asked Sasa.

"Do I have to have a reason?" he said with raised brows, "Let's just say I'm not happy with my government's decision of movin' you bunch of red skins into this territory. I had plans on settlin' down on some land over there when I retire. Had it all picked out, too. But, afore I knowd it, they was movin' the border back a mite east and givin' all that good grazin' land to your filthy lot. Maybe tonight I'm gonna' get some repayment for what I done lost. What do ya say 'bout that, injun?"

"In the first place, I think I have a great deal to say about it, don't you think so Sergeant?" said a voice from the door.

296

"Well, Robert, I was just funnin' with her a little a'fore we kill her. If'n you squint, she looks a mite pretty. I could forget she's red, at least for a while," Willis said chuckling. "Say, you sound different. What's the matter with your voice?"

"Let's just say I am taking off the mask. I happen to be quite educated. Certainly not in the same class of oafs like you and your lot. Now, you are going to listen to my orders and get to it now or we might be sorry. I want all this whiskey taken over to that cut bank," said Robert Reardon.

"But, that's what I been doin all night long. Joseph left a while ago with a load. Can't you see it is almost done? I am missin' at the fort and those ole boys won't cover for me for long," said Willis.

"Never mind about that, and leave the girl alone. I see you have most of it moved out, so that is good. And I see you followed my orders on getting the girl here. Go outside and get that cage with the dog and bring it in here. I want it all to go up in flames at the same time," said Robert.

Willis went to obey, and traipsed on outside. While he was gone, Robert did not bother to look at Sasa. To him she was nothing, a mere technicality. He was going through the drawers in the desk, making sure he got the important things out, when Willis appeared at the door of the shack, huffing and puffing.

"He's gone, escaped. He musta' chewed through the wood, cause he is not there a-tall," cried Willis.

"You bumbling fool. Do I have to do everything for you? He must be out there somewhere," said Robert. Extremely vexed, he stomped out of the shack with Willis in tow to scour the near woods for the dog, taking the lantern with him.

Sasa had begun to lose hope of making it out of this situation alive and she was just beginning to sing her death song when someone crept into the door, quiet and wary. The light from the open door was low and she thought she saw a woman, though she could not say who it was, but it definitely was a white woman. Sasa stayed quiet while the woman came near and suddenly Sasa saw the knife glinting off of the low lamp light from the other room.

"Who are you?" whispered Sasa.

"Never you mind. When I cut these tiez, I expect you to do the rest, 'cauze I won't be here to help you, don't you know?" said Patricia.

"Why would you do this for me?" said Sasa suspiciously, noticing a very pungent smell pervading the room.

"Oh, honey, it ain't for you. I just plan on getting my own for whatz been done to me, don't you know? Throw me out on my ear, will he? Tell me he's gonna' kill me, will he?" Patricia rambled as she proceeded to cut Sasa bonds. "Well, little gal, you best be hightailing it on outta here. As for me, I am gone and you never saw me, do you understandz?"

"Yes, ma'am, and thank you. May the Creator bless you," said Sasa.

The woman was gone in a flash and Sasa could barely believe she was free. Now the problem was to escape from the shack. She could hear the men stomping through the bushes. One relief was that Wheezer had escaped. Just the thought of them burning Wheezer alive made her shudder.

They had taken her moccasins off, but she did not bother to look for them. Her goal was to make it far enough away so they could not find her in the dark. She made it out of the door on silent feet, moving quickly and bent low. She made her move to get to the woods nearby, but when she got there she realized she had picked the wrong direction to travel, for there, through the woods came the men. When they saw her, several curse words were heard, but she did not hesitate, as she turned and ran. She ran as fast as she could on unknown ground, stubbing her toes and scratching her legs as she went.

She had gotten only about fifty yards from the shack when she was pulled back abruptly by her hair, which hurt quite a lot since she had already been hit in the head earlier that day. If she was going to put up a fight, it would have to be now, because once she was inside of that shack, it would be over.

Sasa, began screaming and kicking her feet. When a hand clamped over her mouth to hush her up, she opened wider and bit down hard. The hand was removed and she screamed even louder. As he dragged her toward the shack she grabbed hold of limbs and saplings, anything to slow them down and buy her more time.

"Yahweh, Yahweh, help me Creator, please help me," Sasa yelled.

Chapter 30

The group was careful to follow Jackson's instructions. Yellow Eyes seemed to take no notice that he had seven humans following closely behind him, but he felt safe because of Coyote. Wheezer trotted almost beside Yellow Eyes but back a pace or two. They had traveled quite a way, they were now in an area that Jackson had never explored. It was close to the Indian Territorial border but still in Arkansas, and north of Jackson's ranch.

Abruptly, and in unison, Yellow Eyes and Wheezer halted, the hair on their backs rose. Wheezer's tail stood straight and quivered. Yellow Eyes' ears pricked as he stood with only three paws on the ground. Then like a shot from a starting pistol at a race both animals took off running and the group was hard pressed to keep up with them. However, the closer they came to whatever the animals were heading towards, the better they themselves could hear what the animals had heard. Then, Jackson distinctly heard Sasa call for Yahweh, the Creator, and he knew that he must get to her now, there was not a moment to lose.

They rushed through the forest and burst out close to a tumble down shack. There, almost to the door were two men pulling, and tugging on Sasa to get her inside.

"Stop or I'll shoot," yelled Jackson.

But the men paid him no mind. There were still too many yards away to shoot accurately in the dark, so they held off. But the animals, not understanding what the words meant went rushing into the fray.

Lucius surged forward, hoping to get hold of Robert, because that was the man who had made his life in America a living hell. But, before he could get to them, another figure rushed out of the woods, grabbing Lucius by the throat. To Lucius' surprise, he recognized Joseph and in that odd moment when things seem to slow down and move at a snail's pace, Lucius saw the blade in Joseph's hand, coming down, down, down and striking into his chest. Lucius had no more strength to fight which gave Joseph the opportunity to pull the blade out to repeat the blow. Lucius saw Joseph's arm stop in midair, his hand still up with his knife glinting in the moonlight, but it did not come down again. Instead, Joseph's hand relaxed and the blade fell to the ground. Jackson's own blade protruded from Joseph's back and there is where it stayed. Joseph fell to the side while Anna rushed forward to aid Lucius.

Coyote and Arch ran faster to catch up with Yellow

Eyes and Wheezer, but the animals had gotten to the two other men first. Andrew and Henry were bringing up the rear, as Jackson stopped beside Anna to make sure she was not injured, Jackson then followed and was witness to a terrible scene.

A fierce battle was continuing. Sergeant Willis had one massive strong hand attached to Sasa's hair and was not letting go. Wheezer had made several jumping attacks to Sergeant Willis' neck and face which were bleeding profusely, but had not induced him to give up. On the other hand, Robert, who had the use of both of his hands, had dropped the lantern and the fuel had spilled and began running down the path to the shack. The glass globe broke and the flame transferred to the running fuel which found its way to the dry and brittle shack which caught fire easily.

Arch and Coyote tried to help, but there did not seem a way to get between the men and the animals. They waited for an opportunity.

Yellow Eyes had backed Robert further towards the shack with a snarl that showed every one of his massive canines and his upper lip and nose pulled to the side allowing his mouth to open even wider. His ears lay flat on his head, eyes becoming a reflective blazing furnace which matched the blazing of the shack behind Robert. Then crouching, his head low, his face showing every ounce of his vicious intent, Yellow Eyes leapt onto Robert's chest. The man struggled violently with the wild coyote and succeeded in pushing it away. But, Newton's law, "for every action there is an equal and opposite reaction" proved unerringly true, for the mighty shove which Robert threw the wild coyote away from him, reacted instantly by his body flinging itself in the opposite direction and into the completely engulfed shack. He did not come back out.

Willis still struggled, hoping to get Sasa up to use her as a shield, but Wheezer's attack had bloodied his face to the point where he could barely see. The next thing he knew, two older men, who he had never set eyes on before, were holding guns to his head on either side. There was nothing he could do, but to let go of Sasa and he was taken into custody to be delivered to the Army with a list of his felonies.

As the shack continued to burn, fueled on by the leftover whiskey, abruptly exploding from time to time, like great cannon balls striking the old edifice. Jackson came back to the kneeling form of Anna who held Lucius' head in her lap. She was issuing soothing sounds, trying to keep the man calm. Coyote joined them and examined the wound while the other men looked on helplessly. Finally, Coyote looked up at them with hope gone from this face, and shook his head slowly. The knife had gone through his lung and he was bleeding inside, his chest filling with blood. There was nothing they could do for him, but keep him calm and as comfortable as possible.

The light from the burning shack shone on Lucius' face, glinting off of his light hair and flushed cheeks.

"Anna, I guess I failed you, didn't I? I wanted to redeem meself to show you I was a man of integrity, but I began a wee bit too late. I can say it now Anna, me darlin'. I loved you. I have loved you since the moment I set eyes on you," said Lucius softly.

Anna stroked his hair and moved a few light strands out of his eyes.

"No Lucius, you succeeded. I knew you were not a bad man. You were used terribly and I have no doubt that you would have risen above it. After all, you had always stood up for what you believed in, and you would have come through on the right side. You just needed to know that someone believed in you," said Anna with a quaver in her voice.

Anna looked up at Jackson with pleading and tears in her eyes, but there was nothing Jackson could do but give her support. Lucius was sliding away slowly, but he fought to stay alive long enough to say a little more to his new friends.

"Anna, might I ask you and Jackson a wee favor. Back at me feed store in the desk is an address book with me parents address, it is marked with a red ribbon on the "O" page for O'Malley. Please write to them, me dearie. Don't tell them the bad that I got meself into at the last. Just tell them that I loved them and never in me life stopped the thinkin of them," said Lucius in almost a whisper.

"I will be happy to do that, Lucius. Is there anything you want done with your property in town? Do you have a will we should know about?" asked Jackson.

Before, he answered, Andrew and Henry knelt down by Jackson to lend their support to the dying man.

"Yes, well I never got around to making meself a will. So, Anna and Jackson, unless I miss me guess, you two will be an old married couple soon, so I would like to give you both everything there is," he said, then sputtered blood from his mouth. Once recovered a bit, he said, "There is a safe in the office; the combination is in the back of the address book. I never could remember me numbers," Lucius' voice became strained and weak, but he could still smile at his little joke. "All the important papers and information are there. No, don't say you won't take it. And believe me when I say, my parents are not in need of it, but it is all I have to give to the two people who helped me redeem meself, before I met me maker," said Lucius as he erupted into a violent fit of coughing which transformed into a horrible gurgle and then silence and his body went limp. A good man, gone from the frontier.

Anna sat, still with Lucius' head in her lap, stroking his hair and her tears dripping onto his silent face. Blood smeared the front of her dress, but she did not care. She was sorry she had not gotten to know him better. Looking up into Jackson's sincere face, she took his hand and looked into Jackson's eyes. They knew Lucius had been right in the end.

When the little group broke apart, several of them with tears streaming from their eyes, they saw an encouraging sight. Sasa and Coyote sat on the ground together while Wheezer and Yellow Eyes, holding them down with their paws, licked them from stem to stern, with Arch Flint looking on laughing his fool head off. And far off in the distance they could hear the faint sound of a bugle. The roaring blaze would light the way.

Chapter 31

"Stop, stop," cried Sasa as she ran to keep up with Wheezer and Penny while they played chase in the yard.

The two Jack Russells had become fast friends and, if it was possible, became even more mischievous than before. Adding Penny to the mix certainly livened things up quite a bit. Sasa quit trying to catch them up and came to an abrupt stop at the lodge where Medicine Man and Poison Woman were adding some grass bundles to the side of the lodge. Coyote and Yellow Eyes were off exploring.

"Do you want some help Grandmother and Grandfather?" asked Sasa.

"No, daughter, we are almost finished. You may stay and have some tea with us in a few minutes though. We expect Coyote to be back soon and we can all sit and have a good visit before Coyote leaves," said Poison Woman.

"Leaves? He is leaving us? He did not say anything to me about that," said Sasa.

"No, he would not probably. He has been talking to his Wakan Tanka about what he should do next, but I will let him tell you himself," said Poison Woman.

A few moments later, Coyote arrived with Yellow Eyes beside him. These days Yellow Eyes stayed close to Coyote. They were bonded, like one. Coyote trotted up to Sasa, smiles engulfing his face.

"I am happy to see you Sasa," said Coyote. "I have been wanting to talk with you. Can we go and sit below the brush arbor?" he said.

They sat on a blanket in the patchy shade of the arbor. Sasa looked worried at Coyote. He shyly looked away. It was not easy for him to reveal his inner feelings.

"Sasa, I must leave now. I must go back to my own people. They need to be told about what is to come and I am made to believe that this is what Wakan Tanka has sent me here to learn. I feel honored to carry this message back to my people. But, it will be very hard for them to believe me. But, I must tell them about the herding of the tribes onto land that is different, about the food allotments and the starving of your people and mostly about the white man's whiskey. They must know what has happened to the nations who drink the white man's drink which they call the drink that makes men crazy," said Coyote.

"Have they already been given the drink?" asked Sasa.

"Yes, but not in the amounts that is happening here. Not in my village, but I have heard it said that for many years, the French traders would come from the North and they would bring the drink with them. They never had

307

enough of it to do much damage and it made a night of trading a joyous occasion. What they do not know is how the white men use that drink to get what they want. They want land, our land, and when they give us the drink, we cannot fight them off. The drink makes us weak.

"I believe my people need to plan for that time, and it will come soon. That is why I must go now for winter comes earlier there than it does here," said Coyote.

"Will you come back to us?" asked Sasa.

"I do not know the answer to that question. It is up to Wakan Tanka. I like it here, very much and Jackson offered to teach me how to work on a ranch. My people do not do anything like that, but I see the Cherokee and Choctaw. I see that they are better off when they know how to feed their families. Someday, if our lands are taken from us, I will need to know these things. My people will not want to hear what I have to say, who knows, they may kill me for telling them. They are the strongest Indian nation and have been undefeated in battle. It will be hard for them to see that the white man can do it. I am sure, they will laugh.

"I am going to go to both tribes, the Blackfoot and the different Sioux nations. I will tell them about the Cherokee, the Creek, the Choctaw, the Chickasaw and the Seminole of Indian Territory. I will tell them about the once mighty nation of the Osage, a feared nation, and what they have been reduced to. I will tell them about the thousands that are no more. Only then will I be able to come back and if Jackson still wants to teach me, I will stay," said Coyote.

"I will miss you very much, Coyote. I hope you will come back," said Sasa sincerely.

After the small group had their tea, Coyote picked up his items of travel, collected his picketed horse and began to walk away. But, he heard a whine and turned around to see Yellow Eyes standing expectantly.

"Yellow Eyes, you are my brother. Where I go, you go. I will share the food I catch and the water I drink. And you will be the proof I need to show my people that I bring a message that is true. So, come, Yellow Eyes," said Coyote.

Yellow Eyes turned around to look at Sasa and Wheezer. Sasa nodded her head as a gesture of acceptance. Wheezer came forward. Yellow Eyes lowered his head and Wheezer began to clean Yellow Eyes' ear briefly, then Yellow Eyes trotted off to catch up with Coyote. Sasa truly hoped he would come back someday. Medicine Man and Poison Woman stood outside their temporary lodge watching him go.

"He will be back," said Medicine Man.

The days that passed, after the discovery of the shack and the men behind the murders, caused the little community of Van Buren to buzz with stories about the night the murderers were caught. Jackson, Sasa and Anna were regarded as heroes. The Army took no real part in the clean-up of the burned out shack, burying the dead, returning the bodies to their families or searching for the stash of whiskey the men had hidden, and they also did not bother to investigate any further into who else may have been part of that group of whiskey sellers. They were naive to think that it would all stop now that the ring leaders were dead or in prison. The cache of hidden whiskey was never discovered.

Sergeant Willis faced court martial for his part in the illegal sale of whiskey in Indian Territory and for murder and attempted murder. Of course, Sasa could not bear witness against a white man because an Indian could not testify in court, but, on the night in question, the others in the group had arrived in time to see Willis try to drag Sasa into the building with the intent of setting it ablaze. With Jackson, Andrew and Henry as witnesses, because of their connections back east, the court was forced to not overlook the murder of two Indians and the attempted murder of Sasa. Willis was sentenced to hang.

Unfortunately, the whiskey trade barely slowed its pace during the ensuing weeks. There was always someone ready to take the risks and break the law when there was a profit to be made. The soldiers at the fort continued to take a large part in the selling of whiskey to the Indians, right under the nose of their commanding officers.

The drinking establishments in Fort Smith grew very cocky about the fact that the Captain could not prevent his own men from participating in the sale of whiskey to the Indians and that the Army would not adequately back him up. It became somewhat of a joke. But, the tables turned one day when the Captain went to one particular saloon owner to demand that he stop involving his men in the illegal trade. The saloon owner ordered his ruffians to beat the Captain to a bloody pulp, to the point that he almost died and had to be carried to the fort's infirmary. The very same soldiers who had been disobeying orders did not take kindly to their commanding officer being almost beaten to death. That night, some of them rolled one of the mobile cannon on wheels several blocks into the town.

While the crickets were chirping and the frogs were croaking the soldiers quietly loaded the large cannon with extra powder first, then put a number of pieces of iron shrapnel down the long black barrel. They then positioned the gun directly in front of the saloon doors while the merchant and his wife slept peacefully upstairs. Once the heavy six pound ball was rammed down into the shaft, they lit the fuse. When the cannon fired, it could be heard for miles around and as the smoke dispersed, amid the screams of the merchant and his wife who were in danger of falling from their beds to the street below, the cannon was seen, being rolled back to its home on the Fort Smith parade grounds. The shot had taken out several support beams and joists, demolished everything in its path and seriously undermined the ability of the building to hold up its own roof.

When the merchant complained to the captain and wanted to bring charges up against his men, the Captain replied that if they had not been selling bad homemade whiskey to his men, the incident would not have happened and so therefore they were the makers of their own calamity.

Even though the elimination of the three criminals from the scene did not change much in the town of Fort Smith, that event sent waves of change through Jackson's life and that of his friends. Lucius had broken the ice between Anna and Jackson to the point that they could not retreat from the issue, even if they had wanted to.

"How long have you known you were in love with me, and why didn't you tell me?" asked Jackson one day while they were watching his mules in one of the corrals.

"Silly. A woman does not walk up to the man she loves and announce it like the town crier. I had to wait for you to decide that you wanted me," said Anna, holding out a handful of grain to one of the new arrivals.

"Oh, I wanted you, but I just could not imagine you would want to live here on the frontier running a mule ranch," said Jackson as he turned to gaze at her.

"Thank you for deciding that for me. Why in heaven sakes do you think I stuck around when I could have gone back to my high society life anytime I chose to?" said Anna a little bit peeved by his obtuseness.

"Ah... I guess I was not thinking about that, or much else it seems. So I suppose you won't meet me at the church unless I break down and ask you," said Jackson, smiling.

"I think you already know the answer to that, Jackson," said Anna as she stepped closer, putting her soft hands on his chest and looking up into his eyes.

As they stood by the corral in their long and ardent embrace, a new colt stuck his head through the fence and nudged her arm for a treat. They parted laughing.

"I guess I had better get used to that, hadn't I?" said Anna.

They were married not long after to the great satisfaction of Sasa, Wheezer and Penny, not to mention Andrew and Henry. They planned a trip to go east to Boston where both Anna's and Jackson's mothers lived so their mothers could have the satisfaction of meeting their spouses, but decided to wait until Sasa finished her studies and Anna could then introduce her into society.

As for the inheritance they received from Lucius, they decided that they would liquidate the land and property and put the money in a trust for Sasa so that she could pursue whatever goals in life she desired. But, that would be some time in coming, for there was more trouble brewing in Indian Territory and Sasa would be sorely tested by her loyalties.

Andrew Halley and Henry Neugent remained lifelong friends. They traveled to Fort Gibson so they might better see what types of financial help was needed in Indian Territory. It would be the first of many trips. They also met their friend Nathan Boone who had been given the command of the fort. They too would experience some close calls on the frontier as America went west and trampled everything and everybody underfoot, especially the native peoples.

Wheezer would stay close to Sasa and he now had the added responsibility of showing Penny the ropes and Sasa would soon see that there was any amount of dangerous situations that two Jack Russells could get themselves into, especially when there are bad people roaming the frontier.

Sasa could now look to the future with Wheezer and Penny by her side. She hoped with all her heart that Coyote and Yellow Eyes would make their way back to her and her family. One never knew what might happen in the future. It is something that only the Creator, Yahweh could know, but she did know one thing, she would always try her best to help her people, regardless of the danger. Sasa, Wheezer and Penny walked toward the house to get washed up for dinner. It was the end of another day on the new frontier.

The End

Author's Note

The passage of time has not lessened the magnitude of what the introduction of whiskey has cost the native tribes of North America. There is no doubt, in the author's opinion, that whiskey played a huge part in the subduing of the native tribes. Without the effects of that devastating liquid, it might have been possible for certain tribes to prevail against the U.S. Government and hold out for better treaties and enable them to keep much of their traditional lands. But, history sadly shows that whiskey and other intoxicating liquors do not mix well with the Native American's make-up.

Current estimates of alcoholism on various reservations in North America show that as much as seventy percent of their populations are enslaved to alcohol's effects. Is it any wonder that progress for some of these peoples is at a virtual standstill? Poverty, depression, suicide and many other devastating ills plague our Native American reservations. It is sad when we can look back at the not too distant past and see how it was introduced and used by the white man to accomplish what guns, murder and war could not.

It is even sadder still to know that a nation which calls itself a Christian nation cannot find a way to reach out and offer a hand up to the Native peoples of America, especially considering the fact that the first colony that landed in America would have starved and all its people succumbed to disease and death had the Native Peoples not taught those settlers how to live in the new land.

It is the author's belief that our consciences as individual people could testify against each one of us when the time comes to give an accounting of ourselves. My we be able to show that to the best of our ability, we have shown love and consideration for our fellow man/woman no matter what race they are or what the color of his/her skin.

Kitty Sutton

About the Author

Kitty Sutton was born Kathleen Kelley to an Osage/Irish family. Both sides of her family were from performing families in Kansas City, Missouri and Kitty was trained from an early age in dance, vocal, art and musical instruments. Her father was a Naval band leader. During the Great Depression, her mother helped to support her family by tap dancing in the speakeasys even though she was just a child; she was very tall for her age but made up like an adult. Kitty had music and art on all sides of her family which ultimately helped to feed her imaginative mind and desire to succeed.

  Kitty married a wonderful Cherokee artist from Oklahoma, in fact the very area that she writes about in her Wheezer series of novels. After raising her family, Kitty came to Branson, Missouri and performed in her own one woman show there for twelve years. To honor her father, she performed under the name Kitty Kelley. She has three music albums and several original songs to her credit and is best known for her comical, feel good song called It Ain't Over Till The Fat Lady Sings. Kitty has been writing for many years and in 2011 we accepted her manuscript of an historical Native American murder mystery. First in a series of stories featuring Wheezer, a Jack Russell Terrier and his Cherokee friend, Sasa, it is called, *Wheezer And The Painted Frog*. Kitty lives in the southwestern corner of Missouri near Branson with her husband of 40 years and her three Jack Russell Terriers, one of which is the real and wonderful Wheezer.

If you enjoyed *Wheezer and the Shy Coyote,* or if you have questions, or constructive criticism, you may contact Ms. Sutton at kittyandcompany@centurytel.net.

Wheezer and the Painted Frog, Wheezer and the Golden Serpent, and *Wheezer and the Giveaway Child* can be found at Amazon, Barnes & Noble and fine booksellers everywhere.

Also, visit Kitty's website at:
www.kittysutton.weebly.com

Be sure to check out the other books by Kitty Sutton in this series.

Wheezer and the Shy Coyote
Wheezer and the Golden Serpent
Wheezer and the Giveaway Child
And soon to be released
Wheezer and the Road to Gold